SNIP

ALSO BY DOC MACOMBER

The Killer Coin

Wolf's Remedy

Snip

(A Jack Vu Mystery)

by

Doc Macomber

Floating Word Press, LLC
Portland, Oregon

Floating Word Press, LLC.
1017 SW Morrison Street, Suite 215
Portland, Oregon 97205

Floating Word Press logo is a registered trademark. For information about special discounts for bulk purchases, please contact Floating Word Press, LLC Special Sales at: 1-877-356-9673 or fwp@floatingwordpress.com.

COVER DESIGNED BY DIVERSITY DESIGN STUDIOS
Editor: Jim Hendrickson
Author photograph copyright © 2008 by Serge A. McCabe

Manufactured in the United States of America

Printing Number
10 9 8 7 6 5 4 3 2 1
First Edition

Library of Congress Control Number: 2008925177

ISBN-13: 978-0-9785717-2-6

This book is dedicated to the City of New Orleans

... and to those who saved her ass

ACKNOWLEDGEMENTS

At Floating Word, I'd like to thank my editor, Jim Hendrickson, for his friendship and masterful, yet at times brutal, editing.

I'd also like to give many thanks to the following individuals for their insightful comments during the development of *Snip*: Sergeant Charlie Fender of the Portland Police Department for his assistance with police procedures; Lenny Perrone for his expertise with firearms; Bill, LeAnna, John Hixson, and playwright, Bill Johnson, for their many helpful comments on character and scene development; Annette LH Smith for sharing her equestrian knowledge; Laury Swan for her thorough courtroom analysis and attention to details, Harry Jones, Karl Gillespie, Suzanne, and Jimmy for first reads and encouragement; Jennifer and Jason Rodgers of Columbia Motorcycle for their contined support.

And, without whom this book could not have been written, to my treasured companion, the very adorable and talented Birdie. Her endless readings, innumerable rewrite sessions, and overall general advice and unflinching patience were deeply appreciated. I also owe her much gratitude for turning me on to Bluegrass and always providing the enthusiastic light at the end of the tunnel.

1

A cool drizzle trailed down Willy's leathered neck as
he settled back and waited for the sky to clear. From
shore, he could barely make out faint tug-like sounds
motoring on the Ohio. Leon told him the old boat appeared
to be barging wheat containers upriver. Sure enough, he
finally heard the unmistakable bark of the tug's engine as it
muscled around the turn at the forks, a landmark he could
no longer see.

As the wind shifted, Willy inhaled an oily diesel stench
and the pungent odor of rotting garbage collecting along
the riverbank. He shook his head.

"Twenty years ago this river smelled like fine perfume.
Now all the sweetness is plum gone."

Leon swung round on his folding chair, grinning at his
malcontented friend. "That's 'cause you're sittin' over your
damn creel. Dead carp smells a might better."

Willy wiped his nose and shifted the wicker tackle box
under his skinny buttocks.

"You think my lures stink?"

"Somethin' does."

"Think it's the whiskey?" Willy teasingly patted his tackle box.

Leon pawed around in his front pocket, pulled out a container of chewing tobacco and removed the tin lid.

"I could use a stiff drink. But, I ain't reachin' between your bony legs for it."

"Not until the fish bite." Willy shifted in his folding chair yet couldn't get comfortable. "Them's the rules."

"I should've had Fay spike the coffee."

Leon packed his wet gums, returned the can to his pocket, and gazed out at the winding river.

Willy figured his friend would give in and ask again. But to his surprise, he didn't. Instead, there was only the soft sound of slapping gums and the quiet comfort in knowing Leon had to wait.

"Gotta stretch my legs!"

Willy carefully patted the ground until he found the handle of his white cane. He picked it up off the dirt, unfolded it, and slowly stood. He meandered a few yards along the riverbank, tapping the red tip along the mud, deciphering subtle nuances, and checking the ground for debris. When he heard his creel creak open, he stopped suddenly, flashing a pair of nicotine-stained teeth at his friend.

"If you're fishing for the bottle, I've got it!" He heard the creel shut.

Now satisfied, Willy took his time circling back. When he returned, he folded his cane, tucked it between his legs, and felt around for his fiberglass fishing rod. He found it stuck in a pocket of mud; a hole he'd made for himself. He ran his hand up the Mitchell reel until an index finger discovered the taut monofilament.

"Willy," Leon eyed the whiskey flask sticking out of his friend's shirt pocket, "what's eatin' you?"

"Nothin' worth discussin'."

"I know better. You've been pissin' and moanin' all mornin'. They cut off your disability again?"

"No."

"That's not what Fay said."

"Fay don't know jack."

How could Willy explain the weight of a lifetime of missed opportunities? He sank into this "what if" depression, each time sucking him further into the muck, the rescue line always hovering just at the tips of his frantic fingers. Today the "what if" was his sight. Yesterday it was his flaccid cock, as useless now as a hunk of thick rope. Would vision and a hard-on really have changed the course of his life, as meandering and unpredictable as the river snaking by? Doubtful...

During breakfast somebody other than Leon had noticed his foul mood as well. Fay, the young waitress who slid Willy his plate of biscuits and gravy across the counter, had suspected something immediately.

"You're wearing one sour-ass face this morning," she said. "What's up? Little Oscar depressed?"

"None of your business, Fay. And my pecker's fine thank you. Go fill our thermos with some of that chicory 'cause we're in a hurry. And this time don't scrimp on no sugar."

Leon butted in. "Willy ain't hisself today."

"Shut up, Leon!"

Sure enough, Fay had felt pity for him, because on the way out he'd been able to cop a feel of her fine ass. The last attempt, she'd nearly broken his finger. A blind man wearing a splint on his pussy finger don't look so good. People talk...

Willy sulked. It hadn't helped that some asshole had knocked down his markers along the trail. The sticks were how he counted steps to the water's edge. That was just plain spiteful.

A heavy vibration against Willy's foot snapped him out of his funk. Leon jumped up, staring at the bending tip of his friend's fishing pole and reached for it. Willy whirled around like a frisky rat and rapped Leon's fingers with the blunt end of his cane.

"Hands off!" Willy jerked hard and set the hook.

"Well – what'ya waitin' for? Reel it in!"

Leon rubbed his reddened fingers as he jittered along the riverbank like an electrified eel, gawking at the arc in Willy's rod.

"Reel damnit!"

Shimmering water droplets flew off the line as it circled precariously around a rock, threatening to saw it in two.

"I'm tryin' damnit! Grab hold a me!"

Leon slipped behind his friend, wrapping his arms around Willy's skeletal waist while veins poked out along his forearms as he struggled to hold on. Blood raced to his legs in urgency as both anglers dug in their heels and labored to pull the obstinate fish ashore. For ten exhausting minutes they reeled and kept a steady pressure on it.

"Mother Jesus! It's a fat fucker!"

The two hauled and heaved until their dinner finally hit the shore.

"Well – go see what I hooked."

Leon blankly stared. A gnarled snag had lodged itself against the riverbank.

"You hooked a whopper all right."

"Hot damn!" Willy squealed.

"First a drink." Leon snatched the flask from Willy's pocket – one quick swig before exposing the awful truth.

"Hey…" Willy swatted at Leon as he took a long pull of the amber liquid.

"Have a nip yourself while I haul in your trophy," Leon said, finally surrendering the whiskey.

Willy's line was wrapped tightly around the far branches of the slimy log. Leon grabbed hold and grunted laboriously as he tugged it ashore. The log was hung up. Leon dug his feet in and groaned hard as it finally surrendered and climbed the waterline. For a brief moment it seemed quiet enough to hear a tadpole fart.

An odd something, about the size and color of a dolphin, broke the surface and lodged against the slimy bark. But, it was no fish. Leon crept down for a closer look.

Willy grew impatient. "Well! What is it?"

A woman's head floated on the surface, the current tangling her long hair round a branch, while her lifeless torso bobbed against the shore.

Leon turned ashen. He couldn't swallow. Scuttling back up the riverbank, shaking his head, he grabbed the flask from Willy's hand, twisted the top off and guzzled. Tired of waiting, Willy tottered a few steps closer to the waterline, but stopped shy, and turned back.

Leon flopped down on the muddy bank. "Willy – you done caught you a white girl."

"What do you mean caught me a white girl?"

Hand-over-hand, Willy clumsily followed his fishing line down the bank toward the water, until his left hand encountered the log. He pawed along the wet bark until his other hand entangled a fistful of hair.

The body continued its gentle slosh against the riverbank. Most of the torso was now out of the water face up in the mud. Brunette hair floated on the surface like strands of a jellyfish. At most, the body had only been in the water overnight. The icy temperatures of the Ohio thwarted decay.

Leon watched from a distance, his body quivering.

"Leon, describe her to me."

"Willy – I don't know. She's all slimy, covered in river rot. And, she's got on some kind of uniform."

"Leon! Get your scrawny ass down here. What the hell you mean – a uniform? Like a waitress or something?"

The slight swell of the river, forcing the corpse from its murky depths, gave the lump of bones a mysterious life-like quality all its own. Leon tried to be strong as he cautiously rejoined his friend.

"No. Looks like some kind of military uniform."

Spittle ran down Leon's chin. He swiped it off and watched Willy gently caress the poor girl's face.

"Leave her be," Leon whispered. Leon had no fascination with the dead. Willy, however, was a creature of sensation and wanted to feel every square inch of the corpse. Afterall, it wasn't everyday an old black man garnered from the river opportunity to run his hands over a white girl.

Leon stood back as his friend's fingers traced the girl's face, plucked a blade of river grass from her mouth, and tossed it aside. Then, Willy slowly worked his way down the body. He particularly liked the buttons on her suit and the ribbons on her breast pocket. It certainly was a military uniform. His hand slid down her ankle and discovered she was missing her right shoe. She had on nylons, but the little toe had torn through the sheer material.

"She wearing nail polish?"

"What difference does it make?"

"Is it red?"

Disgusted, Leon walked over and quickly examined the girl's foot. "It's more pink than red."

"What color is the uniform?"

"Blue."

"Air Force then," Willy said.

"We gotta call the cops."

"Look, if we call the cops they're gonna ask us plenty of questions. Couple niggers like us? They'll probably throw us in jail for killing this white girl. Even if they don't, they'll sure's hell find out about your unpaid tickets and yank your license. Then I'd have to take the bus everywhere. Can't do that no more."

"We gotta do something. We can't just leave her out here."

"You could push her back in and let nature sorta ... take its course."

"I ain't touchin' her!"

"You prepared to pay them tickets?"

Leon scratched his head and stubbed the toe of his boot in the dirt. "Guess not."

Willy washed his hands in the river and then stood up straight. "OK, then. I'll say a prayer for her and you push her back in."

"Willy – I swear I'll leave your nigger ass here. You walk away from that poor girl this instant."

Leon found Willy's lure, cut it loose, pocketed it, and trudged over to collect his fishing gear.

Willy, detecting the fear in Leon's voice, knew he was finished. So, he silently prayed for the girl as he moved to gather his own tackle. Leon slipped the cooler over his shoulder, handed Willy the folding chairs, then took his friend by the arm and led him up the trail.

As Willy walked through the tall grass, he reckoned he now had as good a reason as any for his solemn mood. Their favorite fishing hole would never be the same.

2

As Jack Vu reflected on the wreckage of the Arctic Wing no longer moored in New Orleans harbor, he pondered the role boats had played in his life. They had previously been harbingers of significant change. As a Vietnamese teenager, a fishing boat had carried him to safety on his escape from the Killing Fields of Cambodia. Now, it was unclear where Katrina's winds had blown him with respect to yet another vessel.

Vu parked his yellow Vespa at MaCuddy's Boat Works and entered through the front gate where he was boldly confronted by the barking drool of two Dobermans chained to a post near the main office. The dogs strained against their collars as he finessed past and climbed the rickety steps to the front door. The office was a dented, single-wide trailer with boarded windows and rainbow colored rust stains trickling down the aluminum siding. Vu knocked, waited, and knocked again, but no one answered. All he heard were the distant sounds of hammering and grinding thundering from the boat yard.

Leaving the office, he followed a dirt path which led through a hundred or more boats in various stages of disrepair. Yachts and sailboats stood perched on stilts back to back. Many had caved hulls, broken masts, hunks of missing fiberglass, and pretzel twisted outboards. Running gears stuck out of cockpit centers, cables were sheared off, ports shattered, and everywhere rigging wound like knitting balls in heaps. The yard resembled a war zone, a familiar visage for Vu. He searched for his own boat, the Arctic Wing, and feared the worst. If only he'd stayed aboard during Katrina, perhaps the damage could have been prevented.

He found her along the northern portion of the yard. The ninety-five-foot motorsailer built of wood and metal in the late sixties rose defiantly above the other hulks. Her large wooden hull was elevated by a battery of stilts, which exposed three gaping cannonball-sized holes. Her main mast was broken near midpoint and hung askew by its rigging. When Vu first found the Arctic Wing after the storm, the 22' foot Ziggy Bee jutted out near midship. The Bee's fiberglass bow had pierced the Wing's wooden deck during the storm. Fortunately, that area of the boat previously stored underwater marine radar equipment which had recently been sold off. The equipment had once been used to document seafloor conditions as part of a small government research project whose funding eventually dried up.

Although the Ziggy Bee had been removed from the Arctic Wing before transport, none of the dried river mud, branches, or garbage now filling her deck had. The living quarters below deck were even more deplorable.

Vu knew the boat was a wreck. Yet, for a resourceful guy used to living in sparse wartime conditions, he thought he could save her. If the owner of the salvage yard would allow it, he hoped to clean the interior and move back aboard. He missed the warm cradle of the teak, the squeak of the wood, the clanging of the halyards. He treasured the intimate cocoon that held his heart and in which he and Betty had found a life worth living together. The Arctic Wing's survival felt akin to physical validation of their unlikely pairing.

From behind Vu, footsteps crunched across the gravel. He turned. An exhausted man with a shaggy beard and greasy overalls approached, clutching a hammer.

"Tough to look at, ain't it?"

Vu nodded. "Have you been able to work up a repair estimate on her?"

"She's rebuildable alright, but it's going to cost you a pretty penny."

"I was afraid of that."

The scraggly man stuck out his hand. "Name's MaCuddy. I remember you. Been so many wrecks brought in over the last few months, can't keep the owners' names straight. We haven't seen this sort of business since Hurricane Camille in '69."

"I'm Jack Vu."

"That's right. You're the military guy."

"Air Force, stationed at the Joint Naval Base."

"How's life in the barracks?"

"I miss my boat."

"Bet you do. She's a spacious one. A little unsightly down below, but nothing a few days of elbow grease can't fix." MaCuddy turned and studied the boat as if trying to remember the work she needed.

"She's in need of major hull reconstruction and deck work. Some of her electrical is in pretty bad shape. The mast needs replaced, as will her main sail. She's not water tight topside. You've got that crater in her aft cabin, but she'll survive. Can't say that for most of the boats in this yard. The New Orleans Marina faired the best of the three, probably because it was surrounded by Municipal Harbor and all those high-rise condominiums. One marina suffered near 80 percent losses. You're lucky, considering…"

Vu noticed fresh stitches on MaCuddy's forearm and that the black hair had not yet regrown. MaCuddy looked stout and powerful, the type of old tar not to piss off. He walked up to the Arctic Wing, tapped on her hull with his hammer, jotted on a clipboard, and then looked back at Vu.

"No dry rot. That's good. We'll need a check from the insurance company or cash before we begin."

"When will you have a total figure for me?"

"In about ten seconds." MaCuddy flipped through his clipboard and located the document. His bushy eyebrows crunched as he finished his mental calculations. "Give or take a few hundred, I figure we can get her back in the water for thirteen-five, depending on whether we can locate hull material that'll match the existing planking and that I can have a new mast carved. You want a wooden mast, don't you?"

"Yes."

Vu didn't have insurance or thirteen-thousand five-hundred dollars, neither did Hyun-Ok, who actually owned the boat but lived in Tokyo. Vu had been living aboard cheaply while Hyun-Ok decided if she wanted to convert it into a floating hotel. Her insurance agent had recently informed Vu that their company would not be liable for damages. He'd received an e-mail earlier in the week from the owner saying she was done dropping money into a hole in the water. He was on his own. The title was his. She'd send it over. Vu had some serious decisions to make.

"There's no insurance coverage. I have about six-thousand in savings. Would you consider payments?"

"No." MaCuddy lowered his clipboard and looked Jack in the eye. "Cash up front only. Been our policy for forty-six years."

While Vu's mind mulled limited financial options, two men emerged from one of the wreckages behind MaCuddy's back carrying an outboard motor. Vu's acuity immediately deemed the men out of place. They kept their heads down and skulked in the shadows as scavengers, not employees. Vu recognized their furtive movements because he too had stolen as a child, if only to survive.

"Turn around. Do you recognize those men?"

MaCuddy glanced over his shoulder. "Hell, I've got so many people running around this place, I can't tell one from the other." He stared at the men and then shouted, "Hey, you two!"

The men ignored him, but walked faster.

MaCuddy dropped his clipboard on the ground. "Hey!

Stop!"

The men took off running and Vu gave chase. He almost caught up to them near the main entrance. But, they saw Vu, dropped the motor, and made a last dash out the gate toward an old pickup parked on the side of the road. Vu copied the license number on a small notepad just as they sped off.

MaCuddy trotted up, winded and limping, his face twisted in rage. His jaw twitched as he angrily jerked up one fallen strap on his overalls.

"Shit, they got away. They'll just come back. The bastards." He rubbed his fresh scar and looked disgusted.

"Is that souvenir from a recent run in?"

"That's why I got them dogs. Can't defend myself like I used to."

"I take it this is a regular occurrence around here?"

"Getting worse every day."

"Those two are probably part of a larger crew. I might be able to help."

After a few deep breaths, MaCuddy regained his senses. Vu pocketed his notepad.

"What is it you do for the Air Force again?"

"I'm an investigator."

"You mean like a cop?"

"More or less."

"You carry a gun?"

"Yes."

"Then you should have shot them bastards."

Vu remained silent. MaCuddy wiped a sleeve across his sweaty brow. "Well, whatever you are, you just saved me six hundred bucks and plenty of explaining to another customer. I'm obliged. In fact, I'll even take that off the amount you owe me."

Vu got an idea. "I'll tell you what. I'll agree to watch this place in the evenings if you'll allow me to move aboard and keep an eye on things in exchange for a reduction on repairs."

MaCuddy stared intently at him. "You want to live here?"

"Yes. I need a bit of privacy to spend some quality time with my woman."

"What about her place?"

Vu flinched at the memory of kissing Betty goodbye in her childhood bedroom filled with music posters and high school science awards. Closing her door quietly and walking down the hall he'd encountered her father. And, as they nodded to each other in passing, the racial disapproval was alarmingly evident in her father's eyes.

"Lost it in Katrina. She's living with her parents."

MaCuddy thought it over. "You afraid of dogs?"

"No."

"Are you a saucehead?"

"An occasional beer or sake."

"Sake? What in God's name is that?"

"Rice wine."

"What about your gal?"

"She works for the police. Having her around at night means the cops would be close by."

MaCuddy scratched his head. "How much discount we talking about?"

"I'll give you six-thousand dollars down payment and you let me do some work of my own to bring down the remaining balance."

MaCuddy gave it some more thought. "Fine. You can move in tomorrow."

"Great."

The men shook hands. As they walked back toward the office, Vu knew Katrina's winds had blown him through MaCuddy's shipyard gates for a reason. How would this new arrangement turn out? He paused.

"One other thing. I need to borrow your dogs."

3

The historic twin spires of Churchill Downs glistened in the late afternoon sun. Along the infield, dust started to settle. The ninth race was about to begin. The next round of horses trotted onto the track. While the horses paraded by the crowded grandstand, a few spectators scribbled hasty notes into their Daily Racing Forms and dashed off toward the betting windows.

Out on the track, veteran jockey Patti Knot – known among racing circles as "Goldilocks" – pulled up to the gate early, sensing her young mount might give her some trouble. She firmly held the reins and coaxed the skittish chestnut colt into the chute as the gate locked behind. Patti quickly removed a gold coin from her silk pocket and kissed it for luck.

Laughter broke out.

The male jockey from the adjacent chute flashed his pearly whites. "Well, if it isn't Goldilocks," he said. "I thought you retired."

Patti's eyes darkened. A seasoned professional with nearly twenty years on the pro circuit, her career had recently plummeted. Getting rides at her age was becoming increasingly difficult, but retirement was not an option. She needed more money to assemble her dream. A win today would move her one step closer. Meanwhile, the career of her tormentor, Brad Black, had skyrocketed. Thirty-one wins this season, but who was counting?

Patti focused on her mount. Blazing Saddle was a spirited two-year-old. She didn't need him coming unglued out of the gate. From past experiences she knew he was notorious for breaking right out of the chute. A collision with another horse could be disastrous.

The starter checked the gate. All jockeys signaled to ready. Patti's calves tensed in the irons. The brisk air stung her nostrils. She double-checked her goggles, readied her whip at her side, and tightened the reins. Seconds later, the bell sounded.

Blazing Saddle broke perfectly, flying straight out of the gate and immediately found his stride. Ten horses thundered down the dirt track passing the first post. Patti and her mount were hung on the outside, sandwiched between Lucky Star and Ocean Seven and running in third position. Brad's mount, Sea Breeze, a two-year-old filly, was in the lead, hugging the key position along the inside rail. Ocean Seven's jockey nudged forward to second after the third post. Patti held on tight, not giving an inch to the angry jockey beside her or the thousand pounds of bone and muscle barreling down the track at better than thirty miles per hour – with the fourth-place jockey shouting: "Move over bitch!"

It was exhilarating.

With less than three furlongs to go, Blazing Saddle seemed determined to win. The colt impressed Patti with his stamina and drive. Very few two-year-olds had this kind of competitive edge. She held the whip and crept up on the lead horse.

Patti and Brad volleyed for the finish line. The crowd screamed and the horses grunted with exertion. Brad repeatedly raised his whip and brought it down hard on the number one horse. Side-by-side the two horses beat down the track. Fist-sized dirt clods whizzed through the air. Brad raised his whip again, this time striking his opponent. The stinging bite of rawhide on Patti's left buttock startled her, breaking her concentration. In vain, she flashed daggered eyes at her nemesis, but Blazing Saddle had lost momentum...

Sea Breeze crossed the finish line by a length, followed by Ocean Seven. King's Ride captured the show position, with a tired Blazing Saddle sadly finishing fourth.

Back in the stables, Patti climbed down from her mount and handed him over to the groom.

"He did OK," Bobby said, reaching for the reins.

Patti nodded and removed her helmet and gloves. She felt a fresh scratch on her cheek and checked to see if it was bleeding.

"Yeah – thought we had that one," she said finally.

"What happened on the home stretch?"

"He lost his stride."

"That's not what I meant."

Patti ignored the questioning eyes. The track official probably had it all on camera, but she would deal with it in her own way. After a moment, the groom led the horse toward the shed row.

Patti's legs tingled as the muscles readapted to terra firma. She fell behind a few paces, taking one final look as the spirited chestnut turned the corner and disappeared behind the stables.

Inside the Jockey Club, Brad opened his locker. Several jockeys walked up to pay accolades and swap friendly puns, which were all part of winning.

"Saw you spanking Goldilocks," another jockey said, smiling.

Brad put his towel down and slipped off his robe, unveiling layers of rippling chest muscle. He stood straight, stretched the kinks from his back and cracked his neck. "She was begging for it."

One of the newer jockeys said, "She's got a fine ass."

"Yeah – if you like dark meat."

Brad ignored the stilted laughter and pulled a pair of slacks from his locker. Making fun of women was widely accepted in his profession, but racial comments left all but the newest star-struck beginners uncomfortable. As the room silenced, he turned around to see Patti standing directly behind him. She was casually dressed in blue jeans, cowboy boots and a turtleneck sweater. Her Brazilian ancestry was glowingly apparent in her fine maple skin. She surveyed him through intelligent eyes, but was unimpressed by his physique.

Brad closed his locker door.

"So you don't like dark meat? Probably too juicy for you." The other jockeys stifled laughter while shuffling closer to the action they all sensed was brewing. Collectively, most agreed that Goldilocks was one of the few women jockeys who merited respect. She'd been in the game longer than most.

Across the room a jockey entered, chatting on his cell phone. His instincts perked as he encountered the tense standoff. Quickly, he hung up.

Patti stood a confident five-foot-one – no fat, pure muscle. Years of conditioning had honed her body with countless sit-ups, pushups, weight training and horse races. Patti flippantly tossed her golden braids like twin whips cracking the still air.

"Look, I'm sorry about the lash. Guess I missed my mark." Brad's voice held as much sympathy as a scorpion when about to sting a frog. "No hard feelings?"

Patti clenched her fists. "Absolutely not. I look forward to whipping your ass next time around."

The room laughed. Brad mistakenly dropped his guard to join in the joke. Like a consummate professional, Patti saw an opening and effortlessly lunged inside. Fists flying, she connected with Brad's jaw. A cell phone clicked, capturing the shot. Brad's eyes glazed over as he reeled into the locker, his legs folding beneath him. Patti smiled derisively at him as another silence enveloped the room.

When she turned to leave, the crowd parted before rushing to Brad's aid. Once outside, Patti relaxed. The tension drained from her body. Decking that asshole was probably not a smart career move, but it sure felt good.

Near the main entrance of the track, an old Chevy pickup

pulled into the handicapped parking area and killed its engine. Willy stared out the windshield and slapped the dash.

"Leon – you callin' the police ain't gonna bring that girl back! It's just gonna get us in trouble. We don't need no more trouble."

Leon had been listening to his friend's arguments during the entire drive. But, his mind was made up. He glanced around for a payphone near the entrance, though they were becoming increasingly obsolescent thanks in part to cellular phones. His eyes tracked a blonde woman striding in their direction, but her presence didn't register with him.

Leon grabbed the door handle. "Fine. You wait here while I go make the call."

Willy unfolded his cane. "I'm going to find the crapper," he shouted. "You do what you want."

Willy pushed open the passenger door and climbed out. As he unfolded his cane, he heard Leon's door open and slam shut. Willy didn't wait for his friend.

"Willy – wait up!"

Willy raged across the lot, unaware of the large trash receptacle looming before him. Seconds later the blonde grabbed him, averting his collision with the dumpster. As she pulled him safely aside, Leon hustled up out of breath.

Willy turned toward his rescuer.

"What the hell you doin', grabbin' an old blind man like that?"

"You nearly walked into something," Patti laughed. Willy brushed the woman's hand from his shoulder and stretched his cane out. The tip banged the solid metal container.

"Don't pay no attention to this man here," Leon said. "He's done lost his faculties."

"You're the one who's crazy."

Leon continued, "I need to use a pay phone, miss. Where can I find one?"

Willy mimicked his friend causing Patti to suppress a smile.

"I believe the payphones are inside. If it's an emergency you can use my cell phone."

Willy butted in, "No thanks. It's a personal matter."

Leon felt his pockets. "Could I bother you for change, miss? All I got's a twenty."

Patti guessed by the look and smell of the crusty old men in muddy trousers that they were probably just eking by.

"I'm a little short myself. But, you can have my change."

She reached into her pocket and pulled out a handful of coins. Her favorite lucky coin was among them. She deftly plucked it out, dropped it back into her front pocket, and then poured the remaining coins into Leon's eager palm.

"Thanks miss."

Willy wrapped Leon's foot. "Yes. Thank you, ma'am," Willy added. "Have a nice day now."

Before she could respond, a limousine rolled into the lot and honked its horn. Patti glanced over her shoulder and frowned.

"OK. Look, I gotta go guys."

She left them to their own devices and hurried toward the car.

After she was out of earshot, Willy rapped Leon's other foot. Leon's loose tongue had gotten them into trouble more times than Willy cared to recall. Leon, who by now could do nothing but stand still for fear of getting hit again, turned his attention toward the young woman. A woman with mahogany skin and blonde hair was not usually his type, but he just may have to add her to his fantasy repertoire.

Leon turned back round. "That's one fine lookin' filly."

"A filly that could identify us."

"If you could a seen those ham hocks."

"I don't give no damn about her biscuits, Leon."

"I wasn't gonna tell her."

"What if the cops trace your call? And, if they start puttin' two and two together – look around. I figure there's a few hundred cameras here. You take a couple suspicious niggers, a fine lookin' woman, and your big ass mouth … shucks … we just as well go to jail now and save the cops the trouble of shooting."

Leon gazed up at the telephone poles and counted six satellite dishes mounted on the rooftops of the surrounding buildings. Doubt set in. He stared down at his trembling hand. Latching onto it wouldn't even hold it steady.

"I'm callin'. You comin' or not?"

4

The gears turned, swinging the arm into position as the town clock pealed two guttural tolls. Louisville City Hall on West Jefferson Street was a colossal eighteenth century hallmark of downtown – three stories of undulating Italianate facades, a mix of brick and carved stone, with a clock tower the citizenry set watches by. Louisville's early agricultural history was apparent in the sculpted husbandry of horses, pigs and cows prominently displayed above the second story windows. Behind one of those windows sat Detective Sam Buck, a rumpled unshaven titan, a true heavyweight, standing well over six-feet-five. Today he presided over a cluttered desk where a coffee-stained newspaper lay open to the morning crossword. This was Buck's third week back as chief homicide investigator, but he still found traces of Afghan sand in his shoes.

"Hey Smitty," he shouted across the freshly-painted, government office, "What's another word for neutered?"

Detective Smitty, a stout, redheaded Irishman, slid back from his keyboard where he was finishing up a report. He stared across the room at his partner.

"What?"

"A 9-letter word for neutered?" Buck repeated, tapping his pencil on the desk.

"Marriage."

"That's eight letters. It starts with a 'C'."

Smitty glanced out the window. On the sidewalk below an attractive woman in a dark suit picked up her briefcase and sauntered across the street. Smitty leered. "Try cunnilingus, mate."

Buck frowned, nudging his glasses up his crooked nose with his pencil. "Cute."

Smitty waited until the lady was gone, then turned. "How 'bout – castrated?"

Buck picked up his pen and wrote down the letters in the blank boxes. "Yeah – that works. So, how was your nephew's wedding on Saturday?"

"Not good. His bride tumbled into the champagne fountain."

"Nice."

"Little lassie is out of action," Smitty said. "Broke a tooth. I told the lad it was a palpable sign."

"Of what?"

"Things to come, or not to cum, if you'll pardon the pun."

Buck craned inquisitively in Smitty's direction.

"Blow jobs, mate. Once they're legally tethered, women will do anything to avoid 'em … even pitch themselves into a fountain."

The phone on Buck's desk rang. Buck stopped grinning, put his pen down and picked up the receiver.

"Homicide."

The caller seemed nervous, possibly African American, with an unusually deep voice.

"Slow down," Buck told him. "Where'd you find the body? The Ohio. It's a very big river, sir … perhaps you could be more specific?" Buck swung his chair around and pointed for Smitty to pick up.

Smitty covered the receiver and punched the lit button on his phone.

"You're sure it was a female?" he continued. "OK, OK. Where are you right now?"

The phone went dead. Buck replaced the receiver and waited for Smitty to hang up as well. "Think it's legit?"

Smitty logged off his computer. "Beats a crossword."

Buck tore off the piece of tablet where he had jotted a few notes and rose from his desk. He shrugged on the tweed jacket slung over the back of his chair and carefully pocketed the note. He removed a .38 S&W Police Special from his desk drawer and slipped it into his shoulder holster. It felt inadequately small compared to his military issue .45 Colt. Smitty turned off the coffee pot and caught up with Buck at the door.

Downstairs in the underground garage, the two men climbed into an unmarked black sedan. Buck controlled the wheel but had trouble buckling the seat belt. It seemed he'd packed on a few extra pounds lately, nonchalantly blaming it on the difficulties of getting back into the groove after his last tour.

He rolled down the passenger window, unbuttoned his shirt a notch, and lit a smoke.

Twenty minutes later, the sedan pulled off the main road onto the shoulder and parked. From a hill overlooking the Ohio River, the two detectives took in the sweeping view of the city in the distance.

"This it?"

"Think so."

They got out of the car and hiked down the steep embankment. A few hundred yards later they stopped. The Ohio wound ahead like a giant slithering python. The trail came to an abrupt end at the water's edge. A small area of scrub grass had been cleared away along the riverbank. Buck searched for what the caller had said were markers – empty beer cans and sticks stuck in the ground. Instead, all he found were a few thorns stuck to his trouser cuffs. Smitty was frowning at the mud on his newly polished loafers.

"See it anywhere?"

"Caller said the trail was marked," Buck said. "I don't think we're in the right place. Let's try further south."

They eventually followed a narrow trail through the tall scrub grass. At the edge of the trail a pair of sticks stuck out of the ground. A torn piece of red cloth was tied around the top of one of the branches.

Buck spotted it first. "I think we found it." He figured it'd be a good spot for fishing. He remembered a similar place upriver where he'd fished as a kid.

Further down stream, something shifted in the water, disturbing a covey of flies which swarmed the shore in beat to the rhythmic tide.

Smitty pointed to where the corpse lapped against the bank. "There's our catch, mate."

5

The melting ice cubes cracked as New Orleans Detective Dorene Gates sat alone in the lobby bar of the historic Brown Hotel in Louisville, stirring a double shot of Maker's Mark. She studied her reflection in the gilded mirror behind the bar, unable to believe what seventeen years of police work had done to her face.

She was no longer the eighteen-year-old ebony beauty from Louisville who had left friends and family – never to look back. The youthful sparkle in her brown eyes, once brimming with hopeful enthusiasm, was gone. What remained was a piercing intellect with no false illusions, honed from years of working homicide. Just an ordinary cop in New Orleans, she was something of a celebrity in Louisville, where coverage of a recent string of murders had made her face recognizable to anyone who watched TV. She'd tracked down and arrested the infamous "Dyke Killer," who had roamed the ravaged neighborhoods of the Big Easy in the months following Katrina, killing at will.

The rough streets of New Orleans had changed more than Dorene's face. No longer was she the chunky lazy kid who got stoned with other low-cast losers from school. Her body was muscular. Her chest and shoulders resembled carved bronze; annealed from years of pumping iron in seedy basement gyms and beating the hell out of shithead criminals. Even the coy sunbursts splaying from the corners of her eyes had been earned the hard way. Only an artist could truly appreciate the hours of lost sleep, death, filth and decay that had sculpted them over the years. And, the grandiose plans for social change were gone. She no longer believed she could change the world. The world operated at its own tempo. Had its own reasons and desires for existing that had very little to do with individual agendas.

The flight from New Orleans that morning had left her mouth dry, and renewed more than just her hatred of flying. She had revisited her high school traumas and inwardly cringed. She'd been a uniquely easy mark and knew her place in the racist Louisville of her youth, yet she hadn't discovered her place sexually. While she never had any interest in black boys her age, white boys intrigued her with their cocky power. They were kings in the school hierarchy. Even the most popular white girls deferred to them. But unlike the good white girls in school, she had something they wanted and she happily gave it. Nicknamed "Black Box" by the white boys she routinely allowed between her legs, she soon found her interest in sex was driven by similar desire – she wanted to fuck women too.

A black dyke of a whore is nobody's ideally suitable high school chum. In the recently integrated Louisville school system, she was publicly shunned by both black and white girls. It had been a lonely confusing period. That is, until senior year with Patti – a sexy Brazilian blonde with dark skin – another misfit.

From sheer lack of other choices, the two fell in together. Patti's ideas of sexual freedom were unimpeded by southern Christian morals. She was young, exotic and driven. She knew what she wanted – to be a world-class jockey. What better place to make one's mark than Churchill Downs? Louisville held nothing for Gates though, and after high school their parting was stoically businesslike. Both had future dreams that didn't include room for each other. Later, she heard Patti had married in order to stay in the States.

Gates took another drink of bourbon, licking the fiery spirit from her lips and smiled ruefully. Her friend was not coming. Patti Knot was backing out. It had been a stupid idea in the first place. What had she been thinking e-mailing her? And attending her twenty-year reunion? Did she really think they would hook up? For the first time in years she had agonized over what to wear for their "date."

What a schmuck...

She asked the bartender for her bill. While she waited, a vendor dropped a stack of newspapers on the bar. She picked up the evening edition of the *Louisville Examiner* and thumbed through it.

As Gates pulled out the Sports section she snapped to attention. Plastered over the front page was her high school sweetheart, the horse nut who went on to become an internationally famous thoroughbred jockey. Apparently, Patti now had a second career as a boxer. That could explain the no show. No use drowning sorrows. Time to head back to the room, take off the cocktail dress, throw on some jeans and find the nearest gay bar. To hell with reunions.

The bartender brought her receipt and a telephone.

"You have a message at the front desk."

Gates tore her friend's picture from the paper, neatly folded the clipping, tucked it into her pocket and signed the bill.

An old ache rose in her chest as she dialed the front desk. She listened to the message and smiled.

A cool evening moon appeared over the Ohio, its silver trail pointing toward the Galt. Gates popped a breath mint into her mouth and headed toward the main entrance. Strolling down her own memory lane, she passed a half-dozen street corner musicians, including bluegrass, rhythm and blues, rap and even, a pretty darn good Elvis, (the younger version).

A sign near the elevator indicated the Louisville Central High Reunion was being held in the West Wing Ballroom. She boarded the elevator with several white couples wearing evening attire. From their chatter Gates gathered they were heading to the same function, though she didn't recognize any of them.

The group rode the elevator to the third floor and exited together. Gates trailed the pack, automatically assuming her inferior high school social status. They followed the carpeted hallway to its terminus with two double doors which swung open. Loud Rock and Roll spilled into the foyer as several people burst through the doorway, laughing. Gates hung back, took a deep breath, then entered the crowded ballroom. Trying not to look overly expectant, her eyes scanned the room for Patti.

Gates figured several hundred people milled about the room, not counting the small half-drunken group near the stage, focused on the four-piece band bedecked in Zebra stripes hammering out lame covers of Rod Stewart hits. Numerous tables and chairs filled the center area and full-service bars lined both sidewalls.

It was remarkable, she thought. High school all over again – the same little cliques – same stuck-ups and suck-ups, same egos and phony smiles, even the same shitty music.

Suddenly unsure of herself, Gates stood awkwardly rooted. Then, a familiar voice penetrated the crowd. Wearing his old letterman's jacket, fifty extra pounds, and a receding hairline, Wayne Lewis sidled up, giving Gates an obvious once over, which she figured complimentary.

"So our famous dyke cop has returned."

Wayne leaned in closer. "After regular servings of my Johnson, only a dildo could take its place, eh?"

"Yeah, Wayne. You ruined me on real dick for the rest of my life." Gates suggestively ran her fingers across his belt buckle. "Let me ask you a personal question. You have a harder time getting laid with that gut of yours?" Slipping her hand down the edge of his pants, she grabbed his tidy whiteys and gave them a firm yank.

Wayne's face contorted, first in pain and then in anger.

"Just an old high school wedgie, Wayne. But, you give me any more trouble tonight, I'll make it my personal mission to…"

"Dorene!" Gates turned toward the older rotund brunette in the peach colored pants suit hurrying toward her, her cheeks flushed with color.

"Mrs. Brown?"

"It's me. I hardly recognized you either. Can you believe this crowd?"

With that, Meg Brown threw her protective arm around Gates and led her away. She'd been her school counselor and quite a hard-ass, but Gates had respected her. She'd pushed Gates to acquire skills for life beyond just discovering her own identity, though she helped with that too. She forced reading and writing down her throat. These assets would help her later in life. Gates had relied on those creative writing skills more than once in her career to doctor questionable incident reports.

"I want no trouble tonight deary. You stay away from Wayne and the boys and I'll see that their wives keep them in line."

"Yes, ma'am."

"Dory, you look good," Meg said affectionately. "Ruth Henry told me you went into law enforcement. That true?"

Gates nodded. Apparently Meg didn't watch the evening news.

"How exciting."

They chatted for a few minutes. Gates pulled out her gold shield and showed it off, aware of her eagerness to impress her old counselor. Meg smiled approvingly.

"Are you still teaching?"

"No. I retired a couple of years ago." A painful sound crept into her voice. "And my husband, Howard, passed on last year." Sorrow graced Meg's shiny blue eyes.

"Actually, to be truthful, it's been a wee bit wicked. But, my two sons help out around the house these days and we're abiding as best we can. Someone once said: 'You have to learn to do everything, even to die.'"

"Gertrude Stein."

Meg raised her head proudly at her former student. "A great

writer and one I'm pleased you remember."

Gates fought down a surge of gratitude. She wanted to thank her former teacher for not giving up on her. But, everything she could think of saying sounded corny. Instead, she gave her another hug.

Mrs. Brown blushed. "Well, I've seen some of your old pals hanging around the back bar. You might want to remind them about the DUI laws in this state."

"Yes, ma'am."

After their goodbyes, Gates resumed scanning the crowd for Patti.

Musing on Gertrude Stein after so many years, caused her to shake her head. "When you finally get there, there isn't any there, there."

Nothing like a reunion to confuse past and present. Where had the time gone?

Before she found an answer, a beaming face appeared midst the crowd – a bouncy high-heeled sexy Brazilian, frantically waving and dicing her way through the wall of bodies.

Hope had arrived.

"Hey Dork, glad you could make it."

6

Later that evening, Gates hobbled to a table, her fuck me
pumps having carved chunks of raw skin off both pinkie
toes. Dancing injuries, however, were small price to pay. In
high school Patti Knot had only toyed at being gay. Now, nearing
forty, she was a sworn in the wool dyke and Gates was enjoying
every minute of it. No awkward pauses, no strained silences.
They'd clicked immediately.

Gates figured they'd spent the better part of the evening
laughing, telling stories and catching up on each other's lives.
Intentionally, both had kept it somewhat light. If this worked out,
plenty of time lay ahead for the heavy emotional bloodlettings both
had experienced since last they met. Still, given their surroundings,
it'd been a remarkable exchange from the moment Patti espied
her.

"C'mon, Dory – let's dance again."

Patti tried to pull Gates out of her chair and drag her back
onto the dance floor.

"I'm sittin' this one out, sugar."

"OK. I'll dance for both of us."

Patti scurried off to the dance floor alone, kicked off her heels and pranced about, half loaded. Her small stocking feet slid across the waxy floor, missing nary a beat. Not a care in the world, Gates thought, but knew differently. The newspaper article had detailed not only her fight, but also her losing streak and recent financial problems.

Stop it, she mentally scolded herself. *Just for tonight refrain from cop mode.*

After the song ended, Patti picked up her shoes and rejoined Gates at the table. She flopped down beside her and planted a friendly kiss on her welcoming lips.

Patti brushed back her bangs. Her almond face glowed. "I'm starving."

"What are you hungry for?"

Patti slipped her hand under the table and rubbed it along Gates' thigh.

"You could help me make weight."

"I bet I could."

Patti withdrew her hand from Gates' leg and stood. "Let's go to my place. I'll fix us some fried bologna sandwiches, just like old times."

"My hotel's closer and they have room service."

Patti smiled mischievously, pulled out her lucky coin and tossed it in the air. "Call it – tits or ass."

"Tits."

Both women watched eagerly as the coin rolled to a stop. Bending down together, Patti squealed first.

"My ass wins."

"Go get your coat, troublemaker. I'll wait for you at the bar."

Patti danced off toward the coatroom. Gates figured she'd grab them both another drink, her kind of meal. She was surprisingly nervous about the upcoming evening. She approached the bar and stood beside a lanky guy wearing a blue sequined suit, nursing his drink. The bartender arrived and took her order.

The guy in the suit wafted cheap aftershave and bushy sideburns in her direction. He adjusted his gold-rimmed sunglasses as though rehearsed and stared at Gates. She quickly recognized him as the Elvis impersonator she'd seen earlier.

"Your girlfriend, she's pretty," he slurred, his breath fumigating the room.

"Sure is," Gates replied. Just another drunk, she figured – a few bourbons shy of lethal.

"She's my wife."

"Not tonight she isn't. Why don't you go get some fresh air?"

The bartender glanced up and stopped pouring. Gates assumed the two knew each other. "Donny – don't start."

"Ask her if you don't believe me."

"That's it," the bartender announced. "Give me your drink!" Donny scooped up his glass and hobbled toward the exit, clutching what remained of his cocktail. The bartender shook his head sadly and let him be.

Gates calmly pulled a twenty from her pocket and threw it down on the bar. She knew Patti had married but assumed she was long since divorced. It's always something.

"Looks like you're earning your money tonight."

"Yep. Reunions pretty well suck."

"He a friend of yours?"

"Was at one time."

"I don't remember him from school." Gates glanced on down the bar.

"Graduated a few years after you guys." Gates picked up the drinks and turned to rejoin Patti.

"If he comes back, keep an eye on him. I don't want that souse following us."

"Will do. He'll be back alright. I've got what he needs most right here." The bartender patted the bottle on the counter.

Gates strolled off toward Patti, who had reentered the room, coat in hand.

"Let's get out of here." Patti smiled as Gates approached.

Gates glanced back over her shoulder toward the bar.

"Something wrong?"

"Nope." Gates snapped out of it. She handed the straight shot toward Patti. "I told the bartender to make it a diet."

* * *

The impressive doors of the historic Palace Theatre opened briskly, spilling the crowd onto Fourth Street. The theatrical performance of *Chicago* had ended its season finale and the audience mingled on the sidewalk discussing the play and offering frivolous goodbyes.

Racing Commissioner Hurt and his wife stepped through the doors. Mrs. Hurt shrugged her fur higher upon her shoulders as her husband wrapped a guiding arm around her and made way through the festive crowd to the valet station. While the couple waited for their car, they chatted with others in line. A familiar man, clutching a rolled up newspaper, strode toward them.

Hurt lowered his arm from around his wife's shoulder. "Hello, Brad."

"Sorry to bother you Commissioner and Mrs. Hurt," Brad Black politely acknowledged the woman while unrolling the newspaper. "I need a word with your husband, ma'am."

Hurt looked at his wife and nodded. "I'll just be a minute, June."

The annoyed Commissioner led Black down the sidewalk to an area where the two could talk privately, away from the thinning crowd. Across the street a waiter cleared tables outside the rustic Ringler's Restaurant. The spicy scent of southern fried chicken lingered like a hazy sunset.

The Commissioner cleared his throat. "OK, what's this about?" he asked impatiently.

Black offered him the newspaper. "Have you seen today's paper?"

The Commissioner passed the newspaper back to Black without even looking at it. "You've disturbed our evening for this?"

"I want Knot suspended."

"That's not going to happen. I reviewed the race tapes and I'm not suspending her."

"Then I'm going to press criminal charges."

"By all means, you have every right. However, I'd think twice about that if I were you."

"Why?"

"Because, rumor has it Knot is going to ride the Derby favorite for the Seemores. And you already know the kind of connections they have."

Black squeezed his fist. His face went crimson for a brief moment and then returned to normal. "I hadn't heard that rumor." He had connections of his own.

"It's never easy to have your pride wounded by a woman. But, I suggest you let it go."

Hurt glanced back toward the street. "My car has arrived."

"Good evening, sir," Black offered, but Hurt was already gone. "Please express my apologies to your wife."

Black waited until the Commissioner and his wife drove away. His smirk hardened. He'd deal with this himself, even if it required a bit of skullduggery.

* * *

Patti heaved a tired sigh and shivered. The air outside the Galt was crisp and the sky clear. Gates glanced up at the stars and pulled Patti's jacket tighter to bar the cold. Leaving the excitement of the dance hall had sullied Patti's mood.

"Twenty years. It's been a long way to the top, hasn't it Patti?"

"It's longer going down...."

Gates put her arm around Patti's shoulder.

"You're pretty edgy," Gates teased. "Something you want to talk about?"

"No." Patti frowned. "It's just been a strange week."

"One that looks like it may just work out pretty well in the end."

Patti smiled as she leaned her blonde head onto Gates' shoulder. Gates felt the warm breath of her sigh and cracked a subtle smile of her own.

She trusted her instincts and didn't pry. If Patti needed to get something off her chest, she would in due time. Actually, it probably wasn't such a hot idea, two women walking the dark streets after midnight, especially after the incident at the bar. Gates reached up and affectionately touched Patti's cold check. "You sure you don't want to take a cab? My hotel is just down the street."

"No. I want you to see my home." Patti sounded sober now. "And my horses, they're my kids. I don't like leaving them alone overnight."

Hell, Gates thought, there was always some impediment to good, clean, remorseless fucking.

Patti grabbed her hand and squeezed. "It's just – well, I've lived most of my life on the road. You can't begin to imagine how many hotel beds I've slept in. Besides, I want this night to be special. Waking up next to you in my own bed would mean more to me than the fanciest suite in the world."

Gates hadn't looked at it that way. She guessed a jockey's life had its ups and downs like everything else. "So where's your Humvee parked?"

Patti laughed. "I'll lead. I'm losing my buzz fast in this cold."

The two women crossed Main Street and eventually stopped in front of a fire-engine red dually with mud streaked quarter panels. Patti reached into her purse and extracted the keys. Gates scooped them up and opened the driver's door.

"You're sure about this?" Patty asked.

"I've gotta a badge." Gates watched her friend climb into the cab. "It's kind of like a get-out-of-jail-free pass. Now scoot that million-dollar ass."

Gates closed the door and stuck the key into the ignition waiting for the indicator light to go out before firing up the big V-8 turbo diesel. Patti told her to head east on Highway 71 and follow the signs toward Lexington. She lived about twenty miles from the city on a ten-acre ranch in the infamous green hills of Kentucky, but the mortgage was killing her. It'd been a tough year on the racing circuit.

Night had become moonless and the stereo droned one lonesome cowboy song after another. Patti leaned her head on Gates' shoulder and detailed the ups and downs of her equestrian life. Even though it was dark, Gates enjoyed the long mellow drive through the countryside. Finally, Patti sat forward and stared out the windshield.

"Turn here."

Gates veered off the main highway and followed Patti's directions. Several miles down she turned onto a gravel drive and paused at a locked gate. Patti gave her the gate code and Gates rolled down the window and entered it on a touch pad. The gate opened. Gates drove through the narrow opening and followed the road for a few hundred yards where it dead-ended at a ranch-style house. Gates parked in front of a double garage and switched off the motor. She couldn't make out everything but there was a nightlight over the door. Adjacent to the house were several outbuildings, a stable, and a fenced-in pasture. Two horses approached the fence when the truck drove in.

Gates climbed down from the cab. Patti slid out and took hold of Gates' hand to lead her toward the fence where her black thoroughbred filly was whinnying. A bay filly with tobiano markings moved forward and nudged her shoulder. Patti put her purse down to remove a couple of apples, and while the horses munched, she gently stroked their forelocks.

"These are my two oldest babies, Starlet and Harlot. Girls, say hello to Dory."

"Do you take care of this place all by yourself?" Dorene realized the question sounded like she was fishing. Maybe she was.

"I manage with some help from Ed, an old friend." Patti grabbed Gates' hand again. "Let's go inside."

Gates turned, noticing a light burning in the barn.

"I keep a light burning in there. You can see it from miles around. I enjoy its inviting glow when I come home."

The bologna sizzled on the grill along with some fried potatoes. The succulent aroma of spiced pork caused Gates' nostrils to flare and transported her to an earlier time. Funny thing, life cycles. Nowadays a good meal was the most satisfying part of her day. Maybe that would change after tonight.

When they had finished their midnight snack, they washed the dishes together, playfully splashing suds and laughing.

Why was a simple chore suddenly so enjoyable?

Later in the bedroom, while Patti checked on the animals, Gates picked up an iron poker and stirred the fire. One of the logs in the hearth smoldered. She crumpled some newsprint and shoved it underneath the log then hunched down and blew on the weak embers. The paper curled, then ignited. The kindled wood took off. A gentle breath had done the trick.

"Having any luck?"

She hadn't heard Patti enter the bedroom, carrying a bottle of whiskey and two glasses. Her hair was still wet from the shower she'd taken after tending the horses. It was pulled back in one long braid down the center of her back and she was barefoot. She wore a silken bathrobe, which stopped seductively shy of her womanhood. Gates, wantonly intrigued, admired her firm legs.

Soft music miraculously spilled out of hidden speakers in the ceiling.

She walked over and handed the bottle to Gates.

"You can have the honor."

Gates twisted the lid, poured both glasses and carefully placed the bottle beside the hearth. Behind her, Patti had pulled the comforter down on the bed. Gates turned to hand Patti her glass and her eyes lit with surprise. Patti had slid the bathrobe off her shoulders. Her exotic skin radiated beauty. Shadows flickered over her tanned breasts like a lush vine of Clematis, zigzagging across the abdomen and down her inner thigh.

"Uhmm…"

A speechless Gates carried the glasses over to the bed, and sat down beside her. Patti held up her glass for a toast. "To reunions." The two clinked glasses and drank. Then, they kissed. The years peeled away as Gates felt herself moisten with excitement. Gates took Patti's glass and set it down on the nightstand with her own. When she turned back around, Patti lay naked against the headboard, her legs agape.

Gates smiled.

Apparently, Patti never trimmed her pubic hair and Gates loved her bushiness. The thick hair briefly reminded her of a horse's mane. How fitting, she thought.

Gates leaned down and combed her fingers through the pubic hair. A hint of moisture glistened beneath.

Gates planted her head between Patti's legs and slowly nibbled. Patti squirmed on the soft sheets like a kitten purring under a soothing caress. Not at all what Gates had expected from the hardcore athlete, but nonetheless a pleasant surprise.

Eventually, Gates sat up, savoring the sweet after taste. Her eyes glowed in the soft light, feverishly hedonistic, her tongue licked the remaining traces of Patti's juice from her lips.

Patti reached up and pinched Gates' erect nipples with both hands while pulling her down. "Come here detective," she cooed.

As Gates' nipple found Patti's lips, the equestrian wrapped her strong thighs around her hips and rode her to the finish like a champion.

7

Vu's fingers silently plucked a mandolin tune on his leg as he cleared his mental bilge and stared out the dark window of his Ford pickup now parked along a deserted street in New Orlean's Ninth District. Katrina's devastation was so enormous he'd felt impotent in its wake. Protecting MaCuddy's Boat Works was something he could do to restore his spiritual balance. Many homes were mounds of debris or open-shelled silhouettes of dreams gone awry. The air belched acrid decay from each pile of rubble. Plants, people, trees, lives, all died here.

The shotgun house had survived, but not without major damage to the exterior walls and roof. Shingles were blown off and a portion of the south wall was caved in. Most of the windows were still boarded over. The house next door and the one next to it were heaps of broken lumber. The streets were pot-holed. Telephone poles were snapped off like twigs. Electricity and water had not been restored to the area. In short, it was uninhabitable. However, this didn't seem to deter the two thieves he had chased the other day at MaCuddy's from camping here. All night he observed other miscreants arrive, stay for a few minutes, then leave. His shadowing of the house had gone on for more than two hours now with no new visitors. His two canine companions sat next to him waiting patiently. Vu picked up a thermos of water, opened the glovebox, and set out a bowl for the dogs.

As he poured, he whispered, "Stay." They eyed the water but didn't move.

"Stay." The dogs remained resolute.

"Drink."

The dogs lunged toward the bowl, one on each side, and lapped up the water until the dish was empty.

"That's good," Vu said quietly as he stroked them and fed them each a treat. The dogs obediently sat back and continued their vigil.

MaCuddy said his dogs, Gimme and Gotcha, were bitches named after his two ex-wives. Unlike his wives though, these dogs were trainable and loyal. Vu was about to test that theory.

"Ladies, it's time."

Vu pocketed a handful of dog biscuits. Next, he removed two military issue wide-spiked dog collars outfitted with special power lights. The lights, placed at intervals to produce a blinding halo when activated, were designed to illuminate and intimidate their prey. Lastly, he grabbed a halogen flashlight for himself and strapped a 9 mm around his ankle.

Vu checked his watch. It was 0300. He climbed out of the cab and signaled the dogs to follow.

Vu had worked with canines when he first enlisted and felt a special connection with them because they were mostly rescued dogs which had survived by their wits. Kindred spirits with Vu. Unfortunately, that dream died when he failed his physical field test. He couldn't pick up his eighty pound German shepherd and boost it over a six-foot fence. His will to succeed was trumped by his slight build and short height. He had to accept that this was not his path and move on to other pursuits.

At the front of the house Vu motioned for the dogs to stop. He pressed his ear against the front door and listened. No sound from inside. Passed out or sleeping, he thought, either was fine.

He stepped back, flipped on the collar lights, and examined his work. Gimme and Gotcha had enormous heads, razor teeth, and evil eyes, all succinctly captured in rings of blinding light. Their image was perfect.

The front door was locked. Vu pounded on it until someone inside roused. He heard footsteps approaching the door. Then, a man's drugged voice shouted, "Go away!"

Vu pounded on the door again. The dogs perked their ears and waited.

"I said – get the hell out of here!"

"Open the door."

"What do you want?"

"What do you think?"

There was a pause. "Buying or selling?"

"Buying."

Vu heard a deadbolt slide and the door jerked opened. Standing in sweatpants and shirtless was one of the two men he had chased at the boatyard. The balding man held a dim flashlight. The harsher light from the intruders blinded him. He blocked the light with his skinny hand. Vu studied his gaunt face. His eyes were bloodshot and he had a cut on the bridge of his nose. He squinted down at the dogs.

"Jesus-H-Christ!" the man shrieked, stumbling back against the wall. Vu pushed the door open and signaled the dogs inside.

"Keep those fuckers away from me…" the guy uttered, pressing further against the wall. Vu snapped his fingers once. Gimme and Gotcha locked onto the man's ankles with their teeth but didn't break skin. The man screamed in terror.

"Where's your pal?"

"In back," the man stuttered.

Vu snapped his fingers twice and Gotcha released her hold. Vu looked the man in the eye and pointed at him. "Don't move."

The man nodded. Vu shined his flashlight down the narrow hallway. He moved through a small living area with a broken sofa and torn easy-chair with the foot rest extended. Boxes marked

"FEMA Relief" were scattered about filled with TV's, CD players, DVD's, clothing and tools. At the back of the room a police-issued motorcycle leaned against a collapsed section of the wall. The wooden floors were tilted and warped.

The bathroom was next on the right with its yellowing tile floor, crusty sink and decrepit toilet. A substitute five-gallon bucket sat on the floor. The bedroom was at the far end of the hall. From the open door, Vu heard snoring.

Lying under a stained sheet was the second man he had chased. Overturned beer bottles littered the floor and an ashtray filled with butts rested on the nightstand. A .38 sat on the small dresser across the room which Vu pocketed.

Vu snapped his fingers. Gotcha leapt onto the sleeping man's chest and growled. The man popped open his eyes and hastily shut them again, unable to see through the blinding light.

"Help!!!"

"Open your eyes!" Vu ordered, staring down at the man.

"I can't. The light…"

"Open them."

Reluctantly, the man did as he was instructed. Gotcha drooled on his chest, lips curled, fangs exposed. The wimp wet the bed.

Vu motioned to him. "Get up! Your buddy's waiting."

The man rose, quivering. Gotcha headbutted his leg to spur him in the right direction.

Yelping from the contact, he moved back up the hallway where Gimme maintained a sentry's hold on her prize. She squealed gutturally with excitement.

"Gimme. Release," Vu commanded. He tossed a treat to her. "Good job."

Vu had both men kneel on the floor so they were eye level with their canine guards. Fearing the worst, both had shut their eyes.

"I'm only going to tell you this once," Vu said. "I know who you are, where you live, what you drive and what you do for money. If you ever step foot in MaCuddy's boat yard again, I will have these dogs chew off your hands. Find another place to do business or I'll be back. Tell your friends. If anything happens to these dogs, I will find you and kill you. Understood?"

Both men, eyes squeezed tight, jerked their heads up and down.

"Good," Vu said. "Now before I leave, I have one other question." Vu tapped them with his gun barrel. "Open your eyes."

The men stared mutely at Vu.

"Which one of you cut MaCuddy?"

The two men looked at each other and remained silent.

"I'm asking one more time. Who hurt MaCuddy?"

When neither confessed, Vu glanced at the dogs. He snapped his fingers three times. Gimme jumped and locked his teeth on the first man's arm. Blood spurted out. Gotcha latched onto the second man. The animals tore the skin but stopped shy of snapping bones. The men yelled, wriggling in pain.

Vu snapped his fingers twice and the dog's maws released. "Good girls." Vu tossed them each a treat.

The men continued writhing on the floor. "You come around MaCuddy's again, and next time, I won't call them off."

Vu backed toward the door and motioned for the dogs to follow. Once outside, Vu killed the lights, leaving the area in total darkness.

They jumped back into the cab of the truck and drove away. Vu turned affectionately to the dogs. "Ladies, there's someone else I can't wait for you to meet."

8

Pain knifed into Gates' eyes as bright sunlight painted an arrow along the wall of Patti Knot's bedroom. She awoke, startled by the unfamiliar surroundings and a loud ringing. Gates rolled over, grabbed her cell phone off the nightstand, and sat up. Her head throbbed.

"This better be good!"

A male voice said, "Morning sunshine."

"Who the hell is this?"

Gates stared at the empty sheet beside her, waiting for the caller to respond. The spot where Patti had fingered her to sleep last night was empty. She smelled her musky fingers. Patti's sex was all over them. This calmed her.

"It's Hill."

"What do you want?"

"That's no way to talk to your partner."

"Hang on."

Gates put the phone down, stood up and stretched. She pulled open the bedroom door and peered into the living room. A note and a thermos of coffee sat on the kitchen counter. She retrieved them and returned to the bedroom. She put the receiver to her ear while studying the handwritten note.

Clearing the frog from her throat, she said, "What's so important that it can't wait 'til tomorrow?"

"Sampson wants to confess – he won't do it to anyone but you. Gentry's pulling out all the stops on this one. There's a flight out of Louisville at 1:25. It'll get you here by 5 at the latest."

"I'm already on the 7:30 this evening."

"That flight puts you in traffic well after midnight. Gentry thinks it'll be too late. By then, Sampson may change his mind."

"If he wasn't sucking so much cock for the mayor's job, this could wait."

"Look, I'll pick you up at the airport," Hill said.

She snapped her cell closed and fell back on the bed, pulling the covers over her head to block out the harsh sunlight.

Why did she have to leave so soon?

Angrily, she kicked the covers onto the floor, sat up and read the poetic note again. The pillow Patti had used lie next to her. She pressed it to her face, inhaling the spicy scent still lingering in the satin case.

Goddamn that girl was fine.

Knowing she had to bail on this new romance hurt.

Gates poured herself another shot of coffee and drank it. Then, she scooped her clothing off the floor, including her badge, watch and loose change from the nightstand and clambered into the bathroom. She turned on the shower and climbed in. The steaming water soothed her tense muscles, yet her fist slammed against the wall in frustration, cursing lousy timing. And, she wondered what a few more hours with Patti might do for her. Standing alone in the shower, she felt sullen, the enveloping waters exacerbating her loneliness.

After the shower, she dressed and donned makeup, something Gates rarely did. Staring against her reflection, she began to rationalize herself back together. There were plenty of weekends ahead. Twenty years on the force and nothing to keep her in New Orleans, her mind raced to work it all out. Slowly, she recovered her tough outer-shell. She found Patti inside one of the stables, mucking a stall.

Gates stood back from the stable door and quietly watched Patti pitch a load of tainted straw into a wheelbarrow. Her arms rippled from the morning workout. Patti stopped to catch her breath and re-tied the strap around her bibs now smeared with damp hay. She kicked a clump of manure from her rubber boots, then glanced up to greet Gates with a warm smile.

"Good morning, sleepy head!" Patti said.

"You're at it early." Gates leaned over the fence and kissed Patti's lips. "Want some help?" Gates stepped back and watched Patti effortlessly heft a bale of hay.

"In a minute."

"I've got to head back to New Orleans this afternoon."

Patti silently re-filled a feed trough with grain and sat the heavy bag down by her feet. "I guess I knew that was coming." She moved across the stall over near the water trough toward a dense rectangular salt block. The hay it was resting on was caked with meldew.

"Grab that."

Patti pointed toward a pitchfork resting against the wall. Gates picked up the pitchfork and joined her inside the stall.

"Looks heavy. What is it?"

"Salt."

"This is easier with two."

As instructed, Gates steadied the pitchfork while Patti shoved the fifty-pound salt block out of the way with her boot. Gates scooped out the damp straw from beneath it and tossed the pile into the wheelbarrow.

"Now see the bale to your right? Break off a big hunk of it and spread it down by my feet."

Gates dumped the pitchfork against the wall and broke off a bristly flake of straw to scatter around where Patti had indicated. Patti jimmied the salt block into place with her foot.

Gates glanced at her hands. "I see why you wear gloves," she said, picking a few slivers out.

Patti swiped her wrist over her sweaty brow, then brushed salt from her boots. "I wish you could stay," she said, sadly, then removed her leather gloves and slung them over the stable door.

Gates walked over and started to hug the small woman, but Patti put her hand up. Gates waited while Patti untied her bibs and hung them. "I really had a terrific time last night."

Patti turned back around and hugged her. "I can't allow you to go just yet."

Patti unbuttoned her jeans, took hold of Gates' hand, and eased it down inside her warm panties. Gates ran her fingers through the mane of pubic hair and massaged the warm mounds of flesh, passionately kissing her. She stared into Patti's eyes. Sadness resided there that she hadn't noticed before.

"After we make love, I'll clean up and take you to the airport."

"I've already called a cab."

Patti sighed, turned around and spotted a pair of grooming shears resting on the fence. Smiling, she quickly retrieved the shears and dashed back over to Gates, handing them to her. Gates grabbed the implement, confused by its sudden purpose of Patti's design. Patti stepped closer pulling her jeans down around her ankles, her panties followed. Her lush bush glistened.

Patti fluffed herself. "I want you to have something, a token to remember me by."

Gates was fascinated by this deviant mindplay. She'd never taken a trophy before, though she'd seen plenty – usually cached by serial killers. She pushed the dark thought aside.

The shears nudged Patti's thigh, which shuddered in response to the cold steel.

"This might pinch a little."

Patti held her breath as Gates tenderly lowered the blades. With one innocuous snip, a tuft of hair spilled onto her eager palm. She held it to her nose, smelling its spicy fragrance. Patti glanced down at herself and pulled up her jeans, smiling.

Gates stared at the clump of hair. Then, she heard the cabbie's horn and frowned.

Patti removed a turquoise handkerchief from her pocket and handed it to Gates, who carefully wrapped her little memento. With so much still unsaid between them, Gates placed the hanky in her pocket. The horn impatiently honked again.

"I gotta go."

"I know. Just promise to come back before our 50th."

9

For the first time in months, Vu and his girlfriend, Betty, shared the privacy of the Arctic Wing's V-berth. It wasn't quite the scene Vu had imagined. Instead of clean silk sheets, they were encased in mud and mildew. Betty's sandals were piled in the corner beside her shirt and shorts. She'd stripped down earlier because she'd gotten too hot mucking the river rot out of the cabin. Vu wore a white T-shirt streaked with grease and a pair of knee-length shorts, the pockets of which were stuffed with various tools. He groaned as he leaned into his screwdriver. The rusted screw broke free and Vu fell back on his heels to rest. Betty continued scrubbing the cabin's teak floor on her hands and knees. He loved Betty's legs. Despite the scuffs on her knees and the streaks of mud that now ran down them like wet paint, they were intoxicating. Long, white, smooth with the fragrance of white ginger, Betty's favorite. Her pampered feet were soft, her toes polished and adorned with several rings. They welcomed Vu as none before.

"Jack that's not my best angle." Betty sat back, dropped her sponge into a bucket of bleach water and removed a rubber glove to pick dried dirt from her pink toe nails. Vu scrutinized her feet.

"Jack, you're getting that look again."

That look, as she put it, meant Vu's mind was somewhere else. Some images connect an individual to others and Vu was having such a moment. Buddhists had a word for it, so did the Vietnamese – in essence, it meant '*seeing*' or '*thay*'. Translated, one's karmic path was connected to all things.

Vu cleared his throat and snatched her foot for a closer look. "It's your toe nails that trouble me."

"That's a relief. It's my ass that troubles me," Betty giggled. She turned over and sat on her foot still in Vu's grip.

"Your feet remind me of someone." Vu closed his eyes and tried to focus. "She had this same color of nail polish."

"Who?"

"I don't know."

"Does she scrub floors too?"

The corner of Vu's mouth pulled into a crooked smile. "Probably not."

"I didn't think so."

"Well, if you could stop envisioning other women for a minute, I could use some help moving furniture. I've got ninety-nine percent of the dirt up. What remains between the slats will just have to stay."

Vu's focus returned. They were almost done. Tonight they could settle in for their first full night together since the storm.

Vu pulled Betty to his chest, wrapped his arms around her back and kissed her, just as his cell phone vibrated between them.

An hour later, Vu rode into a deserted parking lot on the NAS Joint Naval Base and heaved his Vespa onto its kickstand. He was a member of a special investigative unit recently headed by Air Force Major Steven Mitts. This would be the first time Vu had met alone with his new commander and he was apprehensive. Good impressions were hard to make without time to shower, and Vu's wrinkled Battle Dress Uniform (BDU's) didn't help his cause. He merely hoped this Major could overlook disheveled appearances.

Vu entered a nondescript gray building and caught a whiff

of cologne. Across the office he was surprised to see the callow Sgt. Reardon sitting in his small cubicle, wearing a freshly pressed uniform, pecking out a report on his computer keyboard. Reardon looked up briefly and removed his headset.

"Major's waiting for you in his office."

Mitts' office was at the end of the hall. His door was closed but Vu could hear movement inside.

A shiny pair of regulation issue work boots, identical to Vu's, sat outside the door. As he raised his hand to knock, he closed his eyes and slowly inhaled. When he reopened them, he heard a firm, "Come in."

The Major was seated behind a large desk staring into a laptop. The room was covered with files and unopened boxes. Apparently, he was still settling in.

"Sit down, Jack," the Major said. "I'll be right with you."

Vu took a seat and idly glanced about the room, an attempt to control his nerves. As the Major scribbled notes on a yellow legal pad, Vu's eyes suddenly transfixed on a small picture frame sitting on the Major's desk. The photograph was of an army platoon outside a village near Da Nang. A smiling, and much younger, "Private Mitts" proudly held the decapitated head of a grinning Vietcong. The image jolted Vu.

Would it be easier to view if he was the soldier and Mitts the head?

He forced his mind back to the Major's voice. "I can imagine that's a disturbing photo for you," he said, then cleared his throat. "Hard to deny your past if you face it every day."

Was Mitts proud or regretful when confronted with the photo? His strong jaw and forceful eyes revealed nothing.

The awkward disclosure caused Vu to shift uneasily in his chair. The Major closed his laptop and reached across his desk to hand Vu a manila file, which conveniently changed the subject.

"Your previous commander briefed me on few things and said you would remember a young recruit from the Academy named Beverly Dee Sanders. I believe she went by Bevy. She submitted a resume and he contacted her. I also understand you sat in on her interview."

"Didn't she end up accepting a position with security forces, sir?"

"Yes, that's correct. This office had a policy which precluded hiring applicants under the age of twenty-five. As it turns out, an old colleague of mine from West Point knew her and put in a good word with your former commander, but to no avail. Well, this morning I received some disheartening news. Two days ago Lieutenant Sanders' body washed up on a riverbank in Louisville. She was in uniform so the local authorities contacted us. They were able to obtain her dental records and made a preliminary ID. Normally, we'd let the locals handle this since she's only been with NAS a short time. But, I promised my friend we'd look into it."

"How are the local authorities treating it?"

The Major frowned. "There was no obvious evidence of foul play, so they're treating it as an accidental drowning, perhaps suicide."

"Who found the body?"

"Anonymous caller phoned it in. All we know for certain is that her body washed up on the Ohio."

Vu pulled a small green notepad from his pocket and jotted.

"I contacted her supervisor from the 159th," the Major continued. "His name's Captain Freeman. He arranged for a few days leave last week for her to attend a friend's wedding in Kentucky. He also said she was in good spirits when she left. I pulled her file – smart kid. Graduated top of her class and earned her bars upon graduation. Her application listed a home of record as Lexington, Kentucky. Evidently, her parents were in the horse racing business. Look over her file. She's listed a few references that might come in handy. I haven't shared this with the local authorities just yet. Figure we'll wait and see what they turn up. I got to say, Jack, accidental drowning seems a little suspicious. She was invited to the Olympic Training Center for swimming her senior year."

Vu studied the file. "Was she on any medications, sir?"

"I requested her medical file this morning. According to it, she had a prescription for Ortho Tri-cyclen Lo, a common birth control pill. That's all. You'll get the toxicology report from their pathologist."

Vu stared into the dead woman's face, nearly young enough to be his daughter. "And the parents ... they've been contacted?"

"Her parents died the year she entered the Academy. As far as we can tell, she's got no immediate family."

Just like me. If I had washed up after Katrina, would anyone have known to call Betty?

Vu paused. "She's on birth control. Any boyfriend?"

"Negative," the Major answered. "Freeman spoke with several of her co-workers. She dated once or twice, but there's no one special."

Vu made a note, then noticed his hand was abnormally perspiring. "Has anyone visited her quarters?"

"Freeman checked her room. He found nothing useful, but follow up on it. We're getting most of our information secondhand. The detective in charge of the case in Louisville is Sam Buck. He's ex-military."

"Will I oversee transportation of the body?" Vu asked.

"That'll be up to the local authorities."

"I see, sir. Anything else?"

"Look over the file. You'll ship out tomorrow morning. Sergeant Reardon is handling your reservations and has a copy of your orders."

"Yes, sir."

"You'll have full support on this end, but I want your inquiries discreet." Mitts leaned forward in his chair. "I've read your file Vu, and I know about your impressive success rate. However, your methods attract unwanted attention. I want this one done by the book. Is that clear?"

10

Donny Mason lived in a singlewide mobile home on the outskirts of Louisville. The trailer had belonged to his mother who died several years back from a heart attack. Death had also claimed Donny's father, Jim Mason, a long-haul trucker and horse trainer from Idaho who left him nothing but a shed full of empty beer cans, a broken weed-eater, and a love of NASCAR.

Half of the exterior of Donny's trailer was painted turquoise – a project he had tackled one day after purchasing a half-case of beer and a carton of discount spray cans from the local hardware store during its annual going out of business sale. As both supplies dwindled, so did Donny's enthusiasm, resulting in the trailer's current patchwork artistry. The other residents tolerated most of Donny's habits, including his erratic driving. About once a week they would find his 1970 Cadillac parked in someone's front yard or nose first in a ditch. Donny, when he wasn't drinking, was a decent guy. He mowed lawns for the elderly and helped them with chores as best he could. Actually, most folks felt sorry for him. Donny could've become a professional NASCAR driver, had it not been for a beating which prematurely ended his career. Southerners love a good tragedy, and Donny's demise was sadder than most. As consolation, he developed another talent close to Southern hearts. He dressed, and sang, like Elvis.

Donny hunched shirtless at his kitchen table in a pair of stained grey skivvies, nursing a throbbing headache with a mix of instant coffee and cheap bourbon. He wore a pair of black socks. His feet stunk and he needed a shave. His pompadour stood erect like an upended surfboard. His skin was pale and pockmarks speckled his boney chest. Between his elbows, on the Formica table, lay Patti Knot's picture on the Sports page of a two-day old newspaper. Donny rubbed his swollen eyes and stared down at her, grinding his jaws in methodic bovine fashion.

He carefully tore the picture out, walked over and pinned it up with all the others wallpapering his kitchen. Then, he opened the refrigerator and fished among the half-empty bottles of ketchup, mustard, Spam, and sour milk until he found a carton of Minute Maid. He tipped it nearly upside down and sucked the last of the orange juice dregs. When finished, he tossed the empty carton into the sink, lit a cigarette, and resumed the warm roost at the kitchen table.

A few moments later, there was loud banging on his back door.

"Donny!" a male shouted. "Donny – I know you're in there. Open up, damnit! I need you to move your car!"

Donny winced as he pushed himself up, crept over to the door and opened it. The voice belonged to a barrel-chested man in his late fifties with graying hair around the temples.

"Hey George."

George had seen it all before. "You drinking already?"

"I was at a reunion last night."

"Well, you tore out half my gardenias again."

Donny craned around to survey his neighbor's yard. Sure enough, his black Cadillac was parked in the flowerbed.

"Sorry, George." Donny rubbed his whiskers. "I'll take care of it."

"It's the second time this month."

"Let me go find my keys," Donny said, lowering his eyes. He wandered back into the trailer, but when he returned, George was gone.

Donny trudged across the yard swinging his arms from side to side to coax his circulation. He climbed inside his car, started the motor and backed slowly over the curb into his own driveway. Then, he walked over and half-heartedly propped up George's damaged flowers. Several were flattened beyond repair. Donny retreated back inside his house to take a shower. The hot water heater was on the blink and nothing but cold water came out of the tap. Donny shivered, but the icy water sobered him up enough to jump-start a few brain cells and he got an idea.

After searching through the clutter of his closet, he found a clean pair of black trousers and a white shirt. He combed his hair back, doused it with hair spray to hold it in place, donned his best dress shoes and then checked his wallet. There was just enough cash for a bouquet, and a beer if things didn't go well.

Remarkably, the caddy ran fine. It had a few new dents, but nothing his "someday money" couldn't fix. He headed downtown and eventually parked at Ruth B's Florist and went inside. Ruth B was stuffing a bouquet of carnations in a crystal vase at the front counter. She looked up when she heard the bell.

"Well look what the cat drug in," Ruth B said, curling her lips in a smile. "Donny Mason, you're dressed like you just come from church. I know that ain't possible seeings I heard you roar by my place about three a.m. last night."

"Sorry, Ruthy."

"Oh, you didn't wake me," Ruth B said. "I can't sleep lately."

"Me neither."

Ruth B nodded. "So, you come to borrow some money?"

"No." Donny pulled out his wallet and dropped a ten-dollar bill on the counter. "I'll take whatever that'll get."

Surprised, Ruth B stared at the soiled sawbuck. "You want flowers?"

Donny stared at the carnations in her hand. "Something like those will do," he said. "But put some other stuff in with it. Maybe some irises or tulips or a few roses, if you have 'em."

"I'll put something nice together. Just give me a few minutes."

Ruth B carried the vase of carnations across the room, humming as she went. "What color roses you want?"

"Yellow."

"Fresh out, honey. I think I have some pink ones left."

Ruth B disappeared inside the cooler. Donny stood at the card stand and read a few greeting cards, but nothing sounded right. He chose a blank card with a horse on the front, laid it on the counter, and began to scribble. A few minutes later, Ruth B reappeared holding a large colorful bouquet. She walked over and handed it across the counter. Donny smiled. Her expert choice of flowers pleased him.

"Get these in water real soon"

Donny nodded. "Thanks Ruthy."

Ruth B rang the sale up on the register. Donny stuck the card into his jacket pocket and stepped back from the counter.

Ruth B smiled. "Hope she likes them."

* * *

Later that day Ed's dusty GMC pickup pulled up to Patti Knot's stables and parked. A big fellow in work clothes, he climbed out and closed the driver-side door. He ran his hand through his graying hair and put on his cowboy hat snugging the brim. Ed limped over to the fence, greeted Knot's two fillies, then walked down to the house and rang the bell. After no response, he checked the corral. Patti's favorite horse trotted in the corral near the edge of the pasture. He figured Patti must be inside the stables because she was not the kind of hand to leave the frisky colt unattended.

"Patti?"

Ed noticed the tack room door was ajar. A wheelbarrow sat

outside partially filled with muddy straw. Beside it was an uncoiled garden hose.

Ed inspected the stalls first. They appeared recently cleaned. There were two more down on the end where Patti preferred to keep her own horses. The other two were usually rented this time of year. But, times were tough. Just last week, Patti had asked if he knew anyone interested in boarding a horse, which explained the sparse bedding. He knew money was tight.

After peeking inside the tack room and not finding her, he headed toward the last stall on the end. The door was unlocked. As he got closer, he swatted at a few buzzing flies.

"Patti? You in there?"

Someone had dropped a bouquet of fresh flowers outside the stall. As he stooped to pick them up, something else caught his attention.

Panic-stricken, Ed yanked open the door. A few feet away, lying face up on a bed of fresh hay was Patti's body – her head turned toward him, her mouth agape, her purple tongue distended. A leather harness strap cut into her throat. Blood soaked through her shirt where a pitchfork pierced her chest. Her pale hair was soaked crimson and crawling with flies. A torn feed sack lay on its side next to her, spilling grain onto the ground.

Ed recoiled, a crushing pain gripping his chest. He had trouble breathing as if his heart muscle had seized. Beyond the stable walls, he heard one of fillies whinny in the pasture. He swallowed hard and stared at the body again. He knew he shouldn't touch her, but he couldn't bear for anyone else to see her like this. He swung his big arms over her body, setting the flies in motion.

11

United Flight 1013 out of Louisville was delayed. The cheerful clerk at the gate terminal told Gates it had something to do with a flight out of New York.

Gates felt herself begin to seethe. "What about other flights?"

"Let me check."

The clerk punched the keyboard, staring at the screen. "Don't see anything, ma'am. Sorry."

Disgusted, Gates returned to the crowded bar and found a seat in the corner. She ordered a Maker's Mark and waited for the waitress to return. If the flight didn't arrive soon, she would get shit-faced.

The waitress delivered Gates' drink and moved on to other customers. When Gates eventually got around to paying the tab, she reached into her pocket to pull out some cash and instead discovered Patti's handkerchief. The feel of the soft material and the image of wrapping her arms around her little jockey, diving inside those delicate panties, brightened her mood. Picking through the loose change in her pocket, she smiled at the sight of Patti's lucky coin beckoning her. She must have accidentally scooped it up when she grabbed her stuff from the nightstand.

A few more stragglers approached the bar. The TV was broadcasting an NBA game. Gates stared at the screen without much interest and checked her watch. She finished her drink and ordered a double. Half-way through her second cocktail, the noise in the bar escalated.

A local news broadcast had interrupted the game and the bar heckled the TV announcer in response. Gates stared at the screen, mouth agape, and dropped her glass. The crawl read: *"Famous Jockey Found Murdered."* She forced her way to the bar.

"Shut the hell up!"

Gates couldn't hear the broadcast over the crowd, shouting in frustration that their precious game had been interrupted.

"Go to hell…" A drunken businessman nearest the TV had one thing on his mind. Basketball. Who gave a shit about horseracing? Gates strained to hear the rest of the broadcast, pushing her way between the drunkard and the TV.

"Local celebrity Patti Knot – two-time world champion Kentucky Derby Winner, and a major contender in this year's derby, has been found dead…"

The drunkard interrupted again. "Bartender – give me the remote."

"Don't touch it," Gates snapped, slamming her arm down over the man's outstretched hand. *"Ms. Knot's body was discovered earlier today. Police are still investigating – an apparent victim of a brutal attack. More to come on tonight's 5 o'clock news…"*

"Hey, lady. Move back."

Gates ignored the comment and shoved him back. Her legs spasmed and a searing pain gripped her loins.

The drunkard scooted his chair forward. Under his breath he mumbled for only Gates to hear, "Shut your bitch box."

"What'd you say to me?"

Emboldened, the man grinned and leaned his bulbous nose into her face. "I said sit down and shut up, you crazy bitch."

Gates heard screaming and realized it was her own as she planted a fist squarely into the man's face. Blood shot from his nose like a fountain and he reeled to the floor. When he started to rise, Gates lost all control and kicked him in the rib cage several times. The bartender and another patron finally pulled her off.

"Easy lady," the patron said firmly. "You'll kill the guy."

The drunk lay sprawled on the floor clutching his bloody face and panting like a Pekinese. His glassy eyes gazed up, but couldn't focus. Punch-drunk, he staggered to his feet, still leery of his opponent.

"Fucking bitch," he muttered, spraying blood as he spoke.

Gates struggled to break free, ready to strike again when the port authorities scrambled into the bar, walkie talkies pulled, mace drawn, prepared for anything.

When Gates reached into her pocket for her shield, they slammed her against the bar and wrenched her arms behind her back, emptying the contents onto the floor.

"It's my fault she's dead," Gates gasped, as she fixated on Patti's lucky coin.

* * *

The following morning, a late passenger for New Orleans Flight 1191, a non-stop to Louisville, Kentucky, arrived just as the door was closing and hurried down the aisle toward the back of the aircraft. He stopped at a row where the middle seat was vacant. "Excuse me," he said, looking down at the small Asian man occupying the aisle seat. Jack Vu lowered his newspaper.

"Jack!"

Vu smiled up at the large man. The last time he'd seen Detective Bruce Hill from the New Orleans Police Department was on the Margolis case months earlier.

"Hello, Sergeant," Vu said cheerfully. "This is a surprise."

A heavy-set woman in her late fifties occupying the window seat looked up.

"Oh, man, Vu – You're not going to believe it – Gates is in jail up in Louisville."

"How unfortunate."

The lack of sincerity in Vu's voice was obvious. He had butted heads with Gates on several cases and the two clearly didn't get along.

"Hey, Jack – how 'bout scooting over. The middle seat is a little tight for me."

Vu shook his head. "I prefer the aisle."

"C'mon, Jack."

When it was clear he was glued to the aisle, Hill squeezed past and wedged himself into the dreaded middle. The heavy-set woman sighed and shifted closer to the window.

Hill fumbled with his seatbelt and his broad shoulders unintentionally collided with both passengers.

"Jack – trade me places – I'm dying here. My legs are crammed to my chin. C'mon." Hill punched Vu in the arm.

Hill stared at the Asian, but Vu avoided eye contact. The woman in the window seat cringed.

Ignored, Hill slumped back, removed a magazine from the seat pouch, and flipped pages. Perspiration beaded on his forehead. He loosened his collar, then played with the overhead vent. Yes, Vu thought, Hill wouldn't last five minutes in confinement. It would only be a matter of time.

Hill cleared his throat. "I gotta use the head."

Vu allowed him by and while Hill was gone, he quietly slid to the middle seat and fastened the seatbelt. The passenger beside him, put down an *Inflight* magazine and glared at Vu, then pushed the attendant button.

The attendant and Hill arrived simultaneously. Hill flopped down in the aisle seat and smiled at Vu.

"Thanks, Jack. You're a sweetheart."

The attendant waited for Hill to settle in, then reached over and turned off the call light. "Is everything all right?"

The trapped woman answered. "Miss, I'd like another seat."

"Is there a problem?"

"These men are having a disagreement and I don't want to

catch a flying punch."

"He only hit me once," Vu said helpfully.

"Lovers' quarrel." Hill winked at the two women.

The attendant sized up the unlikely pair and accommodated. "Follow me, ma'am."

After the women left, Vu moved to the window seat. Hill wore a smug expression.

"So you're heading to Louisville?"

"Yes."

"What's cookin'? Terrorists threatening to blow up Churchill Downs?"

"A homicide investigation. A young female recruit."

Vu crossed his arms and stared complacently out the window. The plane began its slow bumpy ride across the tarmac. He stowed his paper and closed his eyes, drifting. What were the odds he and Hill would be traveling side-by-side to the same town?

"So, what has Gates done this time?"

"I don't have all the details. She sort of lost it at the airport and broke a guy's nose."

"And you're going to Louisville to bail her out of jail?"

"It's more complicated than that. She says a female friend of hers was found murdered. Some jockey. I'm gonna grease the wheels with the local cops and see what I can learn."

Traveling with Hill to a distant town to investigate separate homicides, Vu smiled at the coincidental thought. He of all people knew there were no coincidences and began to wonder how the two cases might be related.

An hour later, their plane touched down on a cold, dry runway. Vu awoke and gazed out the window at the Louisville terminal.

Hill sat up and stretched his cramped muscles. "Where you staying, Jack?"

"At the Galt."

Hill scratched his nose. "No shit? Me, too."

The terminal was crowded with arriving flights. Outdoors, near the taxi stand, Vu noticed several large groups loading musical instruments into the back of passenger vans. Even more musicians exited the doors causing Hill to inquiry the attendant.

"What's with all the musicians?"

"International Bluegrass Festival at the Galt. Be a few hundred musicians playing there all week."

Vu perked up. "That's where we're staying. Is it open to the public?"

"I heard the awards ceremony is sold out. That's tonight at the Kennedy Center. I'm not sure about the music events. You might check with the hotel."

Hill kicked his bag to the curb and watched traffic go by while Vu walked over to a box, bought a local newspaper, and resumed his place in line.

Across the street, string music spilled from a multi-level parking structure. On the third tier several banjo players sat on the railing and plucked. Vu idly tapped his feet to the beat.

Hill shook his head. "Why Jack, you ol' Salty Dog," he said smiling. "I didn't know you were a bluegrass fan."

"I first heard Bill Monroe in Vietnam," he explained. "An American GI left me his record collection when he shipped out. I listened to blues, bluegrass, jazz and rock."

"Hell, I was raised a skillet licker," Hill exclaimed. "Blue Sky Boys, Uncle Dave's Fruit Jar Drinkers, Texas Playboys, Snuffy Jenkins, Foggy Mountain Boys – not to mention God himself, Ralph Stanley. My dad used to pass moonshine with neighbors and pluck 'til dawn."

The memory of it brought a smile to Hill's face. He pulled out a cigarette and packed it down.

"When I was thirteen," Hill continued, "I borrowed my Uncle Earl's five string. Tried to teach myself to play, but I didn't have the ear. One day after school, I fed it into a wood chipper. Best thing that ever could a happened. You play?"

"I play the mandolin," Vu said. "But I'm still learning."

"So you're a fan? Who would've known?"

The attendant flagged a taxi to the curb. Hill stomped out his cigarette, picked up his suitcase and followed Vu toward the cab. The two climbed in.

Vu glanced around for a seatbelt. "What'd your uncle do when you told him you'd destroyed his banjo?"

"He beat the hell out of me," Hill said flatly and then directed the driver. Vu buckled up and stared at the driver in the rearview mirror. His dark face resembled a lion's – large nose, hairy ears, bushy mustache, one that curled down past his lips when he spoke.

The cab sped out of the airport. "You say the Galt?"

Hill nodded, and slapped Vu's leg. "Damn good to see you again, Jack."

Vu made no reply, just smiled. "You say it's about a twenty-minute ride?" he asked the driver.

The driver nodded. "How 'bout the radio?"

"Sure," Hill said. "Find us some music."

"How long you staying in Louisville?"

"We're not sure," Vu replied, then changed the subject. "Along the way, will we be passing the downtown police precinct?"

"Yeah, it's on Jefferson. I'll point it out, even give you a mini-tour on the way to the hotel."

Before long, the cab entered the heart of downtown Louisville. The expansive Galt Hotel and its twin towers beckoned at the end of Fourth Street. The Ohio River shone in the background.

"That's the downtown police station there," the cabdriver pointed to a monstrous concrete building out his left window.

Both Vu and Hill glanced out the window. As the cab crawled along, pedestrians meandered out of shops, filling the sidewalks along Muhammad Ali Boulevard. The driver pointed out other local landmarks.

"At night these streets are lit up in glorious neon. If you look up, you'll see a memorial to Muhammad Ali. He's one of my favorites because he fought his way to the top of the white man's world."

Vu suspected not everyone around here felt that way. "Raising up the blacks" was not something average Southern politicians cottoned to. He imagined the political fight that must have taken place over putting these "colored folk" on public display.

"The downtown core has stayed intact," the driver continued, "Over there, the towering spear-like spire of ornate stone, is the Cathedral of the Assumption, built over one-hundred-fifty years ago. Up ahead is the 20-story Kentucky Home Life Building, a prestigious address in the heart of the financial district. My brother-in-law worked there as a custodian. Most of the cast-iron storefronts along Main Street, and the old tobacco warehouses on Market, are being preserved."

Up ahead, Vu noticed a newer glass monstrosity.

"What's that?"

"Fourth Street Live. Basically, two blocks of high-priced chain restaurants, a bowling alley, and an outdoor stage for live music."

Hill added, "I bet the City Council liked the new construction."

"Yeah, but for some of the older shop owners, it's been nothin' but headaches. If we could just figure out what to do about them addicts and thieves causing trouble on the streets now, things in this town would be pretty nice."

Vu jotted a few notes, as the cab pulled up in front of the hotel. A uniformed attendant hustled out to catch the door and the men climbed out. After spending the last few months in a military barrack, Vu was looking forward to a room with some privacy.

Hill slapped Vu's shoulder and flipped a coin to see who would pay the fare. Vu won. Smiling, he turned and stared at the river flowing past the hotel.

In the distance, Vu could see a few people checking out an old steamship. "That a big attraction?"

The attendant shielded his eyes from the sun. "The Belle of Louisville. She's been paddling tourists up and down the Ohio for nearly a century. If you get a chance, you might try the dinner cruise. Gives you a real feel for old Kentucky."

Hill paid the driver while the young porter retrieved the

luggage from the trunk. Vu insisted on carrying his own bag. Reluctantly, the attendant surrendered the suitcase. Hill stuffed his wallet back into his pocket, left his bag in the porter's capable hands and followed Vu toward the main entrance.

Inside the crowded lobby, the two stopped at the front desk and spoke with a harried clerk.

"Did you say the reservation was under Mr. Vu?"

Vu nodded. "I have a confirmation number. Would you like to see it?"

"According to our records you cancelled that reservation yesterday."

"That's impossible."

Hill stepped up to the counter. "Is there a problem, miss?"

"Sir, I show your reservation," the clerk assured him. "But Mr. Vu's reservation was cancelled. You're with the IBMA group, correct, sir?"

"No," Vu said, and flashed his credentials. The clerk glanced at the official ID and then checked her screen again.

"I'm sorry, sir – but we don't show any available rooms. Our records indicate you cancelled your reservation and the room was booked to another party."

"You checked my confirmation number?"

"Yes – it's all in order. It shows that a Jack Vu cancelled the reservation on-line."

Vu coughed, removed a handkerchief from his pocket and blew his nose. The porter glanced up at Hill and shrugged, while the clerk stared blankly.

"May I speak with your supervisor?" Vu asked.

"You can bunk in with me, buddy," Hill blurted.

Vu rubbed his forehead, his vision of a private room and bath evaporating. "I'll try another hotel."

"Sir, I'm afraid this weekend all the hotels are at capacity with the IBMA convention. I could make a few calls for you. But, I tried earlier for another guest and there were no vacancies."

With all the lifeless melancholy of a man being led to the

gallows, Vu turned to Hill. "I guess I'll take you up on your offer." Inwardly, he couldn't help but wonder what cruel karmic debt was being paid.

The clerk picked up the phone and spoke with housekeeping. She hung up after a few moments, looking newly poised.

"They'll bring in extra towels and a roll-away bed, gentlemen."

The room was smaller than both had expected. It had a double-size bed against the wall, a dresser and a large TV set. The bathroom was cramped, but clean. No tub, just a shower and small basin. The view from the window was of a public courtyard with a waterless fountain.

The porter laid Hill's suitcase on the bed and stepped aside. Hill pulled a couple of dollars from his wallet and tipped the porter, who nodded and left. Vu glanced around and then rechecked the bathroom. When he returned, Hill reached for the phone.

"Jack, you want anything?"

"A bigger room."

"I'm ordering up a bottle of Maker's Mark. Relax. It'll be like boot camp all over again."

12

A bearded and balding Frank Ruttle was sucking air through his teeth when Homicide Detective Sam Buck and Sergeant Jack Vu walked into the cold room. For nearly twenty-seven years Ruttle had been chief medical examiner for the Louisville Police Department, an odd man who preferred to work alone. That was probably the main reason most interns didn't stick around long. He belched, passed gas and unabashedly scratched his ass on cabinet handles. He watched Court TV, engrossed by cop shows, on a tiny black & white television with the volume always cranked up. It blasted from the corner of the room, perched atop several cases of formaldehyde. Despite personal habits, his razor techniques were among the best. He attributed them to a grueling eight-year stint as a medical officer in the US Army.

"Frank – this is the fellow from the Air Force, I mentioned earlier," Buck said.

Ruttle pulled off a rubber glove and extended his fat hand toward Vu.

"Yes, yes, the Sanders case. Welcome," Ruttle boomed. "Good flight?"

Vu shook the man's sweaty hand. "I would have preferred an

F-15."

Ruttle laughed. "When I was in the Army, I got around mostly on Blackhawks. Not nearly as fast, but nonetheless thrilling."

Buck had obviously heard the medical examiner's spiel before. He casually picked up a micrometer from the counter and thumbed the dial. "I was telling Sergeant Vu that we're probably dealing with a suicide."

Ruttle slipped his glove back on and studied the pitchfork lying on his work stand. He retrieved the micrometer from Buck and measured the diameter of one of the forks, then noted it on a chart. "Possibly," he said. "Does she fit the profile, Sergeant?"

At this early stage, Vu was not jumping to any conclusions. "She was an academy graduate with a bright future ahead of her. There's no indication she was in trouble. And, I understand, she was an excellent swimmer."

"Had she received orders for overseas?"

"No."

"And she got along OK at her base?"

"Yes." Vu cleared his throat. "May I see the body please?"

Ruttle made no reply, but stared at his notes and then back at the pitchfork.

"Of course. Just one second while I finish." Ruttle shuffled over to his work area. A woman's body was lying on his table – mid to later thirties, Vu thought. Dark exotic skin – about five feet tall, well built – probably an athlete.

Ruttle took a thin probe, inserted it into one of the four puncture wounds in her chest, and measured the distance to chart it. Next, he picked up a calculator and punched in some numbers.

"You any good at physics, Mr. Vu?"

"My degree was in Administrative Justice. Not all Asians are wizards at math."

Ruttle looked at Buck. "Well, I'm shootin' from the hip – but my guess is it took quite a thrust to create those puncture marks. That rules out children and a good portion of the female population. I suspect our killer is a male."

"I thought you said yesterday that the prints lifted from the murder weapon were female," Buck countered.

"Ah, yes, I did say that. I should check with my assistant and see if he's found a match. Excuse me gentleman, I'll be right back."

Vu turned to Buck. "So this is the jockey I read about in the morning paper?"

"Bad week for women around here," Ruttle commented, shuffling toward the door. "First your girl – then Ms. Knot –plenty of unhappy folks in town. Not to mention some disappointed bookies."

With Ruttle gone, the room seemed oddly quiet. Something about the jockey's body troubled Vu.

"Who discovered her?"

"Sanders or Knot?"

"Ms. Knot."

"A ranch hand by the name of Ed Lynch."

"Do you have a suspect?"

Buck adjusted his glasses. "She was last seen with a cop from your neck of the woods." Buck read from his notes. "A Detective Dorene Gates – works out of the 8th precinct." Without acknowledging his prior connections to Gates, Vu moved closer to the body for a better look. "They were attending their twentieth reunion. We spoke with the staff. Most indicated the two were hot for each other. I think something must have gone south and Gates whacked the girl – then lost it again at the airport trying to leave town. Witnesses said she would have killed that guy too, given the chance."

"Detectives have been known to crack."

"I'll know more when we get the lab results."

Vu made no further comment and calmly mulled lingering questions. He would telephone Hill as soon as possible.

Across the room, Ruttle burst through the door frowning and waving an empty clipboard. "Nothing yet, Detective. Mostly partials. My assistant seems to think he can pull a good one from the murder weapon. The pubic hair was a match." Ruttle dropped the clipboard on the counter and put on a fresh pair of gloves. "Now then, gentleman, shall we take a look at Ms. Sanders?"

Vu nodded. *Pubic hair?*

He watched Ruttle move to a bank of stainless steel compartments. About half way down, he pulled a drawer out. A white sheet covered the corpse. After removing the sheet, he stepped back, allowing Vu to examine the body.

"I found no abnormal contusions, no fractures or excessive bruising," Ruttle explained. "There was water in the lungs. So she was alive when she hit the water. I found superficial hemorrhaging around the eyes and minor bruising on the bottom of her right foot and her right hip. The body came in missing a shoe, which might explain the bruising. The hip injury is superficial. It could have happened during the fall or after the body was in the water. This time of year there's plenty of flotsam in the Ohio. I don't see signs of trauma though. My guess is she entered the water from a height of approximately twenty to twenty-five feet. That would be consistent with the impact bruising on her foot."

Vu noticed some old scars on her chest and a fresh red smudge on her sternum. The source of the scars was a mystery. The smudge appeared to be some kind of imprint.

"I was wondering about that myself," Ruttle added quickly. "I photographed it. It came from her dog tags."

"So she could have been pushed backward and fell?" Vu made notes.

"They were pre-mortem, so that's a possibility."

"What about the scars?"

"No idea, though they look to be quite old."

Vu dispassionately studied the body from head to toe, until his eyes connected her pink toenail polish with his earlier troubling vision of Betty's.

Buck walked over rubbing his forehead. "I spoke with the Corps of Engineers this morning. They indicated river flows of approximately three knots to the south that night. That could place the point of entry somewhere northwest of Clarksville. We found the body a mile east of the JFK Bridge. There are several bridges upriver and any number of accessible vantage points she could have jumped from."

"No new leads on who phoned it in?"

"No."

Vu took one final look at the girl.

"May I see her belongings?"

"Of course," Ruttle said. "I have them over here."

Vu followed Ruttle across the lab. The items were laid out neatly on a counter by the window. Ruttle quickly related each. "One standard issue US Air Force Dress Blues uniform – a blended wool material procured from Indonesia. A Firm Fit C-cup brassiere. One pair of torn pantyhose. One standard USAF issue, size 7, black leather shoe."

Vu scanned the items. "What about a hat?"

"No hat. Either she wasn't wearing one, or it fell off."

Vu picked up the polished dress shoe and double-checked the size. He put the shoe down. "Any jewelry?"

"A pair of earrings and a wristwatch. Oh, one other thing," Ruttle added. "When I checked the nail scrapings, I found small traces of furniture polish. And a smudge on the sleeve."

"Like Lemon Pledge?"

"Thicker – more like teak oil."

Vu heard his stomach growl. He looked Ruttle in the eye. "What was the time of death?"

"The body had been in the water roughly eight hours. The cold temperature could affect my reading of the liver. I suspect – and don't nail me to the wall on this – time of death to be around ten-thirty pm."

"What about medications or alcohol in the blood?"

"I found traces of aspirin. Her blood alcohol was .05 percent. That's slightly below the legal limit in the State of Kentucky."

"No barbiturates or opiates?"

"None."

"Semen?"

Ruttle shook his head. Vu jotted down a last note and then glanced up. Buck, who'd been rather uninterested in the corpse until that moment, moved closer.

"Something the matter, detective?" Vu asked. Buck was still studying the girl's face. He shook off whatever it was and sighed. "She reminds me of another suicide."

Vu sensed a solemn change in the detective. "If we determine it was suicide, do you think they might be connected?"

Buck's eyes hollowed. "No. Her name was Rebecca. She was my sister."

13

Vu folded his legs into a lotus position on the park bench, closed his eyes and drew in deep breaths, allowing the air to slowly escape while he waited. Except for a few stray pigeons, a pair of squirrels and a painted stone horse, the small park near the precinct was vacant. An earthy aroma seeped into the air from the freshly cut grass as the morning sun evaporated droplets of dew. The bench where Vu sat faced the river. But, he was momentarily uninterested in views. Eventually, footsteps approached, their heavy cadence recognizable. Sergeant Hill's gait, like that of a seasoned boxer pacing the ring was unmistakable.

"Jack – what's so important?" Hill stooped to re-tie his shoe.

Vu opened his eyes and looked surprisingly down at the normally towering detective.

"Sit, please." Vu unfolded his legs and slid over.

Hill rose, only to flop back down beside him, and cracked his neck.

"Have you spoken to Dorene yet?"

"No. They're giving me the run-around. The old 'she's being transferred from a different facility, an overcrowding problem' bullshit." Hill fitfully stubbed the ground with his toe. "Something's up."

"You're right." Vu pulled out his notebook. "I found out some information at the morgue this morning. It seems Gates is suspected in her friend's murder. They apparently have lab samples which indicate she handled the murder weapon. She was the last person seen with the victim. They haven't matched all the prints yet, but it's likely. Gates was also linked by pubic hair, somehow."

"You're certain they were talking about Dorene?"

"One investigator seems confident your partner is the prime suspect."

"Who?"

"His name is Sam Buck. He is also the detective working the Sanders death. He had no idea I knew Detective Gates."

"This isn't good. Gates hasn't exactly impressed the cops in this town and that guy she beat up is pressing charges. But murder? Her? No way."

"What do your superiors think?"

"Our Captain wants her head on a silver platter. The DA isn't talking. Things could get a might sticky at home, especially if we need any support."

"The consensus is the jockey was well-liked and worth a fortune to the local bookies. I would urge you to suggest she hire an attorney."

"Gates doesn't exactly take advice. But, I'll see what I can do."

"Many of Ms. Knot's fans are upset that she's dead. Consequently, I'd watch your step nosing around town."

Hill stood. "Nobody back home said anything to me about Gates murdering someone." His forehead creased in thought. "I've got an appointment to meet with a Detective Smitty in an hour. I wonder how much smoke he'll try and blow up my ass."

14

Smitty was alone scribbling notation in the margin of a report when Sergeant Hill poked his head in the door. "You Smitty?"

Smitty put his pen down and sat back in his chair. "What can I do for you?"

Hill extended his hand. "I'm Detective Hill, from the New Orleans Police Department. We spoke yesterday."

Smitty stood up and shook hands. "I'll be right with you, chap. There's coffee on if you want."

"I'll pass."

"Have a seat," he said. "I'm just winding up here. Give me five minutes."

Smitty went back to work. Hill glanced around the office while he waited. Finally, Smitty slid back from his computer screen.

"Now then, I suppose you want to talk about your partner downstairs?"

"So she got in a bar fight with some drunk. What's the big deal? Why hasn't she been released?"

"We're holding her on a more serious charge."

"Which would be?"

"Suspicion of murder."

Even though Vu had warned him earlier that this was a possibility, Hill acted surprised. "Murder?"

"That's right, mate."

"Who?"

"Her former tart, Patti Knot."

"I'd like to review the case file if possible."

"Ah, most certainly you would," Smitty said. "But, it's out of my hands. DA has it locked in his safe."

Hill stood up straight. His towering presence didn't intimidate the Irish detective. "Look, I thought our offices had a mutual understanding."

"And so they do, but … your office wants nothing to do with Detective Gates. They've washed their hands of her, so to speak."

Hill sat back down. Smitty had just affirmed his earlier fear that he was alone on this one. Though efficient and well thought of because he was a team player, he didn't know if he could handle the virgin territory of going solo. "Tell me what you can."

"We found her prints on the murder weapon. We can place her at the crime scene around the time of death. We found a tuft of the jockey's bush on her person. A little too kinky for me, mate. The clippers we found at the scene also have her prints on them. Guess she's a trophy hound."

Hill frowned. "Did you say she cut off the vic's pubic hair?"

"That's right, mate. Had a little lock of it tucked in her pants."

Hill turned and glanced out the window. A recycling truck was emptying bins on the street below. "As a courtesy to the department, may I view the crime scene photos?"

Smitty scratched his freckled nose. "I'd have to get the nod first."

"Damn it, I've worked with Gates for two years. She's a good cop."

"Easy Detective – my twins at home don't care if she's a good cop. They just want daddy to bring home din-din every evening. And the wife would be none too happy if I came home unemployed. Nothin' personal mate, but your partner fell in her own shit-pot. Patti Knot was well liked in this town and plenty of folks were banking on her to win the Derby this year. Key word here is bank. Money mate. Knot was a long-shot on the books, but some thought she was due to turn it around. They planned to ride her all the way to the bank come Derby Day."

"Look – with or without your help, I'm going to get to the bottom of this."

"Sure, mate. You go right ahead. I'd expect nothin' less from my partner." Smitty concentrated on his computer again. "Be a good lad now and close the door on your way out."

Hill flinched at the condescending dismissal. When he was gone, Smitty reached for his phone.

The basement of the Louisville City Police Station was cold, damp and reeked of urine. Three holding cells made up the eastern portion. The guard station was along the west corridor, coupled with a control room where detainees could meet counsel without leaving the secured area. Several barred windows hung open at ceiling level to ventilate the stench. A cell door was open and a janitor was mopping the floor. The cell across the hall held a young black prostitute, street named Annie Oakley, who had bragged to Gates about "capping a homeboy nosin' her pimp's bid'ness." Gates passed the time swapping war stories with the crack whore, but soon tired of her manic jabber. Earlier Annie had sworn her cell floor was coated in pepper spray. She stopped suddenly, grabbed the bars, and glared at the janitor.

"Yo – mop boy!" she yelled. "Cop me a cig!"

The janitor was deaf to the whore's request and continued his even mop strokes. After the floor was thoroughly wet, he wrung the mop out and began the process all over again. Gates scratched her thigh and flipped through a soiled copy of Sports Illustrated she held open on her bunk as she tried to comprehend Patti's death.

"Hey – you deaf, Butthead? I need a cigarette!"

Gates stared up.

"I'll make it worth your while." She ran her tongue seductively over her lip."

Gates slammed the magazine closed and sat up. "Put a lid on it sister."

The woman slumped back on her bunk, mumbling profanities. The janitor rang his mop out for the last time and wheeled the bucket out of the corridor. He left through a secured door at the end of the hall. Awhile later, the door reopened and a figure appeared at Gates' cell. Her partner rested his hands on the bars and peered inside.

"How you holdin' up, Dorene?"

Gates jumped up smiling. Hill reached through the bars and squeezed her hand. Gates returned the hampered embrace until both suddenly recoiled, embarrassed by their unexpected exchange of emotion. Gates stepped back and crossed her arms.

"Where you been?"

"Getting the run around."

"Look, I was wrong to kick the shit out of that drunk asshole, even if he deserved it, but come on, I've learned my lesson."

"You don't know, do you?"

"What?"

"They like you for Patti's murder." Hill knew his partner. He watched her eyes narrow and then waited for her jaw to set, a sure sign she had processed the information and retrenched. After momentary silence, a muscle began to strain along her neck.

"Did you speak with those pricks upstairs?"

"They're not granting me access to anything. Not even as a departmental courtesy."

"Contact Gentry – see if he'll make a call."

"Gentry won't help. He's too pissed. Sampson walked."

The whore in the other cell shouted: "Hey, man – you got a cig?"

Hill turned and glared at the ravaged face leering through the bars. "What I got is a need for privacy."

The whore cowered back to her bunk for a second time.

"OK Gates, start from the beginning."

Gates swallowed hard and lowered her voice. "I met Patti in high school. We had a brief fling and then went our separate ways. I hadn't seen her since. When the reunion came up, I thought it would be nice to see her again, so we made arrangements to get together." Gates paused. "We hooked up. I was at her place when you called."

"What happened next?"

"I went out to the barn and said goodbye."

"Before or after you sheared her pubic hair?"

"Cut me some slack here. It was consensual."

"That may be a tough sell to a Southern jury."

Gates rolled her eyes.

"They have your prints on the murder weapon."

"We cleaned a stall together. I handled the pitchfork. What's my motive? Love gone bad?" Gates leaned closer. "Someone set me up."

"Dorene, you need to get an attorney ASAP. Do you know anyone here?"

"Let me think." Gates closed her eyes. "I only had two people who really knew me that I could trust. One of them is dead." Gates looked at Hill. "This sounds pathetic, but my high school counselor, Meg Brown, has always been there for me. She was at the reunion. She's retired now, but she's lived in the same house on Tomahawk Drive for as long as I can remember. Her husband's name was Howard."

Hill watched Gates' jaw muscles work.

"She'll help me."

Hill digested the information. "I'll contact her."

Gates' face showed a brief flash of hope.

"OK, let's rehash it. Anyone see you together?"

"Sure – at the reunion."

"After?"

"No."

Hill paused. "Who else had access to the property?"

"There's a locked gate. But it's a big place. Anyone could have easily cut across the field behind her place or jumped the fence. I've been through this a hundred times already."

"What about a spare key?"

"No key. It's a coded gate. Patti did use a key to open the front door though. I don't know if she keeps a spare outside. You'll need the code to open the gate. Did you bring a pick set?"

Hill winked.

Gates leaned forward and whispered the code into his ear. Then, she moved back.

"It's about ten miles from here, due east. Take highway 71 until you see milepost 37. It's a gravel road." Gates was visibly shaken. "Christ – I can't believe I'm in this fuckin' mess. Search every square inch of that place."

"Take it easy." Hill touched Gates' shoulder. Out of habit, he reached for his notebook. Despite the gravity of the situation, he couldn't help but smile.

"What?" Gates asked, miffed.

"Guess you really did it up this time."

"Look, so I'm a lesbian, but I'm not a killer."

"OK – settle down. How'd you get from her place to the airport?"

"A cab."

"Did the driver see you together?"

"No."

Hill scratched his head. "I'll check with the cab company anyway."

Gates thought it over. "Wait a second – there was this guy at the hotel – I blew him off as a drunk."

Hill's eyes brightened. "Go on."

"At the reunion, I was in the bar and this drunk approached me. Real jerk. Looked like an Elvis impersonator with a comb shoved up his ass."

Hill checked his watch. "And?"

"He said he was Patti's husband."

"Patti had a husband?"

"I didn't ask her."

"Was he following her?"

"Could have been."

"So what happened next – after encountering the ex?"

Gates frowned. "C'mon Hill, Patti never said he was her ex."

"OK, OK. What happened after that?"

"We left."

"You see him again?"

"No. We left in her truck."

Hill made a mental note. "You're sure he didn't follow you?"

"I'm not sure of anything at this point." Dorene paused. "I didn't see anything inside that house to indicate she was married or even living with a man."

"OK. I'll investigate Patti's marital status."

The guard announced that their time was up. The muscles in Gates' face tightened. "Hey – one other thing. Check the local Sports page. I'm not sure which day it was. Look through all of last week's editions if you have to. Patti's picture is there, along with another jockey. Find out what you can about him."

The sun was setting outside City Hall and the temperature was dropping. Hill buttoned up his jacket and looked around for a quiet place to have a cigarette while considering Gates' remarks. Denied access almost everywhere he'd gone in the last few hours, he visited the Medical Examiner's office, the DA, even the Chief of Police. No one would open up. It was total stonewalling. Knot was a celebrity and the town was protecting her virtue. Broaching the idea of Patti's lesbianism resulted only in vehement denials. He was civilian now, no inside ties, no special favors, no unauthorized leads. He lit his cigarette, aware of his ragged breathing. Nerves, he figured, probably seeing his partner behind bars. He revisited the facts and took a drag.

Every minute counted now. Gates needed him. The media was already painting her as an unbalanced cop with a Patti fixation.

Dyke love gone awry. It was strange how lives unraveled and intersected. Hill's strict Southern upbringing included healthy doses of racism and homophobia. The corner of his mouth arced in a smile, as he remembered first getting paired with Dorene. He had been embarrassed, too ashamed even to tell his parents and friends about her. At the time, he thought the assignment was a punishment. They made an odd pair, he and Gates, but they fit together like fist and glove. Her heat, his coolness, anything to save her. That sounded well and good, but the reality was, his own folks still didn't know. His cheeks burned in shame.

He stubbed his cigarette butt and headed off down the sidewalk.

A few blocks away from the courthouse, Hill saw a taxi drive by, which sparked an idea. He pulled out his cell phone and dialed the local cab dispatch office. After ten minutes of inquiries, he'd come up blank. The dispatcher said that there were no records of a cab from their company having picked up anyone at the Knot residence on Sunday.

He dialed information, then spoke with two independent cab companies and still came up empty-handed. In-turn, they referred him to a third company, which didn't pan out either. Evidently, the cops had spread the word – "for DA's use only"– or someone was lying.

Discouraged, he walked for nearly half-an-hour before spotting another cab parked outside the front of a tavern. The driver was reading a newspaper and looked bored. Hill tapped on the window, flashing his badge. The cabby lowered the newspaper and rolled down the window. He had dark features and spoke with an accent.

"What is the problem, officer?"

Hill guessed the driver's accent was from the Middle East. He put his badge away and took out his notepad, flipping through several pages until he found what he was looking for. It was about the only useful lead he'd been able to obtain from the record's clerk. He read the name he'd written down and compared it to the

City permit posted on the dash, relieved by his sudden change of luck.

"Mr. Kurdishson," Hill said. "Do you remember a fare by the name of Dorene Gates? You picked her up Sunday at Patti Knot's home and drove her to the airport?"

The cabby nodded. "Yes, the African American."

"She's Creole, actually," Hill said. "You identified her for the police – right?"

He appeared annoyed by the question. "Yes, yes. It was disturbing. But I have cooperated. What is it you want with me?"

"Did you see anyone else at the house when you picked her up?"

The cabby shook his head frantically.

Hill glared at him. "Think again. You're certain?"

"There was no one else."

"What about Ms. Knot?"

"Only my fare."

"Ms. Knot didn't see her off?"

"No. I've told the police all this. At her hotel I waited while she retrieved her suitcase. Then, I drove her to the airport. This is tragic. I'm a horseracing fan. She was the finest in all America. And this Gates woman murdered her."

Hill glanced inside the cab. "You carry a driver's log, right?"

"Yes, you confiscated that log." The cabby removed a new log from his glove box and handed it out the window. Hill opened it, thumbed through the empty pages – only a half-dozen recent entries. The cabby's eyes narrowed as he watched Hill's disappointment.

Hill returned the log. "How would you like to make some fast cash?" He regretted the words as soon as they left his mouth.

"May I see your badge again officer?"

Hill pursed his lips and slowly wagged his head. He knew he'd reached the end.

The cabby frowned. "This cab is out of service. I cannot help you." He began to roll up the window.

"Wait!"

The driver stared straight ahead and pulled away from the curb.

The cab sped off, spitting gravel.

Hill ducked into the barrage and winced as rock peppered his scalp. *You dumb fuck. You deserved to be hit upside the head.*

15

Vu picked up a stick and threw it into the Ohio, watching the current whisk it away. The sun dipped behind a bank of dark clouds and the temperature dropped noticeably.

"Con song."

"What was that, sergeant?" Buck asked.

"It's the Vietnamese word for river, the great healer."

"Well, it didn't do much for Ms. Sanders."

Vu stepped back from the water and pulled out a small digital camera. Detective Buck yawned.

After snapping photographs of the river, various footprints, and other odd markings in the clay, Vu rummaged through the scattered litter left behind by fishermen. Eventually, he walked over to where Buck stood smoking. A few seagulls had gathered along the shore.

"What's the river traffic like this time of year?"

"Busy. A hundred million tons of cargo up and down annually. That's not including pleasure craft and fishermen. I took a flatboat down once. Not the smartest thing I've ever done. More snags and sandbars out there then you can shake your dick at."

Vu pointed at a marker in the sand. "Is that where you

discovered the body?"

"Yeah."

Vu snapped a few more pictures then put his camera away. For the longest time, he just stared at the ground puzzling.

"We assume two individuals found her," Buck said, breaking the silence. "The evidence supports that. I'd say the caller was in his late fifties, maybe early sixties. Sounded African American on the phone. I imagine they were fishing and accidentally snagged the body."

Vu nodded then pointed out a series of faint trailing arcs in the soil. "Those are unique marks. Made by a white cane I suspect."

Buck walked over and examined the ground. "You can tell the color from those marks?"

Vu cocked his head and studied Buck's face for sarcasm. He found none. "A white cane is a folding cane used by the vision impaired. I believe one of your witnesses may be blind."

"Figures," Buck shook his head. "But, it's a moot point. This clearly isn't a dump site, nor a murder scene. We have reason to believe she jumped from an old railroad bridge, south of town, perhaps gaining access from the river walk. I sent a detective there this morning to check it out."

"What did he find?"

"Nothing yet."

"What makes you think she used that specific location?"

"We spoke to a couple of her high school chums yesterday. Ms. Sanders was planning to attend a wedding for a Marci Stoneham on Saturday. The night before her disappearance, they met Sanders for beers at a pub called Sonny's – on 2nd and Main. The bartender remembered them. For larks, they took a ride downtown afterwards. Sanders wanted to see the old railroad bridge where they used to hang out as kids. The girls weren't all that thrilled about it so they ended up talking her out of it. When they dropped her off at her hotel, they planned to hook up the following night after the rehearsal dinner. Sanders was a no show. But, one of the girls swears she saw her hanging around the river walk in uniform earlier that day."

"And you think she jumped from the bridge?"

"Yes."

"That's quite a reach, detective."

"I'm just following the evidence."

This man was hiding something, Vu was sure of it.

"I'm going to need to interview Ms. Sanders' friends."

Buck consulted his notebook. "Marci Stoneham, 22, Cindy Brewer, 22, and Tami Jones, 23. They reside with their parents and all three recently graduated from Eastern universities. Their parents own large country estates along River Road. Old money. Stoneham's father is an MD at Louisville General. Brewer's father is on the Board of Directors for SAFECO. Jones' father is a corporate attorney for Humana Insurance."

Vu jotted the information. "What about the wives?"

"Educated and pampered with strong community ties. One is a friend of the chief of police. When Sanders didn't show up for the wedding, she let the chief know. Louisville's a tight community. The next day, we got the anonymous call."

"What hotel was she staying in?"

"Marriott on West Jefferson."

"Have you been to the room?"

"Affirm. She checked in alright, but the room wasn't even slept in. No luggage either."

"How do you explain that?"

"I don't."

"When have you known any woman to travel without luggage?"

"I know it's odd, but that's what we've got."

Buck put his notebook away and then patted down his shirt pocket for a cigarette. "Jack – I've looked at everything. If I thought this was a homicide, I'd be on it like a fly on shit. My guess is, the girl had it all worked out before she even got here."

Vu plucked a sticker from his sock. "Why do I get the distinct impression you're not telling me everything?"

"I've given you all the information our office has Vu."

"What about personal information?" Vu countered.

Buck was agitated now. "What personal information?"

"Look, I came from a small town just like this. If you've lived here all your life, you may know something about Ms. Sanders that is influencing your opinions on the case."

Buck paused, nodding slowly to himself, as a decision was reached. "Let's just say ... Beverly Sanders may not have been the strong enthusiastic woman she appeared. She and another kid were attacked and nearly killed several years ago. She may have never ... emotionally recovered. The case was never solved and the files were sealed by the court."

Buck's face told Vu that was all he was going to get.

The two men headed back to the car, but when they came to a fork in the trail, Vu lagged. Buck continued on ahead. Vu noticed someone had placed a matchbook on one of the markers. He removed it and stuck it in his pocket.

"You coming?" Buck shouted.

"Where's the other trail go?"

"Dead ends up ahead."

"And the railroad bridge is north of here?"

"Several miles upriver," Buck said. "Easiest way to get there is from the river walk. It's been abandoned for years, which probably offered her a good location. Kind of hidden away from everything."

Buck fired up a cigarette and watched the trail. Eventually, Vu appeared through the grass. He had his camera slung over his shoulder and hiked along at a slow, steady pace. When they reached the car, Vu rested a few minutes collecting his thoughts. He gave the front tire a couple swift side-kicks, knocking dirt loose from his shoes. Buck impatiently stubbed his cigarette and then checked his watch.

"I go off shift in twenty minutes," Buck informed. "Some place you want me to drop you?"

* * *

The estates along River Road were just as Detective Buck had described, multi-million dollar castles carved in some of the finest Italian stone, half-mile back from the main highway, commanding spectacular views of the Ohio. The estate Vu was trying to locate was at the end of a private lane with an iron gate. Next to the gate was a speaker box, which the cab driver reached for and pushed the small button. A male voice answered, asked a series of questions, and then the gate opened automatically. The cab pulled through and it closed behind them.

The luxurious house sat on a knoll surrounded by guest quarters, two stables, an oval horse track and a groomed pasture with a number of horses trotting freely. A five-car garage sat on the property with a shiny black Porsche parked near a swimming pool. Down at the stables, two young women in leather riding gear climbed off their stallions and disappeared behind a building.

The cab pulled up out front and parked next to a sparkling fountain in the center of the circular drive. Two Irish Setters barked from the back yard and raced down to greet them. The driver slowly turned around. "Some place, huh?"

Someone inside the house parted the curtains and looked out the front window. A side door opened and the dogs were called away.

"Yes, some place…"

Vu told the driver to switch off the engine. The meter could run. He followed the flagstones to the front door and rang the bell. After a long wait, the door opened. A woman with flawless skin stepped out, wearing a black dress and heavy gold jewelry.

"Mr. Wu? I'm Sally Jones, Tami's mother."

"Vu," Vu corrected and offered his card. "Thank you for seeing me."

"We all want to help."

Vu followed the woman through an elegant entryway with marble floors and numerous oil paintings along the walls. The split-level room was divided between a living area with a fireplace and luxurious furniture, and a marvelous kitchen replete with stainless countertops and maple cabinetry. Mrs. Jones stopped outside the kitchen and picked up a glass of champagne from the counter.

"Can I get you something?"

"Tea – if you have it."

A housekeeper appeared from down the hall carrying an armload of freshly washed towels. "Rita, please prepare some tea for our guest."

Rita nodded and disappeared through a side door off the kitchen.

"Let's have a seat," Mrs. Jones said. "The girls will be along shortly."

Vu followed the woman into the living room. She sat down on the sofa and placed her glass on a coffee table. She picked up a remote and turned off the large plasma TV where she had been watching *"Days of Our Lives."* Vu sat across from her in a stiff armchair with lionhead carvings. The chair was so tall Vu had to perch on the edge for his feet to reach the floor. He ran his hand over the carvings, admiring the fine workmanship.

"You've chosen my husband's favorite chair," Mrs. Jones said, plucking at her hem. "I'm afraid he won't be joining us. He's tied up at the office. Have you been to Louisville before, Mr. Wu?"

Vu steadied his face, knowing it wouldn't serve to correct her again. "This is my first visit."

"It's a remarkable place. Every year we host The Derby. We have friends from Europe who stay with us. The town just goes absolutely frenetic for weeks. It's impossible to drive anywhere. On opening day, there's a parade and parties galore. Celebrities flock here. You really should try to experience it sometime."

"I hope to return under better circumstances."

Rita arrived with a tray of hot tea and biscuits. She sat it down on the table and left, allowing them to serve themselves.

Vu picked up the steaming porcelain cup and saucer and rested it tactfully on his knee. "How well did you know Ms. Sanders?"

"We always called her Bevy," she said. "She was my daughter's best friend during middle school. Couldn't separate the two. They were joined at the hip. Bevy's parents trained horses here."

"I saw a number of horses in the pasture."

"We breed thoroughbreds and used to employ Bevy's parents. Bevy came part of the package. She often exercised the horses when we couldn't find a jockey and the girls rode together most every day."

An outer door opened and two slender girls in English riding gear entered the room. A cloud of entitlement consumed them. Mrs. Jones looked up and smiled. "Here she is now. Honey, this is Mr. Wu." Mrs. Jones stared at his card. "He's investigating Bevy's drowning for the Air Force." Satisfied, she turned toward one of the girls. "Cindy, dear – there's some diet soda in the refrigerator. Why don't you fetch two cans and come back and join us. The detective can begin with Tami."

The taller of the two girls stepped forward as if she was going to shake Vu's hand and instead reached for her mother's champagne glass. Her mother slapped her hand away playfully. The second girl sauntered off.

Tami struck a pose for the sergeant. Her puffy lips glistened. She had dark brown eyes like her mother, and with the minor exception of a pimple on her right cheek, her youthful face resembled her mother's flawlessly. She opened her mouth as if she was going to speak just as a purple cell phone clipped to her riding gear rang. She drew it up like a revolver and flipped it open.

"CTRN!" she uttered to the caller, then snapped the cell phone closed and clipped it back in place. Vu, who had risen out of his seat when the girls entered, appeared befuddled and wanted to sit back down, but remained standing. He pulled out his notebook.

He finally said, "Your legal name is Tami?"

Mrs. Jones interrupted. "It's Tamanthelia Ann. We've always called her Tami."

Tami pushed her blonde bangs back. "Mother named me after a horse."

Vu nodded. "Would you care to sit down?"

"Is this GTTL?"

"What?" Vu asked.

"Is this going to take long?" Tami stared at her mother. "I HTP."

This was getting ridiculous. "I'm sorry, what was that second part again?"

"I have to pee!"

Vu smiled. "This is not an interrogation, Ms. Jones. By all means, please go use the toilet."

Tami disappeared down the hall. Vu sat back down and picked up his tea. The second girl, Cindy, reappeared carrying two diet Cokes. She flopped down on the sofa beside Mrs. Jones and stared at Vu like he was an alien. Vu had rerisen in courtesy and sat back down.

"Rita!" Mrs. Jones shouted. "Refill, please."

The Spanish housekeeper reappeared instantly carrying an open bottle of champagne. She filled Mrs. Jones glass and then returned to the kitchen.

"Thank you, dear. Cindy – honey, how was your ride?"

"Fab," Cindy said.

Vu wanted to get the conversation back on track. "Cindy –did either of you know where Ms. Sanders was staying in town?"

Cindy sat forward and put her drink down on the table. Inside her vest pocket her cell phone buzzed like an alarm clock. The irritation startled Vu. Cindy answered the call. "WTF! TTC! RAD!"

Cindy typed on the phone keypad, smiling at the response on the tiny screen. Vu had lost her attention to the device. It was most annoying.

"These girls," Mrs. Jones interjected, "What would they do without text-messaging?"

"Is your daughter returning?" Vu finally asked. Cindy typed. Mrs. Jones sipped champagne. Like a train grinding to a halt Vu's interview was losing steam.

Mrs. Jones sat forward. "Tami!" she shouted. "Tami, dear! Hurry along please."

"What mother?" Tami stormed back into the room.

"The detective is in a hurry dear."

Vu tipped his tea back and stood up. "Please – ladies – could I have the two girls sit on the sofa? Mrs. Jones, I'll need you to refrain from talking while I ask your daughter and her friend some questions."

Cindy typed something quickly, snapped her phone closed, and sat back pouting. Mrs. Jones fidgeted in her seat. "Of course Mr. Wu. If you don't mind, I'll just step out of the room for a moment while you finish up."

Mrs. Jones gracefully unfolded herself from the sofa only to spill champagne. "Oh heavens, look what a mess ... Rita! Bring a towel dear."

Vu sighed and sat back down. He rested his notebook on his lap. Rita dashed in with a towel, dropped to her knees and wiped the puddle of liquid off the floor.

Mrs. Jones pointed at her shoe. "Rita, dear, I think I spilt some on my foot. Yes, I think you've got it now."

Rita dabbed the shoe until it was completely dry and then carried the empty champagne glass into the kitchen. Mrs. Jones trailed after her empty glass. Vu focused on the two girls, who looked blankly back at him.

"What do you think happened to Ms. Sanders?" he asked.

The girls glanced at each other.

"Cindy – let's start with you. Do you think Ms. Sanders drowning was accidental?"

"YOC!"

"Excuse me?"

Cindy sighed. "Yeah. Of course. She was always doing WS."

He gave her a questioning look.

"Wild Shit," Cindy said with a tone of superiority.

Tami glanced at Cindy. "Marci is honeymooning in Tahiti."

"NS!"

"A two-week cruise through the Bahamas. She just texted me."

Vu picked up his pen and clinked his teacup. "Ms. Sanders – your friend from high school? You were friends correct?"

Tami pouted her lip. "She was more Marci's friend than ours."

"Tell me what happened, after you left the bar. I understand you drove downtown to the riverwalk, then later dropped Ms. Sanders at a hotel?"

Tami glanced at her friend. Cindy spoke up, "Bevy wanted to FA on the railroad bridge."

"Fuck Around," Tami added helpfully.

"We talked her out of it. It was late. Marci needed to get back."

"FA? I assume this was something she did often?"

"Yeah," Tami added. "She made all-state in diving, junior and senior year. She was a daredevil."

"So she used to swim in the river?"

"Duhhh… Yeah."

"Where was she staying?"

"Downtown," Cindy said. "The Spenser."

"You're certain it was the Spenser?"

Cindy nodded.

Tami interrupted. "No way, it was the Marriott, Cin … remember?"

"Which is it, girls?"

The girls glanced at each other and shrugged. "Beats me, I was kinda loaded," Cindy said.

Vu pointed at Tami. "Your turn."

"It was definitely the Marriott."

Vu sighed. "Do you think Ms. Sanders returned to the railroad bridge that night?"

Tami shook her head. "No way."

"Why? The police think otherwise."

Tami and Cindy gazed at each other. Tami's phone rang. She

whipped it out and checked the screen. "Sorry, detective, I've got to take this!" Tami sprang up and ran out of the room. Vu was incredulous. Cindy chewed her lip and checked messages on her cell as she waited.

The doorbell rang. Rita appeared from the entryway. "Detective? Your driver outside, he needs money if he is to continue waiting."

Vu stood up and put his notebook away. "Tell him I'm coming."

When he faced Cindy with one final question, she was mesmerized by her phone's text messaging functions, totally oblivious of her surroundings.

He was getting nowhere. He left unnoticed, wondering if all youth FA like these two.

* * *

An hour later, Vu found Sergeant Hill in the lobby bar of the Galt, drinking a beer. Vu saddled the barstool beside him and ordered a cup of tea.

"Have any luck today?" Hill asked.

Vu sighed, and handed the bartender a twenty who had returned with his drink. "No. It was a frustrating day all the way around."

Hill nodded. "Yep, I know what'cha mean."

After the bartender delivered his change, Vu counted it. The tea had cost $3.75. He started to say something about the inflated price, decided against it, then left a scant quarter tip on the bar and tucked the bills neatly into his wallet.

"I saw Gates."

"Was she able to aid in her defense?"

"She could explain her fingerprints on the murder weapon," Hill cracked a half-smile. "And being in possession of the pubes."

Vu would have loved to have heard that one. He forced his face to remain stoic and sipped his tea as various sexual scenarios crossed his mind.

"But, the police won't release information. Pressure's being applied somewhere. And, they think they've got her, open and shut."

"What's Gates' think?"

"She believes she's being framed."

"She is a convenient target."

"I've been thinking. Maybe she's too convenient." Hill peeled the label off his beer. "What if she wasn't the target? What if nobody knew she was there?"

"Wrong place, wrong time?" Vu's mind turned.

"Exactly! I know it sounds lame, but I'm stumped." Hill continued picking at the label. "Nobody knew she was coming. And, it takes time to set up a murder, particularly with someone as visible as Knot."

"As I understand it, a ranch hand found her." Vu took out his notebook where he'd written down the name. "The man's name is Ed Lynch. You should speak with him. He may know something."

"Yeah, like he's going to open up to me."

Hill perked up suddenly. Vu thought it had to do with what he'd said until he saw the young hostess from the hotel carrying a stack of old newspapers toward them. She dumped the load on the bar.

"That's all I could find," the hostess said. "You were lucky, Housekeeping let them pile up."

"Thanks."

The hostess smiled and left. Hill quickly rifled through them. "Grab a few, Vu – we're looking for a jockey's picture. Supposed to be on the cover of last week's Sport's page."

Vu's own case deserved priority. He hopped down from the stool. "I'm going to the room to use the telephone. I'll be back in a minute."

"Jack, just give me five minutes."

Vu sat back down. Reluctantly, he went through each page

mechanically scanning. Down near the bottom of the stack, he found the photograph he assumed Hill wanted and held it up.

Hill took the paper and stared at it. Vu carefully restacked the newspapers.

"Looks like the man in that photograph had motive. You now have another person to contact."

Hill began making notes. "The ranch hand, this jockey, her husband, or ex-husband. She owed money to everybody. But, unless we find a way inside this case, we're still locked out."

A group of rowdy musicians filled up the bar.

Vu slid off his barstool and started to leave.

"You're going?" Hill slammed money on the bar. "Wait – Jack!"

Vu stopped just outside the lobby door while Hill caught up. Music echoed along the corridor.

"I've been giving this some thought," Hill said. "I think we ought to pool our resources."

For a brief moment, Vu wondered which would be more unpleasant – helping Detective Gates, or trying to interview more of Beverly Sanders' textually addicted friends.

16

Captain Lazarus squeezed his firm hand around the phone in unsuccessful attempt to strangle the messenger. "I understand, Commissioner. I'll take care of it."

Commissioner Hurt, director of the Louisville Racing Commission, was on the other end of the line threatening to commandeer, not one, but two, homicide investigations. The Captain could take orders with the best of them, but not from a white man outside the ranks, especially one who had committed numerous felonies and whose sole interest lie in keeping money flowing into Louisville.

"Yes, sir," Lazarus replied calmly. "I will."

It wasn't just the racing industry that profited, the Commissioner reminded him, the annual events and migration into the city for the Kentucky Derby was measured in millions of dollars and vital to the economic life of the town. The two women currently residing in the County Morgue were both connected to the horse racing industry. And, this was no time to shed negative light on Churchill Downs, not with the Derby less than a month away.

Lazarus resented being ordered to bury the file on Beverly

Sanders. Hurt didn't care how, but he suggested accidental drowning would be best. Lazarus hung up the receiver and sat back in his chair.

He knew Detective Buck was leaning toward suicide, which would give Hurt a stroke. Funny how old cases, covered up years ago, had a way of resurfacing only to exude their stench into current affairs. Beverly Sanders' case was legendary in the Police Department. The caste system of the South, and Louisville in particular, was not specific to race. After all, he had moved through his career unencumbered by his black oily skin. There was old money, new money, and a vast social gap between thoroughbred racers and townspeople that was jaw dropping ... even for the hardihood of steeplechasers. The Sanders' case had cost his old boss his job and pension. He didn't intend to make the same mistake.

Sanders he could handle. More incendiary was the potential press regarding Patti Knot's murder. Hurt wanted Dorene Gates charged. While she may have stabbed the jockey, she was a fellow cop and her protection felt second nature to him. Besides, there were plenty of suspects with motives galore in Patti's case, the front runner of which was Brad Black. Coincidentally, he was also a person of interest in the unsolved attack on Beverly Sanders years ago. Bad blood existed between Knot and Black and rumor had it he was set to steal her ride for the Derby. It seemed that had been the underlying message of Commissioner Hurt's call – keep Black out of it at all costs.

Lazarus placed his hands on his desk and slowly pushed himself out of his chair. It was time for a war council with Smitty and Buck. As he entered the squad room, his mind weighed the dilemma of squeezing his detectives without stirring the shit pot any more than it already was.

Across the room Detective Buck was polishing off a donut while wagging his head "No" to his partner. Smitty's face showed frustration.

Lazarus held up his hand, and catching Smitty's eye, called out, "I'd like a word with you two."

After the men entered his office, Lazarus closed the door and took a seat behind his desk.

"You can sit down." Lazarus motioned to the chairs.

"I'll stand, if you don't mind," Buck said, and brushed a few lingering crumbs of powdered sugar from his jacket.

Lazarus knew this wasn't going to be easy.

"So, how's the Knot case coming?" he asked.

"I like the cop for it, but Buck isn't so sure." Smitty glanced at Buck. "Her partner from New Orleans thinks she's been set up."

"And what do you think?" Lazarus looked at Smitty.

"The evidence isn't in her favor."

"Has she hired a local attorney?"

"Not yet," Buck said.

"Well …" Lazarus paused to loosen his shirt collar. "... I just got … off the phone with Commissioner Hurt. He has assured me that Ms. Knot's murder is completely unrelated to horseracing."

"Knot did have that sparring session with Black."

"I can read the paper." Lazarus looked down at his constricting hands a brief moment and willed himself to relax. Do you have anything else to support going after Black?"

"We're just starting to dig in that direction. I'm going to personally pay a visit to Commissioner Hurt this afternoon."

"No, you're not." Lazarus narrowed his eyes at Buck. "And don't go near Black either, not without his attorney present. Hurt said he will make such arrangements for you at a time most convenient to Black."

"Most convenient to Black? You gotta be shitting me." Buck began pacing.

"You already have a suspect in custody, you said so yourself."

Buck stopped. "Are you telling us to stop investigating other leads? I want to be clear about this."

Lazarus ignored the question. "Where are you on the Sanders' case?"

"I think it was a suicide, but I'm having a tough time selling it to Jack Vu, the Air Force investigator."

"What's he think?"

"Homicide or accidental."

"I'd like to go with accidental. Suicide or Homicide both open up shit storms this city doesn't need right now."

"What exactly are you talking about?" Smitty asked Lazarus.

"Before your time, Smitty," Lazarus explained. "Seven years ago, there was an incident in the stables at Churchill Downs. Sanders was raped and Patti Knot's husband at the time was nearly killed. No charges were ever filed."

"Fuck's sake. Could these cases be related?"

"This is a small town, Smitty. Everything is connected in one way or another."

Buck rolled his eyes. "We covered it up then and now you want me to cover up the results of that rape? Captain, the girl committed suicide. I can feel it in my gut."

"Suicides are messy and unpredictable. You, of all people, should know that."

Lazarus regretted the words as soon as he had said them. Buck's head snapped back and his face reddened as if he'd just been slapped. Lazarus sighed. "I'm telling you, look at accidental death."

"And I'm telling you, if I find out that that girl's death had anything to do with Hurt and his stuff-shirted cronies, things will play out differently this time."

Now on the defensive, Buck was even more eager to dig deeper into Sanders' death. This was not going as Lazarus had hoped. Time to play hard ball.

"You might want to reconsider that position, Sergeant Buck. Insubordination could reflect very poorly on your career."

"I'm perfectly willing to take that risk."

"Well, I'm not!" Smitty interjected. He rose to his feet and leaned across the desk toward Lazarus. "Captain, I'm Irish. I'm used to being served shit, and being told to eat it."

Smitty headed for the door, but issued the parting words, "Just don't serve me seconds."

17

Most of the jockeys had arrived at Churchill Downs by 6 a.m. Some had already hustled mounts for the day or were out on the track exercising horses. Others were in paddocks, wandering the backfield or simply resting. Apprentices, or "bugs" as they were called, remained under the watchful eye of trainers who commanded the infield, wielding pocket watches and clocking runs. Still others were down at the stables barking orders or assisting grooms. In short, it was a normal day at the track.

Donny Mason stood near the infield fence and tried to focus, despite a hangover and a punishing recurrence of violent mental images. The casual observer would detect an air of innocence about him. He was a man-child. Yet on rare occasions many found him dangerous. Maybe, it was the way his mind sorted information, how his thought processes misfired and became confused, distorted, delusional, or so his doctors said.

Donny eventually wandered out to the stables. It had been a long time since he last entered that area of the track. He and Knot were an item back then, long before the accident damaged his brain. He wondered if any of them would talk to him. How many would suspect he had killed her – he'd certainly threatened often enough – despite what the reporters were saying.

* * *

Hill reluctantly took a cab to Churchill Downs that same morning. He was unfamiliar with the perfunctory rituals of thoroughbred racing the cab driver tried to explain, and had no more interest in watching the activity once he arrived. He felt like a fish out of water, wandering barns, towering over miniature men and awkwardly squatting to speak eye-to-eye. Through it all, matters deteriorated thanks to an uncontrollable fit of sneezing.

He felt terribly feverish, and was forced to move from the paddock where employees hefted hay into stables causing his allergies to explode. He cursed, rubbing his eyes, until tears clouded his vision. A male jockey burst through one of the stalls nearby, its Dutch door swinging wide. Hill absently struck it with his shoulder.

Jarred by the mishap, he called out. "Hey – wait!"

The jockey ignored him, strutting through the barn like royalty and twirling a riding stick like a baton. Hill eventually caught up to him. "Damnit! Hold up!"

The little man stopped. Out of the shadows, Donny emerged and glanced in their direction, only to withdraw from sight, but remain within earshot.

Hill approached the jockey, staring at his crooked nose and scars. "Sorry to bother you, but I'm looking for a jockey by the name of Black – Brad Black?"

"Yeah, so…"

"I'm investigating a homicide."

The man perked up. "Black's?"

"No – Patti Knot's." Snot ran freely from Hill's nose at this point and he swiped it away. The jockey picked dirt from his own eye and glanced at Hill, nonverbally expressing his surprise that the detective was wasting his time with such silly questions. "Sorry - haven't seen the asshole today."

"Well – what about Knot? Was she well liked?"

"She was a fine rider – let's leave it at that."

Before Hill could continue, he started to sneeze. Turning his back to shield the jockey from the spray, Hill grabbed his sodden handkerchief. When he turned back around, the man had moved on. It wasn't worth chasing him down a second time. He obviously didn't want to get involved.

Hill, unaware a very curious Donny Mason was following him, saw more jockeys ahead. As he caught up to them, his face flushed. He couldn't help breathing down on them, staring at the tops of their heads instead of their faces. Their height was becoming a problem. After another thundering sneeze, one of the horses balked and kicked a stall door.

Hill wiped his nose. "Have you seen Black around?"

"You're scaring the horses," replied a curt jockey wearing blue silks. "Go try the infield." Abruptly, the entourage of jockeys strode away.

"Uh – thanks."

Hill's face and neck were beginning to prickle as he left the stables and crossed over into the grandstand, still unaware he was being watched. From there, he passed two checkpoints where he had to show identification. All around him colorfully clad little people darted about, serious about their work, oblivious to the giant in their midst.

A thick layer of dust hung over the infield. As Hill entered the area, his breathing intensified. His head pounded. His nose, which moments before flowed freely, was now plugged. Hill became a mouth breather, timing questions to his need for oxygen.

A track steward, overhearing Hill's labored conversation with one of the trainers, rose his hand. "Jock you're lookin' for just went to the clubhouse." He pointed over his shoulder toward a towering building near the infield gate.

Inside the glass dome a clerk at the information desk gave him directions. He rode the elevator up six flights to the clubhouse and the doors opened into a dark, cool bar. He took a deep breath, then went out onto the sunny balcony. According to the cocktail waitress, the jockey he'd been looking for was sitting down front with two Japanese businessmen in Italian suits, smoking Cuban cigars.

Hill thanked her and panted along.

All three men gazed up at the detective looming over their box seat. One of the men tapped his cigar ash over the balcony railing. Hill focused on the man in riding wear.

"Excuse me, Mr. Black – I'd like a word with you."

Brad replied, "And you are?"

Hill flashed his badge, which received disinterested grimaces from the table. He briefly explained he was from out of town working a local homicide case.

The businessmen stood up and excused themselves. "We're going to the bar, Brad – join us later, will you?"

After Hill blew his nose, he handed the jockey the clipping from the *Louisville Examiner*. Brad laid the article on the table.

Hill opted to come right out with it. "Nice southpaw."

"Not if you're on the receiving end. Patti was a jealous bitch."

"Of you?"

"Of my purse winnings. So far this year, I've surpassed Julie Krone's record of 2.3 million. Knot couldn't handle it."

"That's why she hit you?"

Brad calmly swatted a fly on his sleeve. "Out on the track I tapped her ass with my riding stick? It was a joke."

"And later on she confronted you. That it?"

"That's right." Brad's jaw tightened. "I should've had the bitch arrested."

In hasty attempt to catch another on-coming sneeze, Hill anxiously pulled out his handkerchief, though one of his cards accidentally fell out, fluttering over the rail. Both men ignored it. "What can you tell me about her death?"

"Just what I read in the papers," Brad said, then turned to greet a sharply dressed couple. "Good morning, Mr. & Mrs. Seemore. Nice to see you both. Oh, allow me to introduce Detective Hill.

Mr. Hill is from New Orleans."

The couple stopped and shook hands, the woman's arm heavy with diamonds and jewelry. Mrs. Seemore was a thoroughbred in her own right, with striking cheekbones. She wore a dress that curved over her slender figure. Mr. Seemore appeared much older up close, perhaps forty-five, and carried himself like a Harvard type. He wore a Rolex, which he immediately checked after shaking Hill's hand.

"What brings you to Louisville, detective?" he said politely.

"Business." Hill's nose wrinkled in a pre-sneeze spasm. The couple turned their attention to the jockey.

Mrs. Seemore smiled at Brad. "You're coming to the party, aren't you Brad?"

Brad smiled and nodded.

"Pardon me, detective, how rude of me. John and I are having a little reception Saturday after the races. We have a new colt to show off. If you're interested, I could give you the address."

"Thank you for the invitation, though I'm not sure I can make it. I'm allergic to horses, hay and grass."

"Sounds like you're allergic to Louisville," Black chuckled.

"We'll see you say, seven-thirty?"

"Absolutely," Brad said. "Looking forward to it."

"You're riding in the third and fifth today, correct?" John studied his racing form.

"Yes. An easy day…"

Hill coughed. Mrs. Seemore held her hand to her face. "You really should go see a doctor about those allergies, detective. I've heard people die from the hives alone."

The couple finally left. Hill sighed and took out his notebook. Brad was starting to walk away when Hill stopped him. "Hang on a minute. When was the last time you saw Ms. Knot?"

"The day she hit me."

"You didn't see her later?"

"No."

"Did you ever visit her property?"

"Yes, though it was a long time ago. I was interested in purchasing that property at one time. Patti beat me to it."

"Can you testify to your whereabouts on Sunday between noon and five?"

Brad acted like it was a game now. "Check with Mrs. Seemore. She'll confirm I was at their farm all day. I left about eight that night, met a girl at the Rubik's Cube downtown for drinks ... then we went back to her place."

"What was this girl's name?"

"Angie."

"Angie have a last name?"

"We were only on a first name basis."

"Where does Angie live?"

"She had a room at the Hilton. She was here on business."

Hill asked for the specifics and wrote them down. "Was Patti fighting with anyone else lately?"

"How would I know?"

Hill paused, studying Black's arrogant expression. "Why do you think someone would want to kill her?"

"Beats me."

"Could her death be connected with racing?"

"Possibly. We're a high strung lot."

"Go on..."

"Look, I've got to go, detective. I have a race. If I knew something, I'd tell you. Ask around, everyone's got an opinion on this murder. You'll have to draw your own conclusions."

The two rode down the elevator together.

"I'm going to need your address and phone number."

Brad reluctantly gave him the information. Hill wrote it down and put his notebook away. Brad didn't offer to shake hands.

Hill felt so lousy he decided to confirm Brad's alibi later. He also didn't notice Donny who had watched the two exit the building, Hill's errant business card firmly in hand.

Back at the hotel, Hill's vision was as fuzzy as his thinking.

Not only had he forgotten to take his pick kit earlier, which he needed to visit Knot's ranch home, but he had struggled outside his room, unable to determine how to open the door. A maid rolling a linen cart down the hall sized him up for an early drinker.

"Here, let me help you," she said. Hill stubbornly persisted on ramming the card backwards into the reader slot without success. Finally, he broke down and handed it over. The maid promptly flipped the card and slid it gently into the slot. The green light blinked and the door clicked open.

Hill noticed the maid was staring at his swollen face. He held up a small brown bag. "I have Benadryl and whiskey. I'm on the road to recovery."

The maid shook her head and left.

Hill closed the door behind him and headed straight for the toilet, bag in hand.

18

Vu had spoken to a dozen different people and needed to process their contradictory statements. Hence, he returned to the hotel room. When he entered, he heard a strange noise coming from the bathroom. The door was ajar so he cautiously poked his head in. Hill's pants were down and he was teetering on the toilet, clutching a whiskey bottle in one hand and a Kleenex in the other.

Vu shrunk. "Excuse me," he said, and began to close the door.

Hill glared at him with devilish eyes, swollen red with fever. "Wait!" Hill quickly popped four Benadryl with a whiskey chaser, and stood up. "Jack, we gotta talk about Gates' case!"

Hill's pants were twisted about his ankles and his shorts hung around his knees. He reminded Vu of an obscene Voodoo charm he'd once seen in the French Quarter purported to attract sexual partners. Hill shuffled toward him, only to be halted by a sneeze so nose twitching it even shook Vu. Vu couldn't believe how quickly Hill's body had deteriorated. He wouldn't have lasted a day in the internment camps in Vietnam.

"When you're finished."

"These fuckin' horses are killing me Vu. It took me an hour to get my contacts out and I'll never get them back in. I can't see shit."

Despite himself, Vu was starting to feel compassionate.

Sensing his pliability, Hill continued. "I've still got to break into the Knot place and I know there are going to be more horses around. Damnit, Jack, I need your help."

"Honestly, I'd help you if I could, but there are inconsistencies with the Sanders' case and I really need to concentrate on it."

"OK. Well, two heads are better than one. Help me with Gates and, I'll help you with Sanders."

"Allow me to consider it."

Frowning, Vu closed the door and took a seat by the window. He wondered how Betty's day was going and called her cell. When she didn't answer, he reluctantly left a message and watched as the wind scattered spring blossoms along the riverwalk below.

A few minutes later, he heard the toilet flush again. Hill stumbled through the bathroom door and flopped lifelessly onto the bed. He held the pillow over his eyes to block out the sunlight spilling into the room.

"Jack!" he mumbled. "I'm spent. Gates' life is at stake here. Can't we work this out? Nobody has to know we're swapping cases."

"Who said anything about swapping cases?"

"If I come near another fuckin' horse, I swear to God I'll put a slug in my head."

Vu thought it over. He stood contemplating the pathetic heap now slobbering on a pillow and mumbling incoherently. He made toward the door, but Hill didn't hear him move.

At the door, Vu stopped. The sick man greatly disturbed him. "I'll bring you back medicine for your allergies."

Hill sat up. "Where're you going?"

"I'm going to get some herb."

"Jack, I don't smoke pot."

Vu frowned. "I never assumed you did. Marijuana actually

aggravates allergies. You're of no help to me or Gates in your present condition. The herbs will help. Valuable time is wasting."

Outside the hotel, Vu stopped to get his bearings. He couldn't decide if the herb store he'd remembered seeing earlier was on Third or Fourth Street. He glanced at the sun and decided on Fourth. His karmic path with Hill was slowly being revealed. Hill had helped him once, long ago. Now, it was time to repay the favor. It was his destiny, as was this case.

Nearby, a dusty and dented black Cadillac sat parked beside the curb. Vu didn't notice the driver, who, after Vu had passed, climbed from the car and headed toward the hotel lobby.

* * *

After reading the card he'd found at the track, Donny Mason was certain that one Detective Bruce Hill from the New Orleans Police Department was trying to get the dyke off.

In his dementia, Donny had gone all out to become the quintessence of Elvis: white leather suit, long tawdry sequined cape, lame boots, gold-rimmed glasses, slicked back hair oozing Brylcreem. By contrast however, his face was markedly devoid of color. And behind the glasses, his piercing eyes mirrored a gleam which only psychotics may possess.

The bellhop chuckled and held the door open. "Afternoon, Elvis."

"Thank you … thank you very much." Donny proudly strutted into the Galt Hotel and approached the reservation desk.

For a man who'd been unable to sleep, living solely on cheap tequila, peanut butter and banana sandwiches, and Snicker's bars, Donny was felicitous and euphoric, even if his thoughts were disturbing.

The young clerk shrieked. "Elvis!"

Donny bowed. "Yes, ma'am. I've got an appointment with a man upstairs. Don't remember his room honey, but he's an important Hollywood type. Look up Bruce Hill on your screen, will ya darlin'?"

The clerk blushed, a big fan of the King. "What was the name again?"

"Hill, honey. Like the sweet hills of Kentucky ... you remember the song..." Donny sang a few bars.

Hill sat up when he heard the door rattle. He figured Vu had forgotten his cardkey. A moment later, a sharp kick against the wood alerted his numb brain, but his head still pounded and his eyes were a blurry mess.

"Jesus, Jack – I'm coming." Even Vu was losing it these days, he thought, as he climbed off the bed and opened the door.

The whiskey had obviously destroyed what remaining ability Hill had to see without his contacts. What the hell was Jack doing in an Elvis costume?

Hill blinked, thinking the image would clear. Then, a searing pain crashed down upon his nose. The King punched him again. He stumbled backwards, and then it was over. The final thought his brain registered was his slow descent to the floor.

* * *

A college kid in dreadlocks ran the Herbal Emporium on Fourth Street. He was polite, knowledgeable and reeked of patchouli oil. As he led Vu down the aisle, he pointed toward a row of plastic bins.

"Wild Chrysanthemum is second from the right. What else did you need?" Vu told him. "Honeysuckle is on the far wall. Schizonepeta? Don't think we carry that."

"What about Bi Yan Pian?"

"We might have a few bottles behind the counter," he said. "What else did you say? Oh, right, Xanthium fruit. Two bins down and green tea, far shelf. What else?"

Vu said he would browse awhile and let him know.

The clerk returned to the register. After he located the pills the clerk put on some new-age music and lit an incense cone. The sweet fragrance wafted through the air, though Vu didn't care for it, nor the electronic music. He quickly collected the rest of his herbal necessities and proceeded to checkout.

The clerk put down the CD case he was reading and rang up Vu's purchase. He bagged each item carefully.

"You want one of our free newsletters?"

Vu declined.

"There's a ten percent coupon inside."

"Save a tree."

Vu wandered back toward the hotel along busy Fourth Street. Suddenly, a keen sense of urgency seized him. His arms broke out in *'gu:sskin*. Goosebumps.

19

Hill groaned on the floor and struggled to open his eyes. A haze rose from the carpet. He couldn't focus on the moving image before him. Then, it all started coming back. He strained to rise and felt a heavy weight on his chest. A rhinestone boot crushed his ribcage.

Grabbing the leg, Hill attempted to wrench it off, but was too weary to defend himself. Donny dropped to straddle Hill's chest, grabbed his throat, and squeezed. Hill's eyes bulged, gasping for air.

"If Priscilla was dead, what would you do?" Elvis roared.

Hill tried to squirm loose, but he was pinned to the floor. His gun was under his pillow. Suddenly, the hotel door opened.

Startled by the intruder, Vu screamed, not in terror, but in furious rage. He dropped his bag and rushed toward Elvis.

Donny tried to fend Vu off and staggered into the dresser. Vu, a black belt in Aikido, kicked him in the stomach. As Vu moved in, Hill rolled to his knees, spouting as his lungs filled with air. Vu, his concentration broken by Hill rising from the depths of the floor like a surfacing submarine, didn't even see the table lamp that Donny picked up and flung at him. It was a direct hit. Vu stumbled over Hill and fell down, his forehead split open.

Donny ran.

Vu struggled upright. "Where'd he go?"

Hill pointed at the open door. Vu stood, wobbling. Between allergies, whiskey, Benadryl and a choke-hold, Hill couldn't budge. He sat cross-legged in the middle of the floor.

Vu uttered. "Stay down."

With no choice but to oblige, Hill gradually shook his head as if explosives were strapped to his forehead and he was deathly afraid to move.

Vu staggered into the hall, but the elevator door was closed. Vu knew he'd never catch the intruder. Elvis had left the building.

Blood trickled onto Vu's cell as he called 911.

* * *

Detective Buck was fondling a new Fender in Denny's Guitar shop on Fourth Avenue; a frequent hangout for him during off hours. The sleek instrument was a perfect fit.

"I'll go find an amp." The owner, Denny Ring, wandered off toward a rack of amplifiers. Buck smiled and licked a furious round of air guitar.

Before the suicide, Buck's sister, Rebecca Ann Buck, had been an avid music fan too. Buck still felt a connection with her every time he came into their favorite store. For years, they'd jammed together. Rebecca played a Nash, always willing to bang away on the "bone yard tunes" as she'd called them: Aerosmith, Led Zeppelin, Def Leopard, AC/DC, an occasional Steppenwolf, or Beatles song. With no wife or kids at home, they were precious memories. She would have been twenty-four this week.

Buck had a younger step-brother living in Ohio, though they rarely spoke now that Rebecca was gone. He felt empty. Even when he played, memories of Rebecca stirred a dull pain no music could ease.

"Hey – Sam!" Denny shouted from across the room. "Come

over here."

Buck turned toward the shopkeeper, just as Smitty burst through the front door. What bad timing.

"I'm being paged," Buck shouted and set down the guitar on the counter. He threaded his way to the front of the store.

Smitty briefed him on the latest news.

"So Jack Vu is staying with Hill, Gates' partner?

"Yep, these two homicides are connected in more ways then one."

"When did Vu call?"

"About twenty minutes ago. Couldn't reach you on your cell phone. Figured you might be here."

"I turned it off. They hurt?"

"Their pride is, but they'll live. Cuts and bruises mostly."

"They ID anyone?"

"Yep, one psychotic Elvis!"

Buck frowned. "Young Elvis or old Elvis?"

"Young."

"Shit. Anyone get a plate?"

"Negative."

"Well, that'll buy us some time. I'll head over to the hotel and take their statements, then meet you back at the barn in an hour."

"We'll have to deal with this right quick, mate. Can't sweep two cops under the rug, despite the Captain."

* * *

The paramedics were leaving the hotel room when Buck arrived. He caught the door as it was closing and peered inside.

"May I come in?"

Vu sat in an overstuffed chair across the room with a fresh bandage around his forehead, cradling a steaming cup of tea. Heeding the gold shield, he nodded. Hill ignored Buck. He sat upright on the bed with his stocking feet propped up, a splint taped to his nose, his eyes already starting to bruise. He nursed a bottle of bourbon.

Buck entered and offered to shake Hill's hand. "I don't believe we've met, detective?"

Hill placed the bottle on the nightstand and wiped his lips. "I met your partner, Irish prick named Smitty."

Buck moved back from the bed, nonetheless disturbed by Hill's cool air. Vu intervened.

"Detective – this is Bruce Hill, Dorene Gates' partner. We're bunking together because the hotel lost my reservation."

"And it's a damn good thing," Hill added, "because he just saved my pathetic ass."

Vu sat up straight and placed his cup on the table. Buck took out his notebook.

Vu said, "I spoke with the clerk in the lobby. She admits giving the intruder the room number."

"Let me get it straight again – the intruder was an Elvis impersonator?"

"Right," Hill said, and gave him the details. "He's a genuine nutcase. He kept yelling, 'if Priscilla was dead'…"

"He say who killed her?"

"I got the distinct impression I had something to do with it."

"Did you?"

"Don't get smart."

"You're certain he was trying to kill you?"

"Absolutely trying to snuff me." Hill pointed to the red marks along his neck. "Look at these. Fuckin' Elvis bastard…"

"How'd he get in?"

"I heard someone rattling the door and thought it was Jack." Hill hung his head.

Buck scribbled in his notebook. "Where did you go today?"

"Churchill Downs," Hill said.

"And…"

"I spoke with several jockeys, a few track officials and a couple patrons."

"You go anywhere else?"

"To the liquor store."

"Piss someone off at the track?"

"Nope."

Buck looked at Vu. "What about you, Special Investigator?"

"I walked along the river walk and made some inquiries."

"What kind of inquiries?"

"I assure you, they're unrelated."

"Anyone follow you?"

"Doubtful."

Buck studied him closely. He distrusted Vu. He made a note then put away his notebook. "This assault disturbs me several ways gentlemen. To begin with, a police officer was nearly strangled in our city. That is a first. The fact that you were attacked here, without provocation, suggests something else. It feels ... personal."

Hill picked up the tiny brown bottle of Bi Yan Pian from the nightstand and washed several pills down with whiskey. "I know where you're going with this."

"Take it easy with those," Vu interrupted. "You should eat."

Hill shrugged and glared at Buck. "You think we instigated all this?"

"Yes, I do."

"That's good. Then it also means someone wants to shut us up."

Buck frowned. "How do you figure?"

Hill hesitated, his face turning the color of snow. He swallowed hard, touched his forehead. "Jack – these pills – I – don't feel so good." Suddenly, Hill jumped up, covered his mouth and ran to the bathroom. Through the thin walls, the men could hear him vomit.

Vu glanced at Buck. "I think we're finished for now," Vu said. "You will keep me informed?"

Buck shrugged. "Yeah, sure..." He took in the broken

furniture, blood, torn drapes and stench.

"Is there something else, detective?" Vu asked.

Buck scowled. "You need to pack. You're changing rooms."

20

Vu couldn't believe his eyes. The new room was even more claustrophobic than the last. A horrid windowless cubicle in the basement, and yet, it was the most secure area of the hotel, according to the manager. No access existed to the floor without a special key. Vu paced off the room. At five, he reached the corner. Sighing, he sat down on its lone chair.

Suddenly, Hill was in good spirits. The pills Vu had given him had him all jacked up.

He turned to Vu. "Hey, Jack – I'm hitting the bar for a nightcap. Want to join me?"

"No, thank you."

"You sure? We could review our notes while we check out the babes?"

"Perhaps tomorrow."

"Hey – one thing I thought. We've got to look into who would profit from Knot's death. According to Gates, she owns a pretty nice spread. It might be motive."

"I'm certain you can obtain that information from public records."

"C'mon, Jack – why do you always have to bust my balls?"

"Quite frankly, I'm too exhausted to bust anyone's balls."

"Whatever." Hill started toward the door, then stopped and grinned. "Don't worry about leaving a light on."

Vu frowned. "I suppose there could be somebody out there with a nose fetish."

Hill tapped his nose tenderly in jest. "Who knows?" he said. "I might get lucky."

* * *

Business in the lounge was slow. Hill found a seat at the bar, ordered a beer and spun his chair toward the dance floor. An attractive woman in a low-cut dress came out of the bathroom, gracefully walked past him to a discreet corner booth and joined her date. When the music resumed, they walked onto the dance floor and began dancing. A few other couples eventually joined in. Hill glanced around. Pickings were slim.

Hill still couldn't get a handle on Jack Vu. Just when he thought he knew what the man was thinking, Vu would throw him a curve. His mood would change and he would grow contemplative. Hill figured it must be cultural. Something inside the little Asian man was shut off from the rest of the world. This isolation vexed Hill to no end.

As he sipped his beer, he focused on Gates' case. She'd really done it up this time, got the whole fuckin' police community bent on putting her away. It just didn't make any sense though. Hill perused his notebook, when it suddenly dawned on him. Gates had mentioned they may have been stalked by an Elvis ringer that said he was married to Patti.

About that time, a man sat down at the bar next to him. Hill paid no attention until the man held out a pack of Camels and offered him a cigarette.

"You find Elvis?" Hill asked.

"Not yet." Buck lit a cigarette.

Hill was in no mood for bullshit.

"How many could there be claiming to be married to Knot?"

"I don't know what you're talking about," Buck rejoined.

Hill chugged his beer and ordered another. "You didn't just show up here by coincidence. What'd you want?"

The bartender, a middle-aged woman, with an unexpected gleam in her eyes after such a long shift, delivered Buck a tall glass of scotch and water, on the house. "Don't usually see you at this hour, Sam. What's the special occasion?"

"Sally, meet Detective Bruce Hill. He's from New Orleans. Here on business."

Sally stared at Hill's lumpy face. "Nice to meet ya."

"Hill's partner is in jail. He believes she's innocent. What do you think, Sally? Should I allow our only suspect in Patti Knot's murder to go free?"

Sally stiffened. "The Chocolate Dyke?"

Hill spun his bar stool around and faced Buck. "You prick!"

Buck countered. "We spoke to your supervisor. She's a loose cannon."

The bartender sensed tension and quickly busied herself with other patrons.

Hill steadied his hand on his glass, but couldn't help feeling the rage boiling to the surface. Two young African American men approached the bar beside Buck and waited to order. Their presence visibly distracted Buck, who quickly sized them up and seemed agitated. He put his cigarette down in the ashtray and rudely slid it aside so that the smoke would drift into their faces. Hill noticed this racial snub, which added to his loathing.

The two men glared at Buck who seemed smugly amused by his antics. One of the men started to reach for the ashtray and Buck confronted him. "Got a problem?" he said loudly.

Hill watched a couple move away from the bar. It didn't take a genius to figure out Buck was a bigot, which could explain some of his actions regarding Gates.

Hill leaned across Buck and dumped his remaining beer on the smoldering cigarette. Buck slid back from the bar and glowered.

Extinguishing one tinder had obviously ignited another.

"What you gonna do about it?" Hill challenged.

"I'm gonna charge Gates with murder in the death of Patti Knot."

Hill threw the first punch and the bar cleared.

Sally, who had years of experience in such matters, pulled a fire extinguisher from beneath the bar, leaned over the counter, aimed the nozzle at Hill and blasted a cloud of white powder. The detective's whitewashed face emerged from the cloud, coughing, his hands frantically swiping chemical dust from his eyes.

Vu stepped under the shower, letting it massage his back and shoulders until he slowly relaxed under the warm water. As his breathing slowed and his neck unkinked, he reached for his toiletries and removed a worn bar of soap. Closing his eyes, he lathered his face and chest, inhaling the scent of white ginger, Betty's scent. He lathered again and sluiced water from his chest, stomach and thighs. His mind replayed intimate scenes with Betty as he soaped and massaged. Steam overtook the mirrors. Ginger filled the air. Vu saw her smile, felt her warmth. His love could only lie fallow for so long. With an aroma of Betty permeating the room, he emerged from the bathroom renewed, reconnected, and grateful. His Zen-like glow lasted only until he towel dried his hair, sparking the fiery sear of stitches on his face.

Reality is overrated, Vu thought, as he limped to the bed.

21

ill never made it home. Vu awoke to this news from Buck at 0100. He told Vu he'd lose the paperwork just as soon as Hill settled down. In the meantime, Vu had work to do.

At 0200 he visited the manager of the Spenser Hotel on Jacob Street, a grizzled character who needed a shave and a bath. The man sat on a stool eating Doritos from the bag, wiping the grease from his fingers on his dirty trousers, and slurping amber liquid from a coffee mug. His beady eyes flicked back and forth while he watched court dramas on a portable TV and half-attempted to read Vu's military ID. The bars over the lobby window gave Vu the feeling he was standing in a pawn shop.

"Beverly Sanders is not on our guest list," the manager insisted.

Vu put his ID away and produced a photograph of Ms. Sanders in uniform. He held the picture up to the bars. The manager was uninterested, glancing only briefly.

"Nope. As I said, never seen her."

"Take another look."

"Mister, I got work to do."

Vu examined the man's hands. The nails were ragged and grey, his skin pale. He was a smoker and probably a heavy drinker.

Vu put the photograph in his jacket. He stepped back from the counter and glanced around the lobby. The walls were painted an institutional green and the carpet was threadbare and filthy. A small table in the corner held a cheap lamp and phone. The few prints hanging on the walls were faded and yellow. This would have been the last place he'd expect a young female to stay. But, it was clear she hadn't stayed at the Marriott, even though she'd made a reservation and checked in.

Why this dive? And why keep the room in the Marriot? How much did her friends really know?

A couple walked through the front door arm in arm and headed toward the counter. The man, in his late fifties, was well dressed. The woman wore stiletto-heels, a short skirt and a low-cut, slinky top. Vu figured it was a business arrangement. Her youthful face had layers of makeup, her long bangs partially hiding bloodshot eyes. The woman reached into her small handbag and removed a twenty-dollar-bill, which she fed through the slot to the manager, who in exchange passed her a room key. Without a word, the woman pocketed the key and led the man upstairs. A few minutes later, Vu heard a door close on an upper floor.

Vu approached the counter again and rummaged his brain to retrieve one of the many *Dragnet* episodes he'd memorized. Aping his TV hero, Jack Webb, had never failed before.

"Nice operation," Vu said gruffly. "You pay taxes on that money?"

The man choked on a chip. He coughed and washed it down with his "coffee". "What?"

"You heard me."

"Nothing illegal about short-term rates."

"Really – let's see what the police think."

Vu wondered if the shakedown would work. The man grumbled to himself, switched channels on the TV and finally, gave in.

"Let me see that photograph again," he said. "When did you

say she checked in?"

"Last week."

Vu took out the photograph and showed it to the clerk. "Look for someone who pre-paid for a week, maybe two."

That seemed to please him. "That narrows it down, let me see here."

The manager flipped through his hotel registry and found two reservations made by women for the time period in question. "Jensen and Larson," he said. "Take your pick."

"They're both still checked in?"

"That's right. And they just paid up for another week."

Vu leaned forward, peering through the bars at the registry book. "What other information do you show there?"

The man ran his finger across the line. "Jensen listed her home address as Minnesota. Larson listed Florida. Look, most of our rooms are rented on a monthly basis right now because of the racing season. The track's temporary housing burnt down last year so they contracted with us to provide rooms to the employees and out-of-town jockeys.

"Keep looking."

The clerk frowned. "Wait – here's one. Hey – her rent was due yesterday. I don't show that she paid."

"What's the name?"

"A Jill Brown from Colorado Springs."

Vu perked up. The Air Force Academy was located in Colorado Springs.

From his wallet, he pulled a twenty-dollar-bill and slipped it through the slot. "Ten minutes – I won't take anything."

The manager looked him over. "Leave your ID."

Vu nodded and slid Hill's business card through the slot. The manager handed him the room key. "You got ten minutes."

Jill Brown's room was on the third floor at the end of the hall. Vu stopped at the door, knocked and waited. Two doors down, a door creaked open. Two dark eyes peered out at him, then the door closed. Vu stuck the key in the slot and went inside.

The room reeked of mold, the musty scent irritating his sinuses. He walked over to the window and attempted to open it, but it was painted shut. The furnishings were old and cheap. The cramped bed in the corner sagged on one side. He checked the closet and quickly began to mentally itemize all of the personal effects within the room. One overnight bag with women's clothing neatly packed: a pair of blue jeans, two white shirts and a new pair of Nikes. Hanging were two items, a pair of women's slacks and a red dress. In the bathroom he noticed an oily ring around the tub, a bottle of bubble bath, shampoo, and liquid soap. On the counter sat a toothbrush, nail clippers, a bottle of pink nail polish, which he focused on briefly, basic cosmetics and a blonde wig combed out and placed on a stand. Nothing extravagant or alarming, he thought, with perhaps the exception of an actor's makeup kit. Many of the items had been used. He stooped over and removed several stained Kleenex from a trash can, inspected the dried mascara and lipstick marks, then tossed them away.

Next, he checked the single dresser. In the top drawer he found two pairs of women's underwear, three pairs of socks, two Harley-Davidson T-shirts, a paperback novel and a holster, but no gun. In the second drawer he found a pair of torn jeans, a flannel shirt, a black stocking cap and a pair of women's cotton pajamas. Beneath the bed he found a used condom. He pulled it out. It had been there at least a month or more. It was covered in dust with a small dead spider curled up inside. He checked underneath the mattress and found two heavy manila envelopes. One was marked "photographs." The other was marked "records."

Vu sat down on the bed and carefully opened one envelope at a time. The first held documents. Vu soon realized this contained a concise unofficial case file. Bevy had been collecting information on someone going back several years. There were pages of official address searches, city and state records, criminal histories, public records and web documents from an ancestry database. Vu suspected she had used her Air Force position to obtain background information unavailable to the general public. There were also official documents from racetracks around the globe.

The second envelope contained mostly photographs. Black and white photographs of jockeys, grooms, track officials, bettors standing at ticket windows, and crowd shots. All were taken with a telephoto lens. The photographs appeared random at first, but then narrowed in focus. Bevy had actually only been trailing a handful of people. There were outdoor photographs of a slaughterhouse, a ranch, a barn and a residence. Then, there were a series of old photographs taken inside a barn, specific close-ups of what Vu assumed was a crime scene: snapshots of a pair of bloodstained and torn women's underwear, a pair of small blue jeans with a torn zipper, a bra, a white shirt with stains on the pocket, traces of blood and semen on the hay where a struggle had occurred. In one of the photos a worn cowboy hat lay on the floor and an uncoiled bullwhip rested on a hay bail. And, there was an old worn saddle lying on the floor, turned on its side. Vu absorbed it all. Bevy had meticulously documented everything – everything about her own rape.

Vu stood up, slipped the manila envelopes inside his jacket, and left the room.

Out in the hall, Vu was locking the door when a Mexican man wearing a Stetson stepped out of the next room. He sized-up Vu for a moment before locking his deadbolt.

"Excuse me?" Vu said. "Did you have any conversations with the girl in this room?"

"No habla English," the man said in Spanish and started to walk away.

Vu caught up to him and said, in the man's native tongue, "Cono zoca, Senorita Brown?"

"Sí, yes," the Mexican said.

"What was she doing here? Did she say?"

"Sí – she wanna find somebody."

"Quien? Who?"

"She not say. I see her last week at the track. She speaks to some jock-ayes."

"Anyone particular?"

He nodded. "Senorita Knot."

"You know Senorita Knot was murdered?"

The man lowered his eyes. "Sí." He shrugged and stared down at his muddy boots. "Senor, something has happen to Senorita Brown?"

22

The next morning, Detective Buck was in his bathrobe manhandling an iron skillet on the stove, not feeling his best due to a few aches and pains from the night before. A glass of tomato juice with a splash of vodka sat on the kitchen table next to an ashtray where a cigarette smoldered.

He knew why Hill had cracked, and was shamed by his own behavior in baiting both Hill and the black men. Everyone knew about Rebecca and the spooks that raped her. Everyone stood witness to her emotional breakdown and suicide. Racial tensions hummed constantly beneath the surface of every southern town and both blacks and whites tried to even the score whenever they could. Indeed, Hill had him pegged exactly for what he was: a stone racist. He'd always leaned that way. As a kid he learned early on he could blame anything on the colored kids and get away with it. Still, he usually knew enough to hide such baiting and intimidation of blacks from outsiders.

Eggs were sizzling in the hot grease and white bread was in the toaster when a knock on the front door snapped him from his musing.

Through the peephole he saw Smitty pacing the porch in a

freshly pressed suit and tie. Buck had not shaved, nor was his hair combed. He stared at his watch. Smitty was an hour early. Buck reluctantly unlocked the deadbolt and opened the door.

"I thought the hearing was at 11?"

Smitty frowned at Buck. "They've moved it up to 10 in order to throw off the press. That gives you fifteen minutes to shit, shower, shave and do something about that shiner."

Buck stepped back from the door, remembering all too well the fight from the previous night. "That doesn't even give me time to get Hill released."

"Yeah, I heard about last night. And so did the Captain. We can deal with that later." Smitty stepped inside the small apartment, glanced around, and wrinkled his nose. "Smells like you're burning toast."

Buck slammed the door and made a beeline for the kitchen where smoke rolled from the toaster. He flipped the stuck lever and popped out two transformed slices of Wonder Bread. They were black. He tossed the bread into the sink while Smitty turned off the burner under the eggs.

As Buck headed into the bathroom, Smitty picked up the tomato juice and chugged it down. Then, humming a raunchy limerick, he found a fork, and began eating the rubbery eggs from the skillet.

The DA, Charles Anbrought, an upwardly mobile trial lawyer, was tapping his wing-tip shoe against the table leg when Buck and Smitty entered the courtroom and sat down. The DA turned to them, frowned at Buck's face and checked his watch.

Buck surveyed the courtroom and spotted Sergeant Vu sitting behind Gates and her attorney, a slender young woman in a black suit. Gates was in orange prison coveralls, her street clothes having been taken as evidence. With her eyes swollen, her hair pulled back, and her hands and feet shackled, Buck felt a twinge of remorse knowing he had deprived her partner from lending moral support. Guilty or innocent, he knew how Gates must feel.

The judge looked up and put his glasses on. "Shall we begin then?"

"Your honor," the DA stood, "Case number 30-06, the State of Kentucky vs. Dorene Gates. Ms. Gates is accused of Murder in the First Degree with extenuating circumstances of Patti L. Knot, one of our most beloved and distinguished citizens. We recommend that bail be denied. Not only does Ms. Gates pose a substantial flight risk, but her access to and knowledge of the legal system, due to her law enforcement background, provides distinct advantage to manipulate the system."

Dorene's lawyer rose to her feet. "Christy McKnight, appearing on behalf of the defendant." She looked directly at the judge. "Your honor, my client enters a plea of Not Guilty to this charge and has already been detained without bail for over 72 hours. Denying bail based upon her law enforcement background only further aggravates the blatant injustice that has been forced upon her. We humbly request that you set a reasonable bail so that Ms. Gates may resume some semblance of normal life after the tragic loss of her friend."

"Unfortunately, murdering and assaulting our local citizens in drunken rage are the only semblances of Ms. Gates' normal life exhibited thus far in our fair city," the DA responded. "By her Captain's own admission, Ms. Gates is a loose cannon with an impressive string of excessive force claims amassed in her personnel file."

"That's enough, Mr. Anbrought." The judge sat back and thumbed through some papers on his desk. "Ms. McKnight, there's substantial evidence here to proceed to trial. As to the issue of bail, whether Ms. Gates is a flight risk or not is immaterial given the evidence before me, which clearly places her at the scene of the crime. I have to agree with the DA. Foresight is always better than hindsight. Your client is fully aware of her survival chances behind bars. Given the evidence, Ms. Gates' history and law-enforcement background, bail is denied. The defendant will remain in custody at this time."

Gates turned and made eye contact with Vu as Ms. McKnight spoke mutedly to her.

"Bailiff, please escort the defendant from the courtroom."

Vu watched as she was led away. When Gates was gone, he glanced back at the judge. *Did they really have enough to convict?*

Outside the courtroom, Vu waited in the hall for the others to exit. He needed to speak with both the detectives and Ms. McKnight. He would leave fate to decide which matter to tackle first. Gates' lawyer was the first through the door. Vu approached her. "May we go somewhere and speak?" he asked.

McKnight's eyes were the color of jade. She nodded. "Follow me. We'll slip out the back door."

She led him downstairs and across the street to a busy coffee shop. They found a table against the back wall and sat down, McKnight positioning herself to watch the crowd. Vu immediately disliked the vocal din of their very public forum.

As people chatted and waitresses shouted orders, Vu leaned across the table toward McKnight. "I assume we would meet in your office or a more private setting."

"It's bad enough I was forced to take this case. But, I am not going to rub my firm's face in it anymore than I have to by dragging you, Gates' partner, or the press back to our door."

Vu could only imagine what a public relations nightmare this case could be to a young associate. This type of case could ruin careers. "Who forced you to take this case?"

McKnight's posture and eyes softened. "My old high school counselor, Mrs. Brown." She leaned forward. "She straightened me out in school. Helped me survive foster care, get through community college, and got me accepted into law school. I told her if I could ever repay her, all she had to do was ask."

Vu cleared his throat. He understood more than she could imagine about payback - the forces set in motion by every action or inaction.

A waitress arrived to take their orders.

"Detective Gates requested that I show you and Detective Hill everything we have." McKnight opened her briefcase and removed Gates' file. Vu shed his jacket and pulled out a notebook.

A cell phone began vibrating against the Formica table. McKnight flipped it open. "I've got to take this."

She slid out of the booth and walked toward the door and out onto the street, speaking guardedly. Vu watched her pace as she spoke.

From cursory reading, Vu could tell that much of this file had been redacted. His visit to the morgue had been more helpful than anything he would read inside. He did, however, jot down a few names and addresses to give to Hill.

McKnight returned to the table and sat down. "Sorry."

"Do you know if Ms. Knot had a will?"

McKnight shook her head. "She probably had several lawyers handling different aspects of her life. I'll see what I can find out."

"It might shed some light on who could profit from her death."

"Well, what's your take on this? You know Ms. Gates. Do you think she was set up?"

"I don't know, but I am certain she is innocent of these charges."

"Then, you and Detective Hill belong to an exclusive club at the moment."

"Hopefully that will change." Vu paused, noticing the wedding band on McKnight's hand. The waitress delivered their order and left.

"Was Patti Knot married?"

"In a way." McKnight studied her hands. "Louisville is a small conservative town. We are fiercely loyal to our own and we keep our own counsel." She toyed with her ring. "Patti Knot married Donny Mason in her 20's. He was a popular race car driver and a rising NASCAR hopeful. She was a thoroughbred jockey on a winning streak. They were the town's Charles and Diana, as near to royalty as you can get for Louisville. One night, he was at the track to pick her up and became involved in a scuffle with some other men. Story is, they were beating and raping a teenager."

Vu felt the hairs on his neck prickle. "Do you know the woman's name?"

"Beverly Sanders."

Vu's stomach tightened. "I am here investigating her death."

McKnight sipped some coffee and lowered her voice even more. "It was my understanding she killed herself."

Vu remained quiet, studying her face.

McKnight continued. "Donny was struck in the head with a pipe and has been mentally impaired ever since. Patti was named his Conservator, and she took care of him financially, though they both lived separate lives."

"Did anyone know she was gay?"

"There were always rumors. Knot traveled alone on the racing circuit. Kentucky, New York, New Jersey, Florida, two trips to Japan, one to Peru. Even raced along the West Coast. I have spoken to colleagues of hers who said she was definitely a lesbian. But, she never came out in Louisville."

"What about long-term female relationships?"

"Most of these jockeys marry or hook up with their own kind. It's easier that way. They spend eighty percent of their time at the track or with horses, which doesn't leave much time for socializing."

"Sounds similar to the military."

"Or a law career." McKnight played with her cup. "I've tried to grasp why Gates would have reason to kill Patti. The evidence supports it, but my gut is that this is one more cover-up, and so says town gossip."

"One more cover-up?"

"No one was ever charged in Donny Mason's beating or Sanders' rape. This is not always the genteel Southern town it appears."

Vu knew that nothing is as it appears.

"As you know, Detective Buck is the prime on this case. About a year ago, his kid sister was raped. The suspects were reportedly three black gang members with criminal records. However, the only witness failed to identify them during a lineup. Once again, no arrests were made."

Vu mentally attempted to connect all these events scattered across a decade.

McKnight continued. "At the time, Buck was deployed with the military and late getting the news. He was unable to come home for a couple of weeks and eventually tried to avoid redeployment altogether, but that didn't pan out. During his last tour, his sister committed suicide. Buck sunk pretty hard. He took some leave, but overall it changed him."

Vu sat back and thought about how the detective had responded the day they viewed Ms. Sanders' body in the morgue. How transfixed he was by the corpse's face. Something struck a nerve. This might also explain his reluctance to move forward on the Sanders' case.

"I want to proffer another item of interest," Vu said finally. "According to a police report, Gates indicated that no one else visited the ranch and that she did not bring flowers with her. If that was the case, how'd the flowers get there? Have you spoken to her about them?"

McKnight fumbled with her briefcase. "I gotta admit Sergeant – what flowers?"

"The fresh flowers Ed Lynch found on the ground outside the stall."

McKnight seemed surprised.

"Someone could have delivered them before she was killed," Vu offered. "But, I highly doubt that."

McKnight opened the file and flipped through the pages. "Shit. Lynch did mention seeing them."

"The police didn't log them into evidence?"

McKnight rifled through the file again. "Apparently not," she said. "Sergeant, do you have any budget for inquiries in this case?"

"You're joking right?"

"What if our office were to pay for your services?"

"I've known Hill and Gates for a couple of years. I've had disagreements with Gates and the way she handles herself; there's no love lost between us. But, something isn't right. I think Buck may have set Hill up to get him out of the way while they tie up loose ends on the case."

"You may be right," McKnight conceded.

"I'm going to try and help get to the bottom of this."

"Good." McKnight studied Vu's face for a moment and sat back. "A word of advice though. Underneath all our Southern charm lies a visceral bed of distrust. Louisville's come a long way, though it's not what I'd call culturally enlightened."

Vu cradled his cup. *What type of town would welcome a murderous black lesbian, a Vietnamese man, and a brawling outsider into their midst?*

McKnight finished her coffee and used the napkin to wipe her mouth. "I'm due back at the office in twenty minutes."

McKnight pulled out her business card and handed it across the table. "Keep me posted." Then, she stood and offered her hand. "And, if you change your mind about my offer..."

Vu jumped up and shook hands. He admired the attorney's firm handshake and slipped the card into his pocket.

"That won't be necessary," he said. "Thank you."

"You're welcome detective," McKnight smiled, "but stay out of trouble."

23

A cross town an escalating groan escaped as perfect teeth bit down on tender flesh. The late morning sunlight shimmered from beneath the master bedroom door of a posh two-story condominium where two bodies writhed in heat.

Atop the king-sized mattress, Mona clawed at the sheets. Sweat rolled down the curvy center of her naked spine while Brad's firm hands held her to his bare chest. Moments later she arched her toned back and thrust her hips forward, moaning a second pleasurable cry.

Afterwards, Mona sat back on Brad's cock, her lips curled with satisfaction. Admiring Brad's muscular chest glistening with sweat, she felt powerful and young again.

"I needed that," she said, her breathing slowly returning to normal.

"Apparently," Black said, with a smug hint of arrogance in his voice. Suddenly, he rolled Mona over and jumped up.

"Brad?"

"Did you hear that?"

"What?"

"The doorbell."

Brad pulled on a bathrobe and checked the window. Out in the drive, Commissioner Hurt was climbing back into his town car. Brad quickly closed the curtains and turned back toward the bed where Mona lay sprawled on the sheets with one tan leg arched seductively upward. She rolled over.

"Who was it?"

"The racing commissioner."

"Ben Hurt?"

"Yeah. I wonder what the fuck he wanted."

"Shit!" Mona slapped the mattress, her afterglow quickly vanishing. "That nosey bastard saw my car parked here."

"Chill, baby. Ben is harmless."

"It's not him I'm worried about."

"I can handle the hubby."

Mona thought it over.

"Maybe he'll divorce you, and then you can be all mine."

"John Seemore doesn't have the balls to divorce me."

She cocked her head at Brad. "Bring me a treat. I'm not ready to face the music yet."

Brad removed a small silver platter from inside the dresser and emptied a vial onto it. He picked up a razor blade from the nightstand and evenly cut the contents into four fine lines. Next, he picked up a glass straw and snorted two of the white powdery lines, then handed the tray to Mona. She snorted the remaining two lines and threw her head back, her eyes tearing profusely. After a few moments, a glow appeared on her face. She licked the platter clean.

Mona patted the sheet provocatively, her heart racing, her breathing irregular. "Let's take another ride."

But Black was gone. The cocaine did that to him. He crawled onto the bed, but didn't mount her naked body like she anticipated. He sat cross-legged and serious, his penis limp and wrinkled. Mona fondled him, but even her warm erotic touch could not engorge his spent manhood.

"If I wanted a limp dick, I could stay home." Mona rolled over and reclined.

Black's fist tightened. A vein popped out on his wrist. He shot a wicked leer at Mona that both frightened and excited her.

Black rolled on top of her, forcing her wrists against the bed. Mona's eyes sparkled with delight. "That's better…"

"We're going to have the husband sign the contract today, aren't we?"

"You know – you may just have to bang me a few more times before the ink is dry on that contract."

"What do I call you after your husband wins the election? Mrs. Governess?"

Mona liked the sound of those words. "Just stick it in."

24

Willy tapped his drumstick against the rim of his snare and listened. Too much glassware in this place, he thought. Makes the sound tinny.

The band was just setting up on the enclosed patio of the Seemore estate when guests began to arrive. Leon breathed in the warm evening air, and gazed out over the patio balcony at a shiny black Porsche pulling into the circular drive. He watched a uniformed valet run out to greet the driver, hold the door open, and assist the young woman from her car. Cindy Brewer had on a short black dress, tall pumps and enough glitter spray to startle a blind man. She waited while a second valet assisted her companion, Tami Jones, from the passenger side of the car. Tami climbed out, smoothed out her white leather skirt, and checked her appearance in a small compact mirror she pulled from her purse.

"Coming Tami?"

Tami hiked up her skirt and bent over to adjust her ankle bracelet, teasing the valet with a glimpse of her long tan legs. "Right behind you, sugar!"

Leon never imagined he and Willy would be playing a gig like this, not in a million years.

Willy, adjusting the height of his cymbal, asked, "That Earl?"

"Nope, some beauties in a fancy two seat coupe. Girls sure is different now days … they're taller and they got them butterscotch legs that done curl your eyelids skyward … and their boobies…"

"Earl better hurry."

"He'll be here – relax. You're gettin' worked up over nothin'."

"He ain't usually late."

"Stop fretting," Leon said. "I'm gonna go fetch us a drink, so you'll stop worrying."

Leon took one more glance over the balcony and saw a man in a dark suit step from the shadows below. He watched the man speak into a walkie-talkie and then walk the perimeter of the driveway. After a few moments, Leon figured he was part of security.

He stepped back from the railing, gently set his horn down, and hustled off toward the kitchen. While Leon was gone, Jim, their rhythm guitarist, finally showed up. He approached Willy and set his battered guitar case on a stool.

"What's happenin' cool cat?" Jim said, smiling broadly enough to reveal a new gold tooth.

Willy turned toward the big black man and his face brightened. Jimmy raised his large hand and laid five on his band mate. "Not much, weather man."

"This one high-class pad," Jimmy said.

"You seen Earl?" Willy asked.

"Not since last night."

"If you got your cell with you, ring the cat."

Jim took off his suit jacket, draped it over the stool and removed a phone from the inside pocket. He dialed Earl's number. Earl picked up on the third ring and said he was five minutes away.

"Hey – who owns this spread?" Willy asked.

"John and Mona Seemore. They got more money than Oprah. Shucks, we impress 'em tonight, this could be the start of something real sweet."

Jim gazed out over the balcony. "You hear about this place yet?"

"No – but I got an idea you're gonna tell me."

Willy joined him on the balcony and had a cigarette. On occasion Willy liked to hear how things looked, though tonight he just wanted to take a few drags of tobacco and breathe the rich country air.

"For as far as the eye can see, man. It's got green rollin' hills, acres of Kentucky Blue, and stables as large as small cities. Maid downstairs told me there are barns filled with broodmares. Mr. Seemore sells mare's piss to some outfit in New York. Makes a fortune. Who would have thought you could sell piss for a profit?" Willy just nodded disinterestedly. "The pad man ... it ain't like no pad I ever seen before. It's a castle, dig? Antique furniture. Oil paintings. Fountain. Marble sculptures all over the place. Man, this dude collects real treasure. I'm surprised there ain't no moat around us. And the garage, hell, there's room enough to build a sound studio."

Willy put his cigarette out. "You about finished?"

"How much bread you think it takes to feed an outfit like this?"

"You see Leon with my beverage?"

"C'mon, Willy, damnit – ride along this here gravy train with me."

"I ain't in no mood."

Jim shrugged and led his band mate sighted-guide back to his drums. After he removed his guitar from the case – an old Gibson that had treated him right over the years – he asked, "You wanna hear how foxy a lady Mrs. Seemore is? I know you wanna hear that."

Willy made no comment. He simply folded his cane, stashed it behind his seat, then picked up a drumstick and rattled a cymbal.

About that time, Mona Seemore strolled around the corner. "Did I hear someone talking about me?"

Willy breathed in the lovely perfumed scent wafting his direction. The scent of a woman could always make him smile. "Jim was just about to tell me what a nice outfit you're wearing tonight, Mrs. Seemore."

Mona, who had on a sparkling red dress and matching heels, adjusted her diamond necklace and pursed her lips. "It's custom made and cost a fortune. How are you set for time? It's seven thirty-five. Shall we say the band kicks off at eight?"

"That'd be fine, ma'am," Willy said.

Jim smiled her direction. "You have a right fine establishment here, ma'am. And I wanna thank you again for hiring us."

"It's my pleasure, boys. I do what I can to support local talent."

Someone in the crowd caught her eye. Mrs. Seemore turned, staring affectionately over her shoulder. Curious, Jim also turned as a short young man in a white suit walked into the living room carrying a bottle of champagne and a bouquet of red roses. His eyes lit up when he saw Mona standing outside on the balcony. She waved.

Mrs. Seemore blushed when the small man handed her the bouquet as he joined them. "They match your dress..." he said cheerfully and gave her a peck on the cheek.

"Brad, you shouldn't have, but I'm glad you did. Gentleman, I'd like to introduce you to Louisville's most talented jockey. He'll be riding one of our thoroughbreds in the Derby this year." She affectionately squeezed the jockey's hand, then changed tempo.

"Brad, meet the Brother Hooch Band."

Jim stepped out from behind a small amplifier and firmly shook Brad's hand. Willy stood up politely and also shook his hand. About then, Leon entered the room with a dapper Negro lugging a shiny guitar case.

"Look who I found sniffing around the kitchen," Leon said. Earl removed his bowler and bowed toward Mrs. Seemore.

"You must be the lady of this fine estate. Ma'am, I'm Earl Lee Roth, at your service."

"Mr. Roth." Mrs. Seemore looped her arm under Brad's and spun him toward the exit. "Excuse me gentleman, I have guests to greet."

Out in the broodmare stable, Mr. Seemore slipped on a pair of rubber boots and fastened his bibs. The air in the large metal building was cold and smelled of manure. He walked past row upon row of feebly emaciated mares tied in narrow stalls. Of the thirty or more horses in the stable, ninety-five percent had rubber sacks strapped to their hindquarters for urine collection. It was a round the clock operation, collecting pregnant mare urine, a multi-million dollar harvest started by his wife's grandfather after WWII.

Dr. Price, Seemore's resident veterinarian, was in the end stall tending to a sickly mare in labor. Dr. Price pulled a thermometer from the horse and grew concerned about her high fever. The horse was panting uncontrollably and wobbly on her feet. Her ribs protruded from her bloated belly. Chances of survival for the mother or the foal appeared grim.

Dr. Price stepped back and adjusted his glasses. "John – it doesn't look good."

"Then kill the foal. We need the mare alive."

"It isn't that simple. It's a breech birth."

"Hook a cable up and pull it out…"

Dr. Price snapped, "That'll kill them both."

"I pay you to keep these horses alive. I don't care how you do it."

A tall white man with a stern face appeared at the stall. "Sorry to interrupt, sir. There are two men outside the gate who aren't on the guest list. They claim they're policemen from New Orleans. One of them said he met you at the racetrack and you invited them to the party?"

"Mona did. Let them in, but keep an eye on them."

"Yes, sir."

The staff member left. Mr. Seemore glared back at the veterinarian. "Well, are you going to kill this foal or am I?"

The yellow cab pulled through the gate and stopped. Detective

Hill and Sergeant Vu climbed out of the back and were immediately greeted by one of Seemore's staff.

"This way gentlemen."

Hill's face was looking a bit better. The splint was gone, his bruising not as apparent. His gate was even sturdy. He'd put on a clean white shirt for the occasion. Vu sported a blue blazer and a butterfly bandage on his forehead. The security man seemed friendly enough and introduced himself. Then, he asked if Hill was from Louisville.

"I grew up down South," Hill said. "Little place outside of Biloxi."

The security guard turned toward Vu, but Vu beat him to the punch. "How about you?"

"Born and bred here."

"How long have you worked for the Seemore family?"

"A while now."

"Are they from Louisville?"

"They're third generation bluebloods. Most of the folk attending this gala tonight are from these parts. It's a tight knit group."

The guard glanced over his shoulder and then turned back to the men.

Soon, the trio was approached by a second security guard, possessing none of the Southern charm of the first. The man pulled out his two-way radio and motioned for Vu and Hill to stop, though they seemed content to listen to the soulful jazz spilling from the second floor balcony anyway. Their stern escort got off his radio and held the door. Hill turned toward the man. "How many guests tonight?" he asked.

"Couple hundred."

"This common?"

"It's a special occasion."

The escort told them to hold up a minute. Mrs. Seemore's assistant was on her way downstairs.

"We'll show ourselves in," Vu said politely and made a move

toward the entrance. The escort put his hand out.

"I said wait."

Vu knew this man was a gatekeeper in a previous life. His karmic journey must have gone unfulfilled, thus he was forced to repeat himself. In American culture, these people are said to have "control issues." He smugly faced Vu, and Vu knew he would not interfere with the man's journey.

Hill broke the silence. "Jack, those herbs really worked. I feel almost normal again."

Vu's lips curled in smile. "An ancient family recipe, but I cannot discuss it. Very secret..."

"Think I should smoke some of it?"

"There's no smoking inside the residence." The escort eyed them as if trouble was about to unleash.

Moments later, a perky young woman in a black dress hustled up. She introduced herself as Becky – Mrs. Seemore's personal assistant.

"They're policemen," the escort explained.

Becky's cheerful expression faded. "I see. OK – right this way, officers."

John Seemore walked out of the stables looking disgusted. He wiped his bloody hands on a towel outside his office. Before entering the small building attached to the stables, he got rid of the soiled towel in the trash. He entered his office and changed out of his bibs and soiled boots and put on freshly polished shoes and a suit jacket hanging beside his work clothes. He checked his nails for dried blood, washed them again in the sink, and then combed his hair in the mirror on the wall. Admiring his stern, handsome features, he knew he had the genes of a thoroughbred. Generations of good breeding – from his great great grandfather who was one of Stonewall Jackson's military advisors, to his father who marched the halls of Yale Law School – he had come from a family of men who were bright, handsome, courageous, and as crooked as the Mississippi.

He flinched as the office door opened and a staff member entered unannounced. It was the same man who had been instructed to escort the policemen.

John faced him and buttoned his tweed jacket. "What's your take on them?"

"They seem harmless enough."

"Well, keep an eye on them."

"Yes, sir."

The man awaited further instructions. When it was clear Mr. Seemore had nothing more to say, he left.

John walked over to his desk, removed a tiny flask from one of the drawers, took a drink and sat down. He put the flask aside and jotted something on a yellow pad, before tearing the paper off and placing it in his front pocket. From the bottom drawer, he removed a small .32 Seecamp handgun, which had been a present to his wife. Her initials were laser-etched in the metal. He'd come home early one day to find her sitting in the living room, intoxicated, pilled, and holding the gun to her head, a depressive condition inherited from her mother. The whole family had been crazy. Nevertheless, they also owned most of Louisville. Some said it came with the territory. After that first episode, he'd taken the gun away and stowed it in his office. The incident was never discussed again.

He checked the magazine, slipped the gun into his outer pocket, and left his office.

The band was taking a short break. Mona, who up until that time had been schmoozing the crowd as perfect hostess, had excused herself, slipping into a bathroom at the far end of the hall. She had a slight headache. It was nothing aspirin, or a few little pink pills secreted away in the medicine cabinet of her private bathroom, wouldn't cure. She found the bottle of pills and swallowed several. Then, she fussed with her earrings, clumsily knocking one off onto the floor. The earring rolled behind the commode.

"Shit!" she said aloud.

She put a knee on the toilet seat and stooped down, her back toward the door, searching. Her eye spotted the glittering object wedged in the corner. Just a little more and she could reach it. Behind her, the bathroom door crept open. A silent figure walked up behind her. She felt a pair of cold hands reach up under her dress. The icy touch on her skin excited, yet startled her.

She grabbed the wrist squeezing her thigh and spun round. A wave of disappointment flashed in her eyes. "John – what the hell are you doing?"

"The guests are asking for you."

"I can't take a little pee without the party falling apart?" Mona thrust his arm aside. "Why are you so cold?"

John stared at her with lustful eyes. "One might ask the same of you, Mona."

"John, let's not start."

Mona stood before the large mirror and refastened her earring while eyeing her husband's reflection. John seethed inwardly.

"After the announcement tonight, we're going to take a little trip, just the two of us," he blurted. "And, we're going to work on this issue."

His wife looked him directly in the eye. "There is no issue, John."

"That's the problem, Mona. You don't see it."

"Our guests are waiting..."

"Just a minute. Remember the fellow Brad introduced us to at the track?"

"Vaguely. He had the allergies."

"Well, you invited him and he brought a friend."

"So?"

"So they're detectives, Mona."

"What are they detecting?" Mona tossed her head.

"Nothing that involves us, right?"

"What on earth are you talking about?"

"Don't play innocent with me." John studied her face. "I deal in capabilities, not intent. You are capable of destroying anything you touch."

John started for the door then changed his mind. "So, Mona, how many pills tonight?"

"Why, enough to keep me smiling, darling."

25

Mona's perfectly manicured hand curled suggestively around the microphone as she brought it up to her lips. "Ladies and gentlemen, if I could have your attention please!"

She stood on the band platform and waited for the crowd to settle. "I have a little announcement to make..."

The crowd quieted and turned their attention to the stage.

"First, I'd like to thank you all for coming tonight. I think we'll all agree the food and music have been splendid this evening. Let's give a round of applause to the catering staff and to Brother Hooch for doing such a fine job." The crowd applauded. "Now, if I could have my husband come up on stage with me..."

Mona searched the crowd. Her husband was nowhere to be seen. She spotted Brad in the corner speaking with the policemen. The crowd grew restless, waiting. "Funny – when you don't want them around they're always at your beck and call," Mona joked. Then, John appeared, from the stairwell, smiling. He'd re-combed his hair, put on a more expensive dinner jacket and was clutching a bottle of champagne. He hurried toward the platform.

"There he is," Mona said, forcing a smile. "Honey – get up here before all these wonderful people lose interest in what we have to say."

John hopped onto the stage. He paused, took a deep breath and enthusiastically beamed at the crowd. His natural stage presence shined. He put his arm around his wife and gave her a kiss on the cheek. The crowd seemed to like this and murmurs echoed throughout the room.

"Sorry, folks – I'm sure my wife will remind me to stick closer to her side from now on."

"That's right, dear. A man's got to know his place. Ladies and gentlemen, I'm sure you've heard the rumor in town lately about the prospect of my husband running for office. We want to put an end to those rumors and let you be the first to hear our decision. Please meet Kentucky's next Governor, John Seemore!"

The room applauded. Mona handed the microphone to her husband and stepped back from the spotlight.

John proudly announced, "That's right folks. It's time this great state of ours had a voice that carried the needs of our time ... and with the help of all of you here this evening I'm just the man to do it!"

The crowd erupted as if hope had come at last.

"Seemore! Seemore! Seemore!"

The only people in the room not clapping and shouting were Detective Hill, Sergeant Vu and Brad Black. They stood off to one side, idly waiting for the applause to die down so they could continue their conversation. Finally, the noise subsided. Brad faced them with a hard glint in his eyes.

"As I was saying, officers, I have no idea what you're talking about. How could I have attacked you? I am at the track until after six every day. There simply isn't time for me to dress up like Elvis, unless of course you think this Calvin Klein suit would qualify."

Neither of them had implied that he was the intruder, but suggested he might somehow be involved. He could have hired the attack to keep them from getting too close to Patti Knot's killer.

"No one else knew I was staying at that hotel except you," Hill said firmly.

"Obviously someone did. As I've said, I don't know what you're talking about. If you'd like to speak with me further about this, my attorney can join us. He's standing over at the bar."

Hill shrugged.

Brad was assuredly pleased with himself. "If it's OK with you two, I'm going to go congratulate my future boss and his wife and grab some champagne? After that we can finish up." Brad brushed some imaginary dirt from his cuff. "I'll meet you out on the balcony – say fifteen minutes? I'll ask my lawyer to join us."

After Brad left, Vu walked out onto the balcony and looked over the railing. A number of guests mingled outside under the clear evening sky smoking cigars or cigarettes. He surveyed the huge estate, taking it all in, and contemplated the wealth that made a place like Louisville tick. He thought about his girlfriend on the Arctic Wing – Betty, his only lover – and wondered if she too was looking up at the stars, miles away.

Vu checked his watch. A couple of band members strolled out onto the balcony and lit up. Vu thought about turning around to discuss Miles Davis with the horn-man, but didn't. Instead, he listened to their idle conversation and waited. Another musician came up from behind and stood against the railing. Vu watched him fold up his cane and set it aside. The man adjusted his dark glasses and tried to light a cigarette. But, he accidentially dropped his matches. Vu picked them up and lit the musician's cigarette. At first the man seemed angry for the intrusion, then changed his demeanor and told Vu he could keep the matches.

"The brothers and me, we got matches comin' out our ears. It's like them club owners think we're some kind'a walking billboards or somethin'," Willy said. "You smoke?"

"My friend does. I'll give them to him."

"You're Asian, ain't ya?"

"I was born in Saigon."

"Nasty thing we did to your homeland," Willy said. "But, sometimes nasty's all we got."

Something about the man's voice interested Vu, as if the sound originated in another time, another place. "My name's Jack. I enjoyed your music."

"Cool... I like a brother who's got rhythm. Most folk are as square as a box."

"Actually, I play the mandolin."

"You don't say?" Willy smiled. "We black folk call those things "midget guitars.""

Vu laughed. He could see his own reflection in the man's sunglasses. "Would you like something from the bar?"

"For starters, I'll take a blonde, a brunette and a bottle of bourbon." Willy coughed a lungful of smoke. Vu stepped back and Willy quickly reached out and grabbed his wrist, still coughing. "Where you going, mandolin man? I was just jivin'."

Just then Hill walked up. He pulled out a pack of cigarettes and before he could find his lighter, Vu handed him the book of matches and said, "Willy – I'd like you to meet a friend of mine, Bruce." Willy stubbed out his cigarette and offered his hand.

"Another mandolin player?"

Hill blew out the match and coughed. "I was raised on the five string. Nice to meet you. You got one mean drumstick."

"Say, you got an accent – where you from?"

"The great Bayou country."

"I knew it ... you boys bass fish in your parts?"

"Once in a blue moon. What about you?" Hill glanced at Vu as if they had stumbled onto something here.

"I only fish when I can't hook a lady for the day. So I guess you might say I've been fishin' plenty lately."

Vu started to laugh at the man's joke when he noticed the matchbook in Hill's hand. Something about it looked familiar – then he replayed Willy's words in his head. Bass fisherman ... hook a lady...

Vu mentally compared the matchbook cover to the one he'd recovered along the riverbank where they located Beverly Sanders' body. They were identical. He looked down at the man's side and confirmed he used a white cane. About that time, Leon walked up toting two cold beers. He stepped up and planted one into Willy's hand. Willy held the beer up to his nose then quenchingly tipped it back.

After he was finished drinking, he said, "Leon – we have some guest musicians in our company."

Leon nodded. "Nice to meet ya."

Vu stood up straight, official looking. "Willy – was Leon with you the other day when you discovered the body along the riverbank?"

Leon choked on his beer. He swiped his hand over his lips nervously and spun round toward Willy, "Damnit – I knew this gig was too good to be true. Willy, what have you gone and done?"

"I done nothin!"

"Then how'd he find out?"

Vu stepped forward. "Because you just told me." For once Willy had nothing to say. "I'm not suggesting either of you had anything to do with Ms. Sander's death."

"Was that her name? Sanders?" Willy asked.

"Yes. Beverly Sanders. I work for the Air Force. Ms. Sanders was one of our recruits. I've been assigned her case."

Leon turned toward Willy.

"Quit staring at me," Willy snapped.

Hill allowed Vu to handle the men while he focused his attention on the crowd. He couldn't see the jockey's face among the many guests inside. This troubled him. He nervously checked his watch. Too much time had passed.

"Jack," Hill interrupted. "You cool here?"

Vu nodded.

"I think the jock split on us."

Vu turned and scanned the crowded room. "I still have some remaining questions for these men."

"I'll go look for Black."

Hill plowed his way through the crowd and disappeared downstairs. Vu turned back toward the two musicians. Other guests within earshot finished their cigarettes and returned inside, leaving only the three standing alone on the balcony.

Leon chugged his beer. "We in trouble, Mister?"

"Why don't we start at the beginning ... tell me what you remember about that day."

Leon swallowed hard. "Go ahead, Willy – you tell 'em?"

Willy put his beer down and lit a second cigarette. "There's not much to tell. I was the one that hooked that poor thing. We were fishin' along the riverbank when I thought I'd hooked Moby Dick himself." Willy paused, thinking. "After I reeled her in we checked her over. She felt pretty bloated, like she'd been in the water all night."

Leon added, "I telephoned the police, used a payphone alongside the road."

Vu thought for a moment. "Go back to the riverbank. Willy, what do you remember before you found the body?"

Willy exhaled smoke. "That Leon stole my whiskey."

* * *

After searching for Black among the guests inside, Hill stepped out into the cool night and looked around. The valets were sitting under an awning chatting, waiting for the party to wind down before they had something to do again. Hill could hear voices near the gatehouse and assumed it was the guards killing time. He thought he also heard someone clambering about near the stables. The security escort had stuck close by most of the evening but was now nowhere to be seen.

Hill ducked between the garage and the residence and followed a fence line. Up ahead he glimpsed a person enter a stable. As he approached the building, he noticed an awful stench and pulled out a handkerchief to cover his nose.

The outside lights clicked off. The area fell into darkness. Hill poked his head in the door, his hand on his gun. A single bulb light burned in the corner.

He moved along the narrow aisle between opposing stalls peering in at the horses. They were stone figures, motionless, their heads hitched to the railings. Most had big balloon looking devices strapped to their hindquarters and the stench was unbearable. A metallic noise at the end of the stable startled him.

As he moved toward the sound, the odor overwhelmed him. He knew death when he smelled it.

In the corner stall, he saw something on the floor. He removed the book of matches from his jacket, lit one, holding it up like a candle. In the flickering light he saw a dead horse – a foal with a long bloody chain wrapped around its ankles, its body a bag of broken bones. The little colt's eyes bulged from their sockets. Yellow mucus crusted its lips. Behind this atrocity lay a second dead horse. Hill presumed it was the mare that had given birth, its birth canal ripped open, where someone had forced the thin skin beyond nature's limit. Blood saturated the stall.

Another horrifying image flashed through his mind. The last time he'd experienced this feeling was on the scene of a car wreck involving innocent children.

He started coughing as he headed toward the door and fresh air. Once outside, he stooped, gasping. His chest hurt. His head pounded. As he regained his breath, he lit a cigarette and headed back toward the front lawn. The security guard who had been missing only minutes before joined him and escorted him to the front gate where he was authoritatively told to wait. He slumped against a bench, like a prisoner awaiting sentencing. He'd seen enough for one night.

* * *

Inside, Vu was trying to paint a picture for the two old musicians.

"Think back. Was it windy? Sunny? Rainy? What sounds did you hear? Were there birds? Planes? Trains?"

Leon broke eye contact and stared out over the balcony.

"Mandolin man, it was overcast," Willy said. "Then we got rain that blew in out of the northwest. After that the sun came out. I remember hearing seagulls and a boat going upriver."

Vu perked up. "What kind of boat?"

Leon closed his eyes, and then uttered: "It was the Belle of Louisville. She was paddling upriver, her engines steaming full throttle."

Willy butted in. "It was no such thing, you drunkard. Mandolin man, sure as I curse this godforsaken planet, it was a tugboat. After it passed, I even caught a snoot-full of diesel fumes, nearly caused me to barf."

Vu scribbled in his notebook. "What else?"

"Poor girl had lost a shoe. Her big toe was sticking out of her stocking."

"I know about the shoe. Anything else – think."

Leon and Willy were deep in thought when Mona burst out the balcony door.

"There you are!" she scolded. "Our guests are ready for more music, gentlemen. Please don't keep them waiting!" Then, she carefully scrutinized Vu. "You're with Detective Hill, correct?"

Vu put his notebook away. "Yes."

"Your partner is outside waiting for you."

Vu found Hill flanked by two security guards. Vu raised his eyebrows. "What happened?"

The front door opened. Mr. Seemore appeared. He marched over to the group.

"Your friend seems to have wandered into a restricted area and frightened our horses. I'm afraid I'm going to have to ask you both to leave. Stan, please escort these gentlemen to their cab."

"Did you find Black?" Vu asked.

Before Hill could answer, Brad strolled up, smiling. "Where'd you two go?" he asked. "I was on the balcony waiting."

"So was I," Vu replied, and turned toward Hill.

Hill shook his head. He didn't have it in him to question the jockey any further that evening.

"We'll discuss our matter with you later," Vu said to Black. He walked toward the gate with Hill.

After the cab pulled onto the main highway, Hill blinked a few times and lifted his head off the seat. "I thought I knew what hell was like, but I was wrong."

26

Vu fumbled with the radio, looking for a station that didn't play country western twang. Obtaining a rental car had been a last minute decision, something he and Hill had both agreed upon late the night before. The B & E was something Vu felt compelled to do, but there was no way Lynch would ever speak to Hill on account of being Gates' partner. So, it was decided Vu would see what he could find out about the physical layout of the place and Hill would search the house. With publicity machines working overtime to convict Gates in the press, they were running out of time.

About a mile from the ranch entrance Vu pulled over and Hill rolled out, a backpack slung on his shoulder.

"Meet you back here by 3 p.m."

"If you aren't here by 1600, I'm coming to find you."

"Fair enough, buddy."

The drive to Knot's ranch had taken longer than Vu expected. However, Ed Lynch was patiently waiting for him at the gate, just as he said he would be. Vu had contacted Lynch, explaining he needed to speak to him regarding the Sanders investigation. As it turned out, Lynch was a close friend of Bevy's parents and had worked with them many years before. Vu considered it fortuitous that Lynch asked to meet him at the Knot ranch. He'd been staying there since Patti's death to keep an eye on things as the authorities had requested. Lynch said he'd already called in several reports of fans and press sneaking around the place. Vu waited for Lynch to unlock the gate, drove the Ford Escort through the narrow opening and parked up near the house.

Lynch was a big man with enormous hands that gripped like steel. His stern eyes sized Vu up quickly, though his voice was friendly. "Have any trouble finding the place?"

"I missed a turn and had to circle back."

"Louisville's the only place I know that burrows the hills first, carves out a homestead, then finds a way to connect roads later. I'm Ed Lynch, good to know you."

Vu formally introduced himself.

"You're an Air Force Investigator?"

"Yes. As I explained on the phone, I was sent here to investigate Beverly Sanders' death."

"I knew Bevy and her parents. Fine people. What I don't understand is what Bevy's death has to do with Patti?"

"I'm not sure either, but Ms. Sanders was seen talking with Ms. Knot the day before she was found dead."

"I see. Well, let's go inside. I'll fix us some coffee and see if I can help you."

Vu hadn't anticipated the invitation inside. "Thanks, but I just had breakfast, so I'll pass on the coffee, if you don't mind."

"OK," Lynch shrugged.

"This is quite a place. Maybe we can talk and you can show me around. We did not have ranches like this in Vietnam."

"Be happy to," Lynch replied, obviously proud of the place.

Vu followed the ranch-hand, surveying the area as they walked. It was much larger than he'd anticipated. Acres of open pasture, white plank fencing, outbuildings, stables, barn and the main house – plenty for a single person to maintain.

"Ms. Knot lived here alone?"

"Yes. When she wasn't on the road. She was trying to get out of racing." Lynch said, his voice cracking. "She wanted to be a breeder and trainer. I helped her with the heavy work, but for the most part, what you see here is all her."

"Who's the nearest neighbor?"

"She's got three really. The Posts live on the west side of the property about a quarter mile down, and the Moss family lives on the east end. There are some trees that divide the two ranches. The Seemores are on the backside, over there across the pasture, say the better part of a mile. It's good grazing country, good for raising cattle or horses. Patti got in before land skyrocketed in these parts. I have a spread of my own about six miles south of here. So it's convenient for me to stop by and keep an eye on the place."

"You two know each other long?"

"Years. She was one of those rare people in life that you took a liking to as soon as you met her." Lynch's eyes lowered and he cleared his throat.

"The first time I saw her, gosh – maybe twenty years ago now – she wore roses embroidered on her racing jersey. I used to call her the Brazilian Rose. I never did like the name the reporters gave her. Her mother died last April. Took Patti by surprise, but she still managed to do fine in last year's Derby. Damn hard worker too. I hoped to see her settle down here and raise a family. Guess it wasn't in the cards."

Vu breathed in the fresh scent of grass. He noticed one of the horses in the field stopped grazing and looked up. The other horses continued wandering the pasture. "Who inherits all this?"

"I suppose that's a question for her attorney to answer."

"Of course. I didn't mean to pry."

Lynch thought it over. "Hell, I don't see what harm it will do to tell you. A few years back, Patti set up a trust in case she was ever injured or killed on the track and couldn't take care of this place. The trust is in my name."

"You're the beneficiary of her estate?"

"No. She had life insurance to cover the mortgage. I'm the

beneficiary on that. The trust covers my care of the property and animals."

"I see."

The man seemed to read his thoughts.

"The remainder of Patti's estate will go to Donny Mason's conservatorship. The court will probably appoint a new guardian to handle that."

Vu stopped and checked his notes.

"Wait. I have that name written here. Were Mr. Mason and Ms. Sanders involved in an accident several years back?"

"Yes. Terrible tragedy. Both were beaten, and Bevy was raped."

"Maybe that was why Bevy looked Patti up?"

"I wouldn't know." Lynch paused. "Bevy's been gone a long time. I don't think she kept in touch with anyone back here, not since her folks passed."

"Would there be any reason for Mr. Mason to hurt Bevy?"

"Gawd no."

"How about Ms. Knot?"

"The only person Donny ever hurt was himself."

"When was the last time you saw Mr. Mason?"

Lynch stopped dead in his tracks. "The police have the killer in custody."

"Sorry." Vu remained calm. "I'm just being an investigator." He crooked a slight smile. "Let's get back to Ms. Sanders."

"Fine, but let's walk over by the stables so I can sit down. My legs get tired easy."

Vu tried to still his anticipation at being led toward Patti Knot's murder scene. That abruptly ended when he stepped into a large pile of horse manure.

Vu's heel skid in the center of the slippery grass turd and Lynch had to grab his elbow to keep him from falling.

"You know what they say about good luck and stepping in shit?" Lynch asked.

"No." Vu stared at his polished shoe mired in goo.

"Me neither," Lynch chuckled. "I'll go get something to clean up that shoe." He headed toward the barn.

Vu hobbled over to the bench. Removing a handkerchief from his pocket, he picked up a stick and began scraping manure from the bottom of his shoe.

It didn't appear the horses had access to this area. Vu wondered how it got here. His mind methodically rehearsed various scenarios as he scraped.

Lynch arrived with a couple of rags that looked in worse condition than his shoe.

"Have you been riding in here recently?"

"Nope."

"This pile looks fairly fresh. Knot's horses are on the other side of the pasture, correct?"

Lynch glanced at the manure. "Can't say I know how that got there. I'd say it looks to be about three or four days old though."

"Did you notice it, the day of the murder?"

"You investigating shit now?"

Vu slipped his shoe back on and walked over to where the horses were roaming the pasture. He studied their defecation. Despite the few flies sprinkling the surface, he thought he could tell the difference between the manure found here and that found by the stable. He stooped down, removed his clean shoe, removed the sock and slipped it over his hand. Then, he picked up a clump of manure from the pasture and folded the sock over it, making a convenient little bundle to carry.

Vu then put his shoe back on his bare foot, and walked back to where Lynch sat, shaking his head. Surely he thought Vu was a lunatic.

Once Vu returned to the bench, he removed his other sock, already fouled from the first mishap, and used it in the same tidy manner to collect a sample from the first pile of manure. Vu stepped back holding his two socks of shit, his miniature trophies.

"You earn your living a funny way, young man."

Vu nodded.

As Lynch walked Vu back to his car, Vu stopped. "They say Ms. Knot was set to ride in the Derby this year?"

"She was offered a contract with the Seemores to ride a thoroughbred named Seven Dancer. A real contender. She was happy at the prospect of riding in the Derby, but not at working for the Seemores."

"Why?"

"Ethical reasons - had to do with their farming operation. But, a win could've made her financial life easier here on the ranch." Lynch paused. "We all make compromises from time to time. Guess Patti had decided to ride for them now and change the world later."

"What kind of operation are we talking about?"

"They raise pregnant mares, collect the urine, and sell it to pharmaceutical companies to be manufactured into estrogen. It's been going on for decades. PETA has been trying to shut down the operations, though there's nothing illegal about it. PETA even approached Patti awhile back and asked her to help. She said it'd be like shooting herself in the foot. So naturally, she bowed out. It's disgraceful, though, the way some producers treat their animals."

Hill felt the tumblers fall in the lock on the side door. He'd checked for signs of an alarm, even though Gates had told him there wasn't one. He stood in a mud room, inhaling the musty stench from work clothes piled on a wooden bench. Muddy books were stacked beneath. He listened for human sounds, but only detected the buzz of the refrigerator. He set his backpack on the floor and replaced the pick set. As his eyes scanned beyond the adjoining laundry room into the center of the ranch house, he grabbed the handle of the pack and withdrew a digital camera.

He knew it was risky, but he might have to hazard using the flash. He'd brought a hood to place over objects, but it would be impossible to totally mask the light if he had the bad luck to be seen from outside at the wrong moment.

He moved into the open living area. The furniture was practical and sturdy, yet the feel was decidedly feminine. Dried flower stems jutted from a vase in the shape of a cowboy boot on the coffee table. Pink rose petals littered the surface below. Soft chenille throws draped over the back of a reading chair. On the table lay a newspaper and a pair of reading glasses. The paper was folded back to reveal the story of Patti decking Black. Photos covered one wall, detailing a life of travel, competition and love. Hill studied each one with the eye of a detective, not a voyeur. Gates was not among them, but he did see one photo wherein Patti was posed with Brad Black and the Seemores. The trophy she was holding read, "2006 Preakness Cup Winner." Black held a smaller version. This photo captured Goldilocks' last major win.

Hill moved mutely along the wall cataloguing her pictorial history, stopping cold at a faded photo of an Elvis look alike, signed, "Love Always, Donny." Involuntarily, he shivered. He was staring into the eyes of his hotel psycho.

Those pricks knew this guy.

Hill wondered what else Buck and Smitty were keeping from him. He continued documenting photos and other items of interest throughout the house.

Walking down the hallway, he stepped over the police tape and entered Patti's office. Her desk was locked, but he easily picked it. Inside were log books for the ranch, detailing income and expenditures. Definitely, more was going out than coming in. And there was another bank journal. This one was a Trust Account for a Donny Mason, showing payments to a mobile home park, a grocery, a drug store, and hundreds of dollars worth of parking tickets made out in her neat penmanship to the Louisville Traffic Court. Each check contained the license number of a '70 Cadillac Sedan de Ville. Hill scribbled furiously.

Time to pay Elvis a special visit before the day is through.

On the desk were the usual piles of papers and bills. He picked up a catalogue for the Louisville Central High School Reunion. He knew there was probably a safe, but he also knew something about women. They often hid things in plain sight for easy access.

Drugs, diet pills, condoms, money, were under the socks in the underwear drawer. Keys were in the jewelry box. He headed to the bedroom, aware the police had searched everywhere before.

He knew it as soon as he saw it. LP albums stacked on the floor formed a table on which sat a sculpture of a horse and rider. He looked closer. It was a plaster replica of Elizabeth Taylor from the movie National Velvet, a childhood memento. Everyone had them. His was a Red Ryder BB gun he'd gotten from his father for his 10th birthday. He sat on the floor by the bed and studied the face of young Elizabeth. As he dropped his eyes, he noticed a bulge under the horse's feet, which caused the statue to sit slightly atilt. He carefully lifted the horse by the chest and rear and set it on the floor. The top album was of Brazilian folk music, but he sensed from its heft that it didn't contain vinyl. He goosed the sides of the album cover causing it to yawn. A thick envelope rested inside. His gloved fingers claimed the prize. It was a contract with the Seemores to ride their horse, Seven Dancer, in the Kentucky Derby. It was signed by Patti, but not the Seemores. Patti had signed it the day before she died.

Hill mined through this rare musical collection. He removed e-mails, personal photos, birthday cards, contracts, safety deposit box keys, and finally, a copy of Patti Knot's Last Will and Testament.

He put them all into his backpack, replaced the album stack and the statue, and headed for the door. He'd just made the turn into the laundry room when he heard the front door open.

Vu stowed his socks in plastic bags in the trunk and drove by the two properties on each side of the Knot Ranch before circling back around to wait for Hill.

Something told him that Beverly Sanders' death and Patti Knot's murder were inextricably connected. He had no proof yet, but walking Knot's property gave him subtle notions, as if the earth had shared a secret.

Back on the main highway, Vu pulled into a White Castle and purchased a bag of hamburgers and two cups of hot tea. After looking at his hands, he decided to use the hot water to rinse them. He dried his fingers on the tail of his shirt before picking up a bun. Then, he ate lunch in the car, listening to bluegrass on the radio.

The light and breezy sounds of a band called Seldom Scene had a remarkable effect on his spirits. He felt lighter than air and his mind wandered. He pined for his girl back in New Orleans, the juicy burger reminding him of her warm lips on his.

Wait. Betty could help. She could analyze the poop. The samples had to remain confidential, so he couldn't take them to Ruttle. But, how should he send her his special "evidence" for analysis? And, what exactly was she to look for?

His mind drifted while the music played and the sun shone down. When Hill interrupted his reverie by opening the passenger door, Vu snapped out of it.

"You won't believe the shit I found in Knot's place," Hill said, tossing his backpack into the rear seat.

Vu chuckled at the reference and handed Hill the bag of burgers with a smile. "I think I found some good shit too."

27

John Seemore checked his watch as two hired hands hoisted the mare's carcass onto the bed of a livestock truck. The men released the chain and allowed it to fall onto the wet pile of remains. Both wiped the stench from their soiled hands onto their jeans.

"That should do it, sir," one hired hand said.

John walked up and closed the truck's gate. "Take this load to the rendering plant in Shelbyville."

"We aren't using the one in Middletown, sir?"

"PETA is camped out on their doorstep. Don't like everybody knowing my business."

John waved them away and went inside his office. He sat down behind the desk and retrieved his phone messages.

After making two quick phone calls to his campaign manager, he rechecked his watch, got up, and opened the door. A Lincoln Town car pulled into the drive and parked. Racing Commissioner Hurt climbed out and looked around.

John stepped outside and called to him. "Over here, Ben!"

Hurt turned and waved. "Howdy, John! Looks like rain, don't it?"

John glanced up at the sky and shrugged. "C'mon inside."

He showed the commissioner into his office and closed the door. "Have a seat," he said, pointing to a leather chair opposite his desk. Hurt glanced around the office as he settled into the chair. John sat down and pulled out a humidor, offering Hurt a cigar. Hurt took one and clipped the end off.

"Well – what's so urgent Ben?" John held up a lighter and lit the commissioner's cigar.

"I heard that two policemen were questioning Brad Black. What can you tell me about that?"

"Routine stuff really. They questioned him about the article in *The Examiner*."

"Listen, Knot's murder has everyone on edge and I don't want this getting out of hand. With the Derby just around the corner, anymore bad publicity for our jockeys could play hell with revenues."

"I liked Knot – she was a damn fine jockey," John said, and sat back. "I think she could have taken Seven Dancer all the way."

Hurt nodded. "Would have been a great financial boost, not to mention the publicity for your campaign."

"Black is taking her slot."

"You happy about that?"

"Do I have another choice?"

"I hope so."

"Ben – get to the point."

"Black's urine tested positive for cocaine."

"I don't believe it." John held Hurt's gaze while his mind scrambled for a plausible explanation. "Name me one jockey who hasn't been injured and I'll show you a clean urine sample. I'm sure it's a mistake. Retest him. Who the hell does cocaine recreationally anymore? They know the rules."

"I'm only giving you a heads up on this, John. That's all."

"Well, I'll talk with Mona about it."

"Where is Mona anyway? She should join us."

"She's in town getting a facial."

"You're sure about that?" Hurt leaned back and blew a puff of smoke toward the ceiling. He seemed to be pondering something.

John thought he heard another car drive in and rose from his desk. After looking out the window and seeing no one, he turned around and faced the commissioner.

"Look, I'm a busy man. Something else bothering you, Ben?"

"Your wife's Jaguar is parked over at Black's condo right now. It's been there a half-dozen times in the last week."

John sat down, shocked by the news. She's been handling the contract negotiations," he bluffed.

The commissioner put his cigar in an ashtray. "Drop the bullshit. I don't care if she's sucking coke or sucking cock." Hurt rose to his feet. "It's gotta stop. We all have too much to lose here."

28

etective Buck slammed the car door and stepped over the curb into the soft yielding carpet of grass. He had stopped at Ruth B's Flower Shop on the way from police headquarters to pick up yellow and red sunflowers, and had driven west on Hwy 64 to Sunny Ridge Cemetery.

The sky promised rain. Buck trekked along the mowed field occasionally glancing down at the headstones when he caught sight of a familiar figure wearing a bright scarf wrapped around her shoulders. She was seated on a small camp stool. A large bouquet of magnolias was arranged on her deceased husband's grave.

"Why Detective," Mrs. Stencil smiled, "it's so good to see you. You haven't been at the services lately. Have you been deployed again?"

"Not recently, ma'am."

Mrs. Stencil cocked her head inquisitively.

"They changed my work schedule again."

Buck sensed she knew it was a lie. But, it was easier to explain his absence at church that way than to tell her about the current state of his "relationship" with God.

"How's your grandson?" he offered, changing the subject.

"He's doing fine. He's been made a supervisor."

Buck smiled and made polite conversation until there was an appropriate pause. Then, he patted Mrs. Stencil affectionately on the shoulder and walked away.

His sister Rebecca's gravesite was near the bottom of the row, in the shade of a tall elm. Buck stooped over and placed the flowers on her marble headstone. She used to love sunflowers. As a child their grandmother had told them that they were so named because they always turned their faces to the sun. Rebecca had renamed them "flowers of the sun."

Buck stood up, closed his eyes, and remembered her smiling face. The family had nicknamed her "Sunny" because of her happy disposition. Laughter and music always surrounded her birthdays, family holidays, and other social gatherings. Sunny had been most happy playing guitar.

A cool breeze blew in and Buck could smell rain in the air. He buttoned his jacket. "Happy Birthday, kiddo," he whispered. "I've missed you."

There was so much left unsaid, and so many questions remained. But, he knew he wouldn't find the answers, not here. Still, he lingered awhile before walking off.

As he worked his way back to the car, Buck pondered and sorted his emotions. Lashing rain against his face slapped him back to reality and he broke into a run.

* * *

The old railroad bridge needed more than a facelift. Her main beams were rusted and the pilings were badly pitted with corrosion. All the crossties between the iron rails were either rotting or had extensive termite damage on the surface. The boards creaked under Buck's heavy steps. Overhead, cobwebs hung down and brushed his shoulder as he walked out to the center of the dilapidated bridge. Eventually, he felt more at ease with the height and the surrounding views. He took in the distant shoreline, the city, and the river winding its way into the distance only to disappear around the bend.

As the rain blew through, the bridge swayed in the wind. Buck grabbed a steel strut for support, peered down over the forty-foot drop into the muddy Ohio River below, and tried to imagine what the Sanders girl was thinking that night. Why go to these extremes if she wanted to take her own life? There were easier means. She was an Air Force cop. She could've killed herself back in Louisiana. Why choose Louisville during a wedding celebration? A fall didn't guarantee success. It didn't make sense. To get to a location that would allow her to slip under the steel beams and hang over the ledge, she would have had to of walked or crawled twenty-five feet or more along rotting timbers. Why not just swallow a bottle of sleeping pills?

Smitty's input would help. At this time of year, the sister thing always surfaced, and it fucked him up. Just because Rebecca couldn't cope, didn't mean that Bev Sanders had suffered the same fate. By all indications, she had recovered and gone on to a successful career. He, on the other hand, was sinking in a bog and unable to navigate.

* * *

Smitty hiked up the small slope and crawled onto the bridge. "Hey! Sam! What are you doin' there, lad?"

Buck turned. He saw his partner standing some thirty-feet away, waving to get his attention.

Buck took one final look at the river below and stepped back. He gazed down at the rotting railroad ties. A hunk of old wood about the size of Sanders' missing shoe would do. He broke a piece loose, tossed it over the edge, and watched it splash into the river current.

Buck stood up and braced himself on the steel beam and headed toward shore. "You're late," Buck said, smiling.

"And you were scarin' the pee right out of me, lad."

Buck slapped his partner's shoulder. "She didn't enter the water from this bridge like we thought." Buck watched the wood, caught in an eddy, swirl in a lazy circle. "The current is too slow. If Sanders jumped from here, her body wouldn't have reached the location where the fishermen found her."

"OK, mate," Smitty said, looking puzzled. "What now?"

"I think Bevy's past caught up with her like we thought, but it played out differently."

Smitty nodded. "Maybe her rapist stamped her death warrant."

"Lazarus ain't gonna like where this is going, but I'm gonna reopen the rape case."

Smitty saw his pension dissolving into the wind. "Slow down, Sam. Let's not lose our heads."

"We could start by interviewing Donny. He's the only witness left."

"Interview a delusional alcoholic Elvis impersonator?"

"We gotta see him anyway. You got a better idea?"

29

The security policeman at the Kentucky Air National Guard Base stepped out of his guard shack as Vu's car approached. The Guard Base, home of the 123rd Airlift Wing, provided worldwide airlifts for the U.S. military. A dozen flights a day flew out of the base to locations all over the world.

Vu rolled down the car window, handed over his ID card, and asked for directions to the Base Logistics Office. The young guard stepped back inside his post, made a brief phone call, and returned to the car.

He handed the ID back to Vu and pointed where Vu should turn. "The office you need is just past the tower on the right. You can't miss it."

Vu nodded and waited for the guardrail to rise.

Being on a military installation always calmed Vu. He drove slowly, checking out the old gray buildings. He passed several hangars. Nearby, four massive airframes sat under the protective eye of armed security policemen patrolling the tarmac. They waved him through as he passed. One of the planes had its rear door open where several maintenance workers streamed in and out.

Vu parked in the lot and got out. He opened the trunk, removed a zippered canvas pouch, and carried it toward the entrance of the Logistics office.

Inside, the main desk was bustling with activity. A flight board behind the desk listed the week's air frame deployments. Two planes were leaving today: One to Homestead Air Reserve Station in Florida; a second to the joint NAF Naval Air Station outside New Orleans.

One of the NCOs glanced up. "May I help you?"

Vu flashed his credentials.

"I have a critical lab sample that needs to be on the 1500 flight to New Orleans."

The NCO glanced over his shoulder at the flight board. "It's tight, but I think we can make it. You'll need to complete this paperwork, and we'll need your commander's authorization."

"Of course. I'll need a secure line."

"Down the hall, second door on your left."

Vu carried his parcel to the office down the hall and closed the door. He picked up the receiver and dialed the DSN number for the Naval Air Station in New Orleans. Major Mitts picked up on the third ring.

"This is Major Mitts."

"Sir, it's Sergeant Vu."

"Vu! Where the hell are you?"

"Sir, I'm at the Kentucky National Guard Airbase outside Louisville."

"I'm getting all sorts of flack on my end. What's the status of Lieutenant Sanders' case?"

"It doesn't appear to be a suicide, sir."

"Go on."

"It appears to be tied to another case."

"What other case?"

"A Patti Knot, the murdered jockey that has been in the news."

"Are you sure about this connection?"

"Not yet, but I think I will have some answers soon."

"I want this wrapped up with no adverse publicity. Is that clear?"

"Yes, sir."

"What do you need from me?"

"Sir, I need your permission to send a lab sample on a flight to NAS that leaves in an hour. Routing should go to a Ms. Elizabeth Caan for analysis."

"Ms. Caan? She new at the lab?"

"No, sir. I'm not using our lab."

"Why not?"

"I want to keep the military out of this. As you indicated, you don't want the military tied to a sensational murder. And, time is of the essence."

"Who is this Caan woman?"

"A discrete business associate and an excellent forensic pathologist from New Orleans. She has been quite helpful to the Air Force in the past."

There was a pause. "They need a completed Form 2?"

"I've already filled it out, sir. They just need your written authorization faxed here?"

"I trust you'll handle this with the utmost dispatch and discretion, sergeant. I don't want this coming back to bite me in the ass."

"Yes sir."

"What's the fax number?"

Vu provided the information and then there was a loud click on the end of the line. Satisfied, Vu hung up and returned to the lobby desk. He placed the pouch on the countertop.

"Major Mitts is faxing his authorization to you immediately." Vu filled in the boxes on the delivery paperwork and attached it to the pouch.

"It'll be tight."

"Do whatever is necessary," Vu said firmly. "The Major needs to receive this ASAP."

The fax machine promptly hummed to life behind the clerk.

Surprised, he pulled the transmittal from the machine.

"This must be some important shit," the clerk mumbled as he checked over the form.

30

Donny Mason ran his tongue along the roof of his mouth, scraping the scum onto his teeth. He had the presence of mind to realize he might have done something awful, though what it was he wasn't quite sure. No amount of alcohol could quiet that sense, nor could it rinse the familiar sour taste in his mouth, which meant his brain had snapped again.

The doctors warned it could happen. Under stress, synapses misfire, sending false signals to the cerebral cortex which controls rational behavior and a rare form of psychosis occurs. The simplistic explanation was if something set him off, he could become extremely violent and have no memory of it. People were skeptical when he tried to explain this irrational schizophrenia. They knew he'd had a terrible accident, the eight-inch scar a visible reminder when his hair was parted on the wrong side. This explained why he kept it combed back and greased down. But, the Elvis thing … well, nobody believed him.

That night, after the beating, the King had visited him in the hospital. Elvis told him to hang on and find the willpower to tough it out. In return, he would help. If he promised to keep the King alive playing his music, Elvis would keep Donny alive.

They were a good match, he and Elvis. Both had drug problems, talent destroyed too soon, scorn from women they loved, and hearts in open conflict with their minds. And, they both loved weapons. It was not uncommon for Donny to be the nicest Elvis on the planet one moment, only to fantasize about slicing someone's gallbladder out with a steak knife the next.

This could explain Donny's outrage when he heard a loud knock on his screen door right in the middle of *The Dawn of the Dead*.

"What? Damnit!"

The door rattled again and a woman's voice could be heard shouting, "Donny, open up!"

Donny clicked the mute button and heaved himself out of a sagging easy chair. Passing the kitchen table, he grabbed a knife covered in peanut butter and answered the door.

The woman standing on the wet stoop was wearing a floral print dress under a clear plastic raincoat. Her beehive hairdo was similarly encased in plastic. He had not recognized the throaty voice. Ruth B adjusted her glasses. "Donny, we gotta talk."

Donny looked down at the butter knife. "I was making dinner, Ruth. You hungry?"

"No. They're havin' a spaghetti feed at the Elk's club tonight. I can't stay. But, can I come in?"

"Sure."

Ruth B reluctantly entered the house, dripping on the worn linoleum. Donny's clutter was nothing new to her. She'd been the only family member who'd checked in on him from time to time after the incident. Ruth B was Donny's aunt from his mother's side of the family.

Ruth walked into the kitchen and opened his refrigerator. A partial half-rack of discount beer stood on the shelf next to a half-empty bottle of rose wine. On the table sat an opened bottle of whiskey and a can of Coke.

"Donny – you're not supposed to be drinking."

"I'm missing my movie, Ruth. What'd you want?"

Ruth B turned to the TV screen just in time to see a silent scream come from a comely blonde as her heart was torn from her chest. Startled, she turned back to Donny.

"I came by because I've been worried about you, what with Patti's death and all."

Donny flopped down at the table and Ruth B joined him. "I'm doing fine, Ruth B, as you can see."

Ruth could see all right – Donny's three-day stubble, bruised knuckles, and his vacant eyes. In the sink were a week's worth of dirty dishes. The trash overflowed onto the floor. There were cereal crumbs, bottle caps and banana peels strewn about the counter. The windows hadn't been opened, which explained why the room smelled like sardines.

"You go to the doctor this week?"

"I've been taking a little break – a doctor vacation."

Ruth B fidgeted around in her chair and couldn't keep her hands still. "Donny, Detective Buck was in today. You know, Rebecca's brother. Actually, he was in twice. Second time he didn't buy flowers, but he asked if I sold any recently to that black woman cop? When I said no, he asked if I remembered selling any on Sunday, the day Patti was killed. I had to think about it for a few minutes, but then I remembered I sold some to you."

Donny's jaw dropped. The mention of flowers punched a small crack in his memory.

"Donny, please don't tell me you went and done something stupid."

Donny rubbed his head. "I done stupid things all my life, Ruth B. What makes you think I can change now?"

"That's not the kind of answer I was lookin' for." Ruth B sat up straight. "What'd you do with them flowers I sold you?"

Donny thought about it. "I kept 'em." Donny then stood up abruptly, walked to the door and held it open. Ruth B got the message.

Donny frowned. "You tell him about me?"

"No."

"Have a nice dinner."

31

Later that night, Smitty was putting on his jacket after completing some paperwork at the station. Buck and he had visited two more locations along the river before hanging it up. They'd managed to dodge most of the rain, but it was really dumping now.

When the office door flung open, Vu was standing in the doorway, frowning, his jacket dripping wet.

"I have some new information on the Sanders case," he belted out.

"Well lad, I'm glad someone has something new," Smitty sighed, left his jacket on and sat back down.

"Where's Detective Buck?"

"Gone spelunking as they say 'round these parts.'"

"Do you know how to reach him?"

"Maybe. New information you say?"

Vu unzipped his jacket and withdrew the two large manila files he'd removed from Sanders' room. He walked over and dumped them on Smitty's desk.

Smitty pushed them aside. "What might I find in here?"

"Information that leads me to believe Beverly Sanders didn't commit suicide."

"Interesting…"

"And, there may be a connection between the Knot and Sanders cases."

This was not news Smitty wanted to hear so late in the day. He checked his watch. "Can't it wait 'til morning?"

"No."

"Ah, but lad, you're on my turf, and my shift is over."

"I had a legal obligation to show you these files. If you're not interested –"

Smitty put up his hand. "Hold on now. I never said I wasn't interested. But the girl's dead. A single day does her no good now, does it?"

Vu scooped up the envelopes and headed for the door.

"Vu, wait up!" Smitty jumped up and ran after him.

Outside the office in the hall, Smitty latched onto Vu's wrist and pulled him aside. "I said hold on now, lad. There's no reason we can't take this matter up under more suitable conditions. The Lackey's Pub is just round the block a bit. What'd you say?"

The owner of Lackey's Pub was an Irishman named Red Lackey. Vu guessed, by the spackling of white in his otherwise red hair, that Red was in his sixties. Jovial, sporting work clothes like most of the other patrons and packing a gut that showed his fondness for product, he plunked down two beer mugs on the bar, smiling at both men. Vu glanced down at the foamy head now spewing over the top of his mug onto the counter like a tiny volcano and searched for a napkin.

"There you be, boys," Red said, smiling. "Just whistle if you need something else."

Smitty picked up his mug and offered to clink glasses. Vu saw more beer slop from Smitty's mug onto the bar, but he didn't want to start off on a sour note, so he clanked glasses and sucked a few slurps of ale.

"There now, this is much better, don't you agree?"

Vu would have preferred to conduct official business in the office. "Sure. Let's move to a table where we can spread out and talk privately."

Smitty reluctantly picked up his beer and moved to a sticky table in the back of the room.

Vu got down to business. "Beverly Sanders was renting a room at the Spencer Hotel under the name of Jill Brown. That's why you didn't find her at the Marriott."

"Jill Brown, eh? I guess we blew that one."

Vu placed the manila files down on a dry spot on the table. Smitty guzzled a large portion of his beer then opened the first envelope. He removed the photographs, thumbing through them quickly, then, put them down. He did the same with the contents of the second envelope.

"Assuming we can piece this puzzle together," Smitty said, "and providing the statue of limitations hasn't run out – she was a minor then, right?"

"Yes."

"Well, lad, then the courts would've sealed the file. Even if we find the persons responsible, we got no grounds for an arrest without her testimony."

"You do if they tie into Patti Knot's murder."

"Now you're stretching it, lad. Let's rethink this. We have hard evidence your copper from New Orleans is guilty."

"It's circumstantial at best," Vu countered, and then tapped the envelopes. "There's motive in there. When Sanders came snooping around, somebody got nervous. She started asking too many questions. I suspect Knot told her something. Someone found out what she knew and killed them both."

"Why you figure Knot and Sanders are connected?"

"A man at the hotel saw Sanders speaking with Knot at the track last week."

"And who might this lad be?"

"He works at the track. He's staying at the Spencer Hotel."

"Was this lad privy to the conversation?"

"No."

Smitty furrowed his brow. "Maybe Sanders was getting her autograph," but even he didn't sound convinced by the posit.

Vu sensed he'd successfully cast a shadow of doubt in the detective's mind. Now, his own plan was cooking.

Vu sat back. "I need to find out more about what Knot knew and how she ties into Sanders' death. I'm heading to the track tomorrow to try and connect the two."

Smitty smiled. "Do you even know the first thing 'bout horses? Or racing for that matter? Or, what about the politics and money entangled in both?"

"I'm a quick study."

"Jack be nimble, Jack be quick, Jack jump over the candlestick," Smitty sing-songed. "You know who they wrote that nursery rhyme about?"

"I've no idea."

"They wrote it about Jack Black." Smitty polished off his beer and slammed his glass down. "He played a dangerous game, too, and died from having his throat cut. He was a pirate, an outsider, just like you."

* * *

A moaning echoed from the basement cell. Gates slapped the bars with her hand. "Shut the hell up over there!"

Gates paced her small cell, cursing her situation. The door to the main cellblock opened. Detective Buck walked in, stopped a few feet from Gates' cell, exchanged words with the guard, and then moved closer. Gates felt her jaw tighten and wondered what the hell this asshole wanted.

Gates made no comment and looked him in the eye.

"I may have overlooked a piece of evidence."

"No shit?"

"Let me ask you something –"

Gates cut him off. "I hear you pulled my partner off the street."

"Let's not get sidetracked."

"Fuck you."

Buck cleared his throat. "There's no record that you bought flowers downtown before you headed out to Knot's place. Where did you buy them?"

"What the hell are you talking about?"

"You did take her flowers?"

"No."

"Flowers were found at the scene. We assumed you gave them to her."

Gates dropped her shoulders and relaxed a bit. "I didn't buy any flowers. I didn't give her any flowers. Hell, I didn't even see any flowers. If you found some fucking flowers, they arrived after I left."

"That may suggest someone visited the ranch after you."

"No shit, Sherlock," Gates snapped. Buck frowned, studying her face a moment as if attempting to determine her veracity.

"When I get out of here, I'm going to do your job and find the son-of-a-bitch that killed her."

"What makes you think you're getting out of here?"

32

The harmonic bluegrass music of Ralph Stanley spilled into the crowded lobby of the Galt Hotel. Electrified musicians and fans swarmed the corridors packed with vendors, reporters, photographers, excited hobbyists, celebrities, politicians, thieves, mothers, sons and daughters. All played, or appreciated, bluegrass.

Vu headed to the basement intentionally oblivious to the music he loved, carrying an armload of equestrian reading material.

Hill had left a note in the room that he was tracking down Elvis. Exhausted and wet, Vu stripped off his clothes and hung them in the closet.

He was wearing a pair of yellow boxers Betty had given him that read, *"Dead Bodies Make Me Horny"*. They had survived Katrina by virtue of the fact that he had had them on when the storm struck. They were now officially dubbed his "lucky" shorts.

He had been trying to make contact with Betty all day, and once again her machine picked up. Vu saddened and started to leave a message. Finally, he heard Betty's out of breath voice pick up.

"Jack! Is that you?"

Dogs were barking wildly in the background.

"Hello, Betty…"

"The girls and I have been playing."

"Betty, be careful with those dogs. They are trained machines."

"Hey did you know that when you snap your fingers they roll onto their backs to have their bellies rubbed?"

Vu was speechless. Those dogs would never put themselves in a vulnerable belly-up position – and one snap was an attack signal.

"They are barking now, but just wait, I'll show you. I'm going to lay the phone down and snap my fingers…"

"Betty, No!" Vu screamed. He heard Betty yell and beg, "No babies … stop!" Then there was silence.

"Betty! Betty! Answer me." Vu was frantic.

"Why haven't you called me?" Betty said in a calm, quiet voice.

"Apply pressure to the wound and lock the dogs out."

"The only one who is going to get locked out is you. I can't believe you haven't checked your messages. I asked you to call back hours ago."

Betty was indignant. Jack was beyond words.

"It was just a little joke, Jack," Betty laughed. "So how's it going?"

Vu swallowed, choking, "Look, I need to tell you something." Vu paused. "Last night Detective Hill and I got drunk at a party and I blacked out. When I rolled over in bed this morning, there was a naked woman between us."

The silence over the phone was deafening.

"Just a little joke." Vu could feel Betty smiling through the phone. "It serves you right."

"Touché, Jack. Ok, tell me what's been going on. Wait … did I tell you how much I miss you?"

Vu felt his heart sink into that quiet zone and he relaxed. He conjured an image of Betty lying in bed naked, draped across yellow silk sheets. "I miss you too, sugar," he said softly.

"Tell me more sweet things…"

"I'm wearing your gift."

"How sexy. Is that all you're wearing?"

"Yes."

"I hope you're alone."

"Betty, I do have a favor to ask."

"Anything, just name it."

"I've sent you some important evidence – two specimens taken from a murder scene – to run at your lab. It should arrive today. You'll receive a call when it does. Can you do that for me?"

"I'll have to be sneaky about it, but I'll get it done."

Suddenly, Hill opened the hotel door and peered in. "Anybody home?"

Vu blushed, jumped up, revealing his lucky underwear.

"Those shorts make me horny, Vu."

Vu held the phone to his chest, shoved Hill back into the hall, and pushed the door closed. "Jack – who's there?"

"I'm sharing a room with detective Hill. It's a long story."

"Jack, you haven't turned gay on me?"

Vu smiled. "I'll explain everything later. These samples are important and I can't use the Air Force lab for this one. It's too time sensitive. I've taken extreme measures to get it to you."

"What is it? Blood? Hair?"

"Horse manure."

"You sent me shit?"

"Actually two piles of shit. I need to know if they came from the same ranch."

"I would have preferred chocolates."

"I'll make it up to you. I promise."

"I'll have to think about it. I suppose I could analyze for different grains."

Hill rattled the door, trying to reenter. It was pointless since Vu had hooked the chain. "Vu, I gotta bleed my weasel," he pleaded.

Vu ignored him.

"Betty, it's essential to my case. Just a preliminary report will be fine. Call, fax, e-mail, I don't care. But I need it ASAP."

More silence.

"OK – but hurry up and get your butt home. I miss sleeping in the V-berth with you. I'll call your cell when I receive the results from your mysterious package."

"Thanks, honey. I love you."

"Vu!" Hill banged again on the door; the sound carried loudly into the room.

"What?" Betty yelled.

"I said I love you, but I gotta go."

"OK, Jack. But put some pants on before you let that homo Hill and his weasel back in the room."

33

The rain had not let up from yesterday and continued its staccato pelt against the wooden roof of the Belle of Louisville's quarterdeck. Captain James D. Roman, a veteran of the old 192 foot steamship, donned his yellow slicker and walked out of the pilot's house to inspect the fore and aft anchor lines. He jotted the results in his log book and was just making way to the engine room when he bumped into Sergeant Vu.

"May I have a moment of your time, Captain?" Vu asked politely, then introduced himself, as rain speckled his glasses.

Roman looked him over, unimpressed, and then pointed to the observation deck. "Let's get out of this rain."

Vu followed the big man inside. Roman had broad shoulders and a square jaw that had braved its share of brawls. The scars were mostly hidden by his neatly trimmed beard, sprinkled with gray. He carried a confidence that only comes from years of experience on the sea.

Roman shed his raincoat and made a note in his logbook, as if he'd forgotten something earlier.

"On the night of the 8th, were you piloting this boat?" Vu asked, reviewing his notebook.

"That would have been our mid-week sunset cruise. Yes – I was in charge that night. We had a private party aboard. About fifty people in all."

"Who was the party for?"

"Humana Insurance executives and their wives. The local business community frequently rents the Belle for private engagements. What's this about?"

Vu explained. The captain listened carefully.

"I'm curious – did you notice anything unusual that evening out on the water?"

"Like what?"

"For instance, did you go near the railroad bridge? Did you see anyone crawling around on it? Or, were there any other boats on the river that night?"

"Let me see. I suppose we passed a few tugs. As far as that old rusted railroad bridge – it was deserted. That's not to say I haven't seen kids up there fooling about before."

"Can you recall the river conditions that night?"

"Turbulent with plenty of flotsam. And a pretty swift current too, 3 maybe 4 knots. If I remember correctly, she was blowing hard out of the East. We had to counter-steer the old gal several degrees. Had to be on our toes."

"Did you see anything suspicious?"

"Like what?"

"I'm investigating a drowning that occurred that night, a young Air Force Officer named Beverly Sanders."

"No sergeant, I did not see a body. In such circumstances, we're required to notify the Coast Guard and offer assistance."

"She was found downriver the morning following your scheduled cruise."

A shipmate in a white uniform appeared and began polishing the brass fixtures. While Vu waited for the Captain's response, he noticed the shiny teak woodwork. He ran his finger along the freshly varnished railing. A hint of oily residue remained on his finger. He smelled it.

"And you think she might have been aboard this vessel?"

"Do you have a passengers manifest from that evening?"

"You'd have to get that from Humana. However, I must warn you – they consider maintaining confidentiality of their guests to be of utmost importance."

"Was there a photographer on board that evening?"

"Probably. There usually is."

"Did you get a chance to mingle with the guests?"

"I don't spend much time with the passengers. As I said, my primary focus is to operate this vessel. And I had my hands full that night." The Captain paused. "Are you actually suggesting this girl may have jumped from the Belle?"

"It's a possibility. I'm unclear just what did happen to Ms. Sanders, but your boat was on the river that night." Captain Roman's face closed on itself, deep in thought. "Would your crew have had contact with her?"

"The kitchen staff might have. They mingle more with the passengers."

"I'll need a list of their names and phone numbers."

"I'll see what I can do."

"Do you mind if I look around before I leave?"

"No. Just steer clean of restricted areas."

Vu handed the Captain his card. "I won't take up any more of your time. I appreciate you talking with me."

Roman shook his hand. "Watch your step down below, sergeant. It can get mighty slippery in this weather."

Vu located the galley midship, two decks below. He found the steamy compartment and heard cupboards banging closed on the other side of the wall as he entered. Standing in the center of the galley area was a barrel-chested black man as large as a hot-air balloon. His enormous body was stuffed into a chef's uniform. He was cursing at a sack of flour with a hole in the bottom that had spilled all over the counter and floor.

"Excuse me?"

The man spun round, eyes blazing. "You the new prep cook?"

"No,"

"Then what you want? I'm busy."

Vu cleared his throat. "Captain Roman sent me."

The black man grinned. "Did he now? I'm surprised he knew where to send you. He's never been in here as far as I know." The black man pointed to the corner closet. "There's a broom and dustpan in there. Get 'em for me."

Vu decided not to argue. He walked over and pulled open the small cluttered closet. A mop handle fell out. Vu caught it inches from his forehead and pushed it back inside. He removed the broom and dustpan and carried them over to the cook.

"He expects me to whip up three hundred dinners by six this evening and I got me a rodent problem that's driving me crazy. You know how hard it is to keep food aboard when you got vermin gnawing everything? Sweep that up, would you?"

Vu glanced down at the pile of flour.

"I said sweep."

Vu did as he was told. He swept the flour into a neat pile and used the dustpan to pick it up. "What should I do with it?"

"Throw it out, what else?"

Vu looked to where the cook pointed his stubby finger. About then, a loud snap startled him. The cook threw up his hands and hustled over to the source. He stooped down and searched beneath the grill. When he finally stood, he was dangling a dead mouse by the tail, its skull crushed by the steel trap.

Vu stepped aside and allowed the cook to dump the rodent in the trash. He followed behind with his dustpan. The garbage can was filled with battered vermin carcasses. The cook washed his hands and returned to the counter. Vu put the broom away and rejoined him.

"You a Health Inspector?"

"No. I'm investigating a recent drowning and would like to ask you a few questions about the night of the 8th."

The large man ignored him and pulled down a stainless steel bowl the size of a small satellite dish. He scooped the flour off the counter into the bowl and then added water from the faucet and stuck his big hands into the doughy mixture. "You give me a hand here, and I'll do the same for you."

Vu stood rooted to the spot.

"Put on an apron and give me a hand and I might remember somethin'. The 8th you said?"

"That's right. It was a private party."

The cook kept mixing. "Go get me ten pounds of butter from the cooler."

"I'll be happy to do that." Vu pulled a photograph from his pocket and laid it on the counter. "But first, I'd like you to take a look at this. She is an Air Force Officer who may have been aboard this vessel that night."

The black man concentrated on his bowl.

"Her name is Beverly Sanders," Vu continued. "White, mid 20's. Until very recently, she was a 2nd Lieutenant stationed in New Orleans. She worked for a Security Police Detachment."

"She in some kind of trouble?"

"The worst kind. She's dead. She drowned that night in the river."

"Whatcha want to know?"

"So you remember her?"

"Yes."

Despite himself, Vu felt excitement at hearing this verification of his theory.

The cook quit mixing and turned to Vu. "I see everything that goes on aboard the Belle. I've been working on this old gal since I was a teenager. Nothin' goes by ol' Rusty without Rusty takin' notice. Now, you gonna get that butter?"

Vu studied the man. His change in posture and demeanor indicated he was weighing what to say next. Vu decided to give him a moment. He wandered around the corner to where he guessed the ship's refrigeration was located. He saw a large stainless steel door and opened it. A blast of chilly air rushed past him as he searched the shelving inside. Through the cartons, bricks of cheese, and stacks of meat, he found a large box with the word "Butter" written on the outside. He opened the top and removed two five-pound blocks.

Back in the kitchen he plunked down one of the blocks of butter on the counter. "What can you tell me about her?" It was a face-off now. Man to man.

"This is confidential, right?"

Vu nodded and slapped the butter brick against his palm.

"She was wearing an Air Force dress uniform. I thought she might have been aboard in some official capacity – to give a speech or somethin'." The cook smiled. "I was on break topside when she came charging down out of the observation deck. Practically ran smack into my big ass. I told her a girl with her kind of looks ought to be in a fancy dress with diamonds and all, not in no uniform. At first she looked like she was gonna tear my head off, so I apologized and she calmed right down. We chatted a bit –talked about the river and the war and such. I told her how to make a Key lime pie that would cause a man to cream his britches and she was laughing before I was finished. Then, the Gov called to her and she headed off in his direction." He plucked the butter brick away from Vu, snapped it in half, and mashed it up with his powerful hands into the large bowl of dough.

"The Governor was on the boat?"

"No, John Seemore – the man that's gonna be Governor."

"He just announced, he's running. The election won't take place for another year."

Rusty shook his head. "You don't know much about Louisville, do you?"

Vu didn't know Louisville, but he understood politics and power. "What was he doing aboard?"

"He sits on the Humana Board of Directors," the cook said, slightly disappointed in Vu's inability to figure this out. "He and his wife were here, along with about fifty other rich white folk."

Vu offered up the second butter brick. Rusty grabbed it and squeezed it like Popeye opening a can of spinach.

"Did you see Ms. Sanders again?"

"No. I was back down here."

"So the last person you saw her with was John Seemore?"

The man's eyes bulged. "Holy, Jesus! You thinkin' what I'm thinkin' – not the Gov?"

"Did Mr. Seemore seem upset when he called to her?"

"No, sir. He was right kind to her."

"What about some of the other guests? Did she argue with any of them?"

"No, sir. Just saw her with the Gov and maybe later with his wife."

"Mrs. Seemore?"

I can't be sure it was them out on the aft deck."

The cook froze, realizing the slip. "I've said too much already."

The cook opened a carton of eggs and wouldn't look Vu in the eye. "You can't be mentionin' this to nobody, sir. Nobody, you understand? I like this job, even though I bellyache 'bout it from time to time. You don't know the way this town works."

Vu knew, all too well.

34

Mona dismounted the stiff saddle and firmly held the reins as she stroked the two-year old chestnut affectionately. The tingling in her thighs felt good. Her muscles had needed a real workout. Although, it'd been nearly a week since she had last ridden, the colt performed beautifully.

"Good, boy!" she said. "You'll be next year's Derby winner for sure."

She walked the tired horse toward an open stall, slipped off the damp saddle and blanket, and slung them over a rail to air. Then, she brushed the colt's lathered coat. She felt sweaty in her heavy riding gear and peeled off her jacket. Her neck and arms were hot and her calves still quivered. She bent over to stretch her back muscles, took a few deep breaths, and tried to clear her head before entering the tack room. From a 55-gallon drum, she scooped a portion of grain and refilled the feed bin, then topped off the water trough with a hose. Next to Seven Dancer, this new colt was her favorite.

She began coiling the water hose, day-dreaming about her latest romp with Brad Black, when her husband walked up from behind and cleared his throat.

"John, back up. You'll ruin your suit."

John stared at her, frustration furrowing his brow. How could he still find her attractive after all she'd done behind his back? He swallowed hard and spoke wretchedly. "How was your spa treatment yesterday?"

Mona tossed the hose into an old barrel and brushed her hands off. "Fine."

He studied her expression, noticing only a slight color deviation around her neck – something that always occurred when she was lying.

"Ben came by yesterday."

Mona stood up straight and put her jacket back on. "Oh? What'd Ben want?"

"He said we might want to find a new jockey for the Derby."

Mona stopped cold in her tracks. "You can't be serious?"

"Brad's urine sample tested positive for cocaine."

Mona rubbed her nose. "That's impossible. The lab must have made a mistake."

The flush on Mona's neck deepened.

"Well, I'm going to have a talk with him."

Mona became solicitous and leaned toward him. "Let me handle him. You've got more important things to worry about. Like your campaign."

John closed the gap and stepped within inches of her finely tanned chest. He could see the throbbing vein in her neck. "You're right – I have more important things to worry about. For instance the other night…"

"You mean when you tried to seduce me in the bathroom? We had guests, John!"

"That's not what I was referring to." His facial expression darkened. "What happened between you and Bev on the boat?"

"Nothing. Why don't you discuss these "suspicions" of yours with the police, if you don't believe me? Go ahead, kiss your governorship goodbye."

John made a move as if he was going to strike her and then

turned to walk away.

Mona raised her voice, trying to convince him. "Bevy apparently became distraught after leaving the ship. You told her what you could. She was depressed, so she took her own life. Plain and simple." John stopped dead in his tracks, spun around, and glowered. Mona reached out and grabbed his arm. "I swear I didn't lay a hand on her."

He stared at her neck. The flush faded. He believed her. She was a lying drug addicted adulterer, but she was no murderer.

35

The air at the racetrack was crisp and the cloudy sky had finally cleared. A good sign, Vu thought, as he climbed from the car. He could see the outdoor stable area where grooms walked horses. Out on the racetrack, a handful of riders were making trial runs. A few early risers stood along the fence, studying jockeys and horses while making notes in tablets. Vu remembered from his reading that this was the norm to get a leg up on the competition and improve the odds of winning.

The guard at the entrance to the Jockey Club was sipping hot coffee and absorbed in *The Racing News* when Vu walked up.

"Sorry, sir – restricted entry unless you have a pass."

Vu looked the man in the eye. "Where do I pick up my pass?"

The guard pointed toward the grandstand. "Last office on your right, just past the betting area."

"Thanks." Vu turned to walk away as a water truck approached. The driver rolled down his window and called the guard over. Vu waited until the man had walked around the cab of the truck. Once he was out of sight conversing with the driver, Vu casually slipped through the gate and skirted the perimeter.

He wandered the stalls amongst various track employees, listening to bits of conversation, followed several jockeys across the paddock, and even stopped to chat with a group of enthusiastic children selling cupcakes near the grandstand to raise money for a project in Patti Knot's honor. Eventually, he made his way toward the private stables.

No one seemed to give Vu a second glance. Security was on hand, but Vu made no suspicious moves and blended well with the environment. The stables and grounds were populated with small foreigners and being Vietnamese had no extraordinary impact on these people. It was an unusual feeling compared to working in law enforcement where Vu's height, features and accent were all noticeable. The resulting stares and judgment were constant reminders of his cultural and racial differences. Despite this new sense of acceptance, after questioning dozens, Vu still had squat. But, his luck was about to turn.

A stable hand, mucking an open stall, was happy to answer his questions. It meant he could take a brief break. He said he was getting too old for shoveling shit. However, his granddaughter had the flu. She usually handled these things, but as a trainer, he sometimes got stuck doing the grunt work.

"What'd you say you wanted?"

"I'm looking for information. Did you know Patti Knot?"

"As well as most."

"How did she get along with the other riders and owners?"

"Fine, I guess."

"No enemies?"

"Maybe one or two competitors. When you get to be her age, you look for ways to avoid trouble, not create it. Actually, most of the owners loved Patti. A couple of jockeys might have felt different."

"I take it you're referring to the recent photograph in the paper."

"Yeah, he probably had that coming long ago." The man put his shovel aside and continued. "It's no secret. Mrs. Seemore wasn't happy with Patti's performance of late. Rumor had it she was going to fire her and get a new jockey to ride the Derby.

"Who did Mrs. Seemore want instead?"

"The punching bag himself, Brad Black. Though you didn't hear that from me, understand? The Seemores have plenty of influence around these parts, and I don't want any trouble."

"Fair enough."

As he was walking away, the man unexpectedly called out to him. Vu stopped.

"Hey – I didn't get your name?"

"Jack."

"Well Jack, be sure and talk to Miki Davis. She and Patti were friends. She might steer you in the right direction. She's out on the track. You can probably catch her at the gate. I saw her practicing starts earlier."

"What does Miki look like?"

"Dark hair, red jersey. Eyes like peanut butter cups. Can't miss her. She's probably the only woman out there."

And miss her Vu didn't. She was cussing up a storm, limping on one ankle, cursing her horse, and pacing back and forth in front of the starting gate while clutching her shoulder. Vu was reluctant to step too close. Four of the gate doors were open, but the stubborn horse refused to move. Vu gathered the animal was to blame.

From a distance he called out, "You all right?"

Miki glared at him. "No, fuckin' horse. Excuse my French, but the little shit bit me."

"Are you bleeding?"

"Feels like it. Could you take a look?"

Reluctantly, Vu moved forward, but steered clear of the horse. Miki secured the animal then turned and pulled her jersey back off her shoulder. "Well?" she asked impatiently. "How bad is it?"

Vu used his handkerchief to wipe the blood off the wound. "It's going to bruise, but he barely broke the skin."

"Great." Miki shook free and turned to stare at him.

"I don't recognize you from around here."

"I'm an investigator with the Air Force. I understand you were friends with Patti Knot. Do you have a minute to answer a few questions?"

Miki crinkled her nose and squinted toward the backfield. "I don't usually talk to cops, but you did do me a favor. You're kinda small for law enforcement? Where you from again?"

"Vietnam."

"You ever think about becoming a jockey?"

"I would make a terrible jockey. Now, Ms. Davis, could we keep to the topic please?"

"Surething. Blast away, sergeant. But, if you ask me, the cops got it all wrong. They ought to be looking for Donny Mason, because in my opinion, he's a stalker. And he probably killed her." Miki shifted her weight. "She couldn't go anywhere without that freak following. He was like trying to wipe wet shit from a boot. He clung..."

"Actually, I am tracking the activities of Beverly Sanders. Did you know her?"

"Everyone knew of her and what happened around here, but I wouldn't have recognized her. She hadn't been here in years. Patti introduced me to her last week in the parking lot. Patti said Bev was trying to solve her own rape."

"Go on."

Patti also said some con down in Florida had mouthed off to a cellmate one night and one thing led to another. Well, the guy contacts Bev, says he'll tell her the name of one of her rapists for some hard cash. Beverly pays the guy, but before she gets the full scoop, he up and splits..."

"Where'd Patti fit in?"

"I don't know exactly. She was married to Donny Mason, the shitheel, back then. I got the impression from Patti that Bev thought she knew her rapist."

"Did she?"

"Believe me, I wish I knew, but I was in a hurry that day – late for a race – and I never saw either of them again."

Over his shoulder Vu saw two jockeys heading their direction. They were each leading a horse. He turned his back and bid farewell to Miki just before Brad Black and another jockey in blue silks walked by and nosed their mounts into the gate.

At the exit to the parking lot, the security guard lowered his newspaper and put his hand up for Vu to stop. Vu turned to the man and waited for him to unlock the turnstile.

"How long have you worked here?"

"Fifteen years next October," the guard said casually.

"Do you remember a rape that happened here nearly ten years ago? It was the evening after the Kentucky Derby. It involved a fourteen year old girl. A man was injured trying to stop the attackers?"

The guard rubbed his fat chin. "Sure. I worked the day shift back then. That was a real bad thing. Punk nearly killed them both." The guard lowered his voice, "I felt real bad for that little girl. Her father was a trainer out here. They hunted for the guy, but never found him."

"You think it was someone local?"

"No. When the Derby runs, we get people from all over. Just in town for a week, then they're gone again. Nothing like that has ever happened since. Good thing, too. Because I'd run a pitchfork through the bastard, just like they did to poor Bevy."

Vu perked up. "Say that again?"

"What? The part about the track workers?"

"No – the other…"

"I said I'd pitchfork the bastard if I caught him."

36

Jack Vu hung up the phone with Ruttle and stared at his notes. The old scars and puncture wounds Vu had observed on Beverly Sanders had been caused by a pitchfork during her rape. Patti Knot had died from the same type of weapon. Detective Buck's sister had committed suicide after a brutal rape. Donny Mason knew them all. Vu closed his eyes and tried to mentally sort his information. Were these events all related, or were they random?

As Vu meditated on the concept of inter-connectedness, Hill was learning that in the world of the rich and powerful, there was no connection with those outside their realm.

* * *

The Ridgewood Country Club was an elite member's only facility with annual dues higher than his annual salary. It was listed as one of the top ten country clubs in America. Its registry was strictly confidential, but included Hollywood celebrities, foreign dignitaries, politicians, lawyers and numerous executives from various Fortune 500 corporations.

The resort was comprised of a five-star restaurant, a lounge, an Olympic-size swimming pool, 18-hole golf course, four tennis courts, a full-size gym with three racket-ball courts and a full-service spa.

After being politely, but firmly, rebuffed at the main clubhouse, Hill scouted the perimeter and jumped the fence at the 8th hole.

Tami's mother had said she scheduled the girls a 1 o'clock tee time. As he had hoped, Hill found Cindy Brewer and Tami Jones out on the golf course, along the sixth fairway, enjoying a lax round in the afternoon sun. Tami wore a tight white knit shirt and matching skirt which showed off her tanned legs. Cindy sported the same outfit, but in red. Tami offered Hill a nice view of her figure as she bent over the back of a golf cart, pawing through an ice chest. He had also watched Cindy put out a joint about two minutes before he approached. They both reeked of pot.

"You want a beer?" Tami asked.

The fact that he'd tracked the girls down didn't even seem to cross their minds.

"I'll pass," Hill said, and glanced around. "This is some place."

"It's OK. I've been to better." Cindy smiled haughtily.

"Who's winning?"

"Tami. She's a three handicapper."

"Not bad."

Tami stepped back and popped the cap on a wine cooler. A white froth foamed out of the top and oozed down her arm. She cursed and shook it off. Some of the foam clung to the front of her knit top, though she wasn't aware of it. Hill kept staring as if he wanted to say something.

"So Detective," Tami said. "What do you want? We told everything to Mr. Vu."

A golf ball whizzed by and landed in the trees. Hill glanced over his shoulder and saw a frustrated golfer throw down his club and stomp off the fairway. No amount of money could get Hill to play the game.

"Vu had a little problem understanding you last time."

The girls looked at each other. "Us?"

"I think it was the "tech-talk" that messed with him."

Tami picked a 3-wood from her golf bag and made a few practice swings. "We were just fucking with him."

Cindy nodded. "We weren't that close to B."

Hill asked, "Was that before or after the rape?"

The question made them uncomfortable.

Hill grew impatient. "Well…"

"We were drinking and partying in one of the stalls. We all got a little crazy," Tami said.

Cindy piped in, "We had a water fight. Bevy's clothes got all wet. She stripped out of them and we were going to go borrow some jockey's outfit for her to wear. Sounds silly to say that now, but we were kids then."

"So you weren't there when it happened?"

"We were smashed," Cindy said. "We had to pee. Then, we ran into some friends and never made it back to her."

"And Bevy didn't know who attacked her?"

The girls looked at each other. "No, she was knocked out, lying face down. When she came to and tried to turn over, she couldn't. She was pinned to the floor with a pitchfork."

"You think this trip had something to do with the rape?"

Cindy looked at Tami and they both shook their heads no.

He could tell the girls were withholding something. He stepped back and watched Tami set up her next shot. She steadied her club and took her time hitting it down the fairway. The shot came up short and rolled into a sand trap.

"What happened to Bevy afterwards?"

"She left town."

Tami bagged her club and picked out a beer this time. After a long drink she said, "Her parents sent her off to a private boarding school out of state. We didn't see her again for nearly six years."

"Did she want to go?"

"She didn't want to stay here. There was a fund started at a local bank to pay for her hospital bill, but there wasn't enough money for that. Her parents couldn't have afforded it. They worked at the track."

"Maybe she got a scholarship?"

"Maybe."

Cindy interrupted. "She didn't get a scholarship. Mr. Seemore paid for it and he offered to get her name changed. He also paid for that other guy's hospital bills." She was looking at Tami now. Some of this was news to Tami.

Hill scratched his nose. The fresh cut grass irritated it. "What other guy?"

"Tami – what the fuck was his name? He tried breaking it up but got beat so bad he turned into a 'tard."

"I don't remember."

Hill stepped in. "Why would Seemore pay?"

"Bevy's parents worked for them. Seemore owned the stall where it happened. I guess he felt responsible."

"What happened to the guy?"

"He's a loser Elvis impersonator."

Hill couldn't believe it. Was he the only one in town that didn't know who Elvis was?

Cindy swatted a bee buzzing around her head. "Before she went away to school, B said someday she was going to find the guy responsible and kill him."

"Did she talk about it last week?"

"No. As far as I know she was here for Marci's wedding."

"And you didn't have contact with her the night of her drowning?"

"No. We partied the night before."

Hill was frustrated with the results, but he'd run out of questions. He noticed the girls were restless to get back to their game or another joint. He couldn't blame them for not wanting to talk about a rape they might have prevented.

"I need the guy's name," Hill said firmly.

The girls looked at each other and shrugged. It was Cindy's turn to take her swing. She was less polished and more dramatic, dancing back and forth in front of the tee, sizing up the distance while inching toward the ball.

Cindy swung, but the drive came up short. A kid wearing a baseball jersey on the next hole witnessed the lame shot and heckled her. Disdainfully, she flipped him off.

Cindy tossed her club into her bag. "Tami! C'mon! What was that guy's name?" Tami, deep in thought, stared toward the kid in the jersey. Hill waited. Finally, she blinked her eyes and blurted, "Mason! Donny Mason."

"I had a major crush on him at the time." She faced Hill. "He was our NASCAR hopeful."

"What happened to him?"

"Everybody thought he'd get better and return to racing, but he didn't. His brain didn't work right anymore.

Tami jumped into the cart and switched on the motor, then called to her friend. "Cin, TTG"

Cindy translated for Hill. "Time to go." Cindy hopped in the passenger's seat.

Hill put his hand on the cart. "Do you know where this Donny lives?"

"How should we know? We don't hang around with retards." Tami stepped on the pedal.

37

V u didn't recognize the guard at the Seemore Estate.

"I'm here to see Mr. Seemore, please."

The guard checked his list and then passed it to Vu. "Everyone must sign in," the guard said, handing Vu a pen.

Vu signed the book and returned the pen.

"Mr. Seemore is out in the south building. Follow the stables and keep walking. You'll see the open door."

The estate appeared different in the daylight. It sprawled across hundreds of acres of pristine land, bordered by a forest of tall trees. A chauffeur was waxing a car outside the garage and a maid was standing near the main entrance to the split-level house shaking a rug. At the back of the house a Hispanic man was cutting the grass with a riding lawnmower. A farmhand met Vu as he walked by the stables carrying some wood and a canvas tool bag. He explained he had spent the morning repairing a hole in the fence along the south pasture.

Vu asked, "Did any horses get out?"

"Not according to my final count," the man replied. "Someone tore a pretty good hole in the fence. Probably PETA. We're hooking up electricity next week. Give them a real surprise."

"That a common problem?"

"Getting to be more of a problem all the time. This hole wasn't more than a week old."

Vu watched the bow-legged worker mosey off. He glanced back in the direction he'd come from. A number of horses trotted around the open pasture. Beyond them, he saw woods and glimpsed what he figured was Knot's ranch through a small opening in the trees. If someone really wanted to pay a visit to either ranch, it was just a matter of trotting across the field.

Vu eventually found the south building. John Seemore was just washing up, his coveralls were greasy, and he had streaks of axle grease on his forehead.

He looked up when Vu entered the small garage which resembled a basic repair shop. An assortment of tools hung from the wall. In one of the two bays an ancient John Deere tractor sat on blocks with its hood open.

"Hello, Sergeant," John said, wiping his hands. "My mechanic has the week off. And wouldn't you know it, old Elsie here throws a fan belt. What can I do for you?"

"Is this a good time to talk?"

John looked at his watch. "I have to check on my operation."

"Mind if I join you?" Vu asked. "We can talk on the way."

"Fine with me. Just watch your step. This is a ranch not a city sidewalk."

Vu followed John outside and waited for him to close the door. Almost immediately, Vu noticed how different Mr. Seemore's attitude seemed from the other night. He was more open and relaxed. Something had happened to calm the man down.

The men crossed a small oval track and met two sprightly girls in riding gear exercising sleek muscular thoroughbreds. The girls waved. "The horse on the right," John said, "is a two-year old. We've high hopes for him. He's a little jittery out of the gate, but flies once you give him the room. Mona has done well with him."

"I was under the impression you bred horses for other purposes?"

"Our primary operation here is breeding mares for the collection of urine. But, my wife has this fantasy about winning the Derby, so we also own World Class Thoroughbreds. They are kept in separate buildings. The two operations are mutually exclusive."

The men continued walking, while Seemore described his primary operation. Beyond the track, past a series of large metal buildings and inside a small fenced area with hay and water, a farmhand led a very pregnant mare around in circles. The device reminded Vu of a merry-go-round with long poles hanging from it.

John pointed to the run-about. "We use that periodically to exercise the foals and some of the older mares after they've given birth."

The men entered the center building. Vu was amazed at the number of horse stalls inside the facility, as well as the lack of natural sunlight and fresh air. They moved along slowly, passing the stalls where each horse had a rubber device strapped to their hindquarters that sagged under the weight of the collected liquid. The straps cut into the horses' hides.

Vu believed that all living things were reincarnated and wondered what previous lives led these animals to this particular fate.

"There are roughly thirty-five mares to a building. Most are pregnant. We try and rotate the frequency of their pregnancies so the horses aren't overworked. Our sole purpose is to collect their urine."

"What's it used for?"

"Estrogen supplement. North America is the only place that still produces pregnant mare's urine for this purpose. It is sold under the brand name 'Premarin.' Many of the manufacturers are going to synthetic. Your animal right's groups are pleased by this. At risk of sounding harsh though, I believe we produce a much better product."

Vu could see why some found the operation repulsive. The

animals had a dismal life, even if it was their karmic path.

"How often is the urine collected?"

"Daily. We transport weekly. Our manufacturer is in Lexington."

"What do you do with the foals?"

"Some are slaughtered. Some are sold off to local farms. Most of the females are raised here and will replace the older mares when they become too sick to produce."

"Do many of the animals become sick or die?"

"Sure. But that's the cost of doing business. Much like war."

"I wouldn't make the same correlation."

"You're in the military. I provide a much needed service – just like the military. There are always causalities on both sides. And, like war, it's very profitable."

Seemore went on to describe the operation in detail while Vu contemplated the unfathomable toll taken in the "business" of war.

"Would you like a beer, Sergeant?"

Vu checked his watch. "Yes, please."

Seemore walked to a refrigerator in the back of the building, removed two beers, and handed one to Vu. "I'm afraid I've done all the talking. So, what'd you want to talk to me about?"

"I don't know if you realize this, but I'm investigating the death of Beverly Sanders."

John rubbed his cheek. "I thought you were investigating the murder of Patti Knot?"

"Actually, the cases may be related."

"Really?"

"Did Ms. Sanders have a conversation with either you or your wife aboard the Belle of Louisville on the evening of the 8th?"

"Yes. That was a private fundraiser. Beverly contacted us and told us she'd be in town for a wedding, so I invited her onboard the Belle for a friendly visit while she was in town. We spoke briefly. As I said, it was good to see her after all this time and to hear she was doing well."

For the first time that day, Vu sensed he was lying.

"Was there any indication she was depressed or in some kind of trouble?"

"No. The news of her suicide devastated us both."

"So, you'd agree her suicide came as a surprise?"

Instead of responding to Vu, John became distracted by something protruding from underneath the tractor. He walked over and pulled out a chunk of wood that had jammed itself into the undercarriage. He stood in the center of the shop for a moment, unsure what to do with the scrap he was now holding. Eventually, he set it down on the workbench.

"What did you ask, sergeant?"

"Her suicide, did it come as a surprise?"

"Yes, especially after all these years."

"Do you think it had anything to do with her rape?"

"I see you've done your homework," Seemore paused and took a long pull from his beer. "That was a very painful time in her life and it's never been discussed since. It was a terrible thing. Derby officials kept the matter from the press as best they could, to protect the girl of course. But, I don't think she ever recovered emotionally."

"Did she happen to mention she was investigating her own case?"

"No. I had no idea."

"My theory is this: Ms Sanders uncovered information, perhaps the identity of the perpetrator, and that's why she returned to Louisville. Unfortunately, she was killed before she could take action."

"That's some theory, Sergeant."

"Maybe she spoke to Mrs. Seemore about her intentions?"

"Doubtful. But you're free to ask her yourself. I believe she's inside the house."

Vu changed the subject. "I understand Brad Black is going to ride your contender in the upcoming Derby."

John frowned. "Mr. Black was not my first choice."

"How long had Ms. Knot ridden for you?"

"A number of years. She was classy, talented and honest. Alas, one must move forward, and this is Seven Dancer's year."

"As you said, there are casualties on all sides, just as in war, but it is extremely profitable."

"That attitude came from my father's side of the family. He stormed the coast of France with the 7th Brigade."

"Detective Hill mentioned Mr. Black was working for you the day Ms. Knot was murdered. Is this true?"

"I was gone on business. You'll have to ask my wife about that." His disdain was apparent. "Brad is on our payroll though."

"And how did Ms. Knot feel about her competitor working for you as well?"

"She didn't like it, but Ms. Knot did not want to work here, so we had to make a business decision. She was a professional and she accepted it. Shall we go find my wife, Mr. Vu? It's getting late."

During their stroll toward the house, conversation waned. Vu figured Seemore had his reasons for withholding information. Perhaps he would have better luck with the wife, though he sensed, having spoken to her at the party, she too would be difficult.

They took seats on the porch and the maid brought more iced beer before fetching Mrs. Seemore. Moments later, Mrs. Seemore stepped onto the porch, looking fit in her tennis outfit and carrying a racket. Vu put his beer down and stood, offering his hand.

"Please – sit," Mona said, "John – I'm running late. I'll see you this evening at the club?"

John frowned momentarily, and then mechanically smiled. "I believe the detective would like to ask you a few questions first."

Mona stood in her tracks and then turned toward Vu, who had remained standing. "What would you like to know detective?"

Vu bowed graciously. "You have a remarkable estate here. I understand it has been in your family for a number of years."

"Yes," she said bluntly. "John married money – as they say."

"Mrs. Seemore, if you don't mind, could you please tell me if anyone was riding your horses last Sunday?"

"Here?"

"Yes."

"Let me see," she said, staring coldly at her husband. "No, I don't believe so."

John spoke up. "What about Brad?"

Mona frowned. "Oh, yes – that's right. He came by around noon and exercised Sun Downer."

"Were you with him the whole time?"

"He's very experienced. There would be no need for me to watch over him."

"And which horse did he ride again?"

Mrs. Seemore pointed toward the pasture. "That one. The overly-zealous colt."

Vu glanced over his shoulder to see where she was pointing. "Thank you, Mrs. Seemore."

The relief on her face was palpable. "On that happy note, goodbye then."

After Mrs. Seemore left, John became morose. He stood, and rather bluntly indicated that he had office work to do prior to an evening meeting. Vu offered to see himself out.

As soon as Mr. Seemore left him in the driveway, Vu circled back around to the pasture which Mrs. Seemore had pointed out earlier.

Situated on the ground near the fence was a fresh pile of Sun Downer's shit. Vu pulled a plastic bag from his pocket, and using a spoon with an ornately engraved G on the handle, carefully scooped from the steaming pile.

38

The dusty pickup pulled off the highway and parked at Rusty's farm. Leon switched off the motor and reached for the open quart beer tucked between Willy's legs that they had shared during the drive.

Leon had been having trouble sleeping recently, unable to get the dead girl off his mind. After a few sleepless nights, Willy suggested they make the rounds and ask a few questions, even if it did go against his better judgment. Leon liked the idea.

Leon polished off the quart, leaned out and tossed the empty into the pickup bed. Willy was already outside, waiting impatiently, rapping his cane against the roof of the cab.

"Hurry up. I gotta piss."

"I'm comin', hold your horses."

The farm consisted of semi-arid land surrounded by hills. There was a small old house in desperate need of a foundation and a metal tool shed. Out back was an outhouse, still in use, and a clothesline strung between two tall oaks where sheets ruffled in the warm afternoon breeze. Rusty's wife still hung out the wash to line-dry once a week. Over the years, they had managed to get the modern conveniences of hot water, electricity and phone service, but never got 'round to building an indoor toilet. Rusty had plowed a small section behind the house for his garden, where the rocks didn't dull his tiller. For years he'd raised vegetables when he wasn't pulling twelve hour shifts aboard the Belle of Louisville. This year he was getting ready to plant pole beans. He was hoeing narrow rows by hand as the men approached.

"Looks like work to me," Leon said, shaking his head at the sweating big black man, laboring in his garden.

"It gets my mind off things and works off this gut of mine." Rusty chuckled, wiping his dirty hands onto his blue jeans. He leaned the hoe against a tree, walked over, and shook Willy and Leon's hands. "Long time no see, boys. You two still juke jiving down at ol' Sax's place?"

Willy laughed. "Yeah, man – we still be jamming on Sundays. You ought to bring the woman down. We got us a new horn-man. Real bluesy cat out of Chicago."

"I'll do that. So, what brings you two out this way?"

Leon cleared his throat and started to say something before Willy interrupted. "Man, I hate to be rude, but I gotta piss like a racehorse."

Rusty pointed to the outhouse, then realized his gesture had no meaning to a blind man. "Be my guest. Leon will show you."

Willy took Leon's arm and followed him sighted-guide over to the outhouse. Willy did his business inside and then Leon walked with him back over to the garden where Rusty was sowing seeds. He put the empty sack on the ground and pulled up his baggy trousers.

"Willy said you know something about the dead white girl we found."

"Who told you that?"

"My cousin Charlie. He works on the Belle."

Rusty brushed some dust from his nose. "So, it was you two that found her?"

"Done won us the booby prize," Willy said, shaking his head.

"A Jap cop paid a visit to the Belle yesterday. Wanted to know what I knew."

Willy folded up his cane. "He's Vietnamese."

Rusty ripped open a second bag of seed. "I see you've talked to him."

Willy frowned at Leon. "Leon just had to play Boy Scout. I wanted nothin' to do with it."

"Cops got long noses," Rusty said. "They can sniff out a rat in a hen house."

"Well, Leon can't sleep now. And it's affecting his playing. The band decided the best thing I could do was see you. Charlie said you mentioned something about the girl the other night."

"This is between us – you hear?" Willy and Leon nodded. "Good, 'cause I can't have this shit getting out. The night before they found Beverly Sanders' body, she had been aboard the Belle of Louisville. I overheard some of the conversation the girl had with Mr. Seemore. She was angry and wanted to know about a jockey. He tried comforting her. Then, Mrs. Seemore, she walked into the cabin and the girl stormed out. I saw her later on the ship's aft deck with Mrs. Seemore, just the two of them. I returned to the kitchen just as the ship hit some flotsam in the water and pitched sidewise hard. I hustled back up to make sure everything was secure. The girl was gone. And, Mrs. Seemore, she's just calmly looking down at the water.

I asked her if she and her friend were all right. She just looked me right in the eye and told me she had been up there alone the whole time."

"You think she pushed her?" Willy asked.

"I know a bunch of niggers like us will never find out," Rusty said. He set down his seed. "Let's go inside and grab a drink. Betsy's here, but don't go talkin' about this in front of her. I don't want her involved."

Betsy, Rusty's second wife, was a stout woman with dark curly hair. She wore a red apron over her floral print dress and was just pulling a pan of crepes from the oven when Rusty walked up and gave her butt a gentle squeeze. He leaned over her shoulder, smelling the sweet scent from the pastries, and kissed her cheek.

"Sugar dumplin', we have guests."

Betsy peeked round the corner into the small living room. "How are you, gentleman?"

"We've been better, ma'am," Leon said. Willy snapped his foot with his cane.

"We've been right fine, Betsy," Willy corrected. "Something sure smells sweet in there."

"Rusty likes crepes. Just lettin' 'em cool off a bit. You all can have some."

Betsy took off her oven mitt and slapped Rusty's butt. "Did you invite these rascals over here?"

"They come on their own."

"Just get back in there and finish up your business. 'Cause when dessert is over, I'm running those boys out so you and me can have us a little dessert before I gotta run off to work."

Rusty smiled. "They'll be gone in five minutes."

Willy sat on a wooden chair with a lumpy cushion, staring at the wall. He kept fidgeting to get his bony butt comfortable. Leon sat on a sagging sofa across from him. It was so low that he had trouble stretching his legs and bending forward to reach the newspaper on the coffee table. He'd been thinking about Rusty's chatterboxing and his mind was awhirl.

Rusty popped through the kitchen door smiling, whistling, and carrying a fresh Mason jar filled with clear liquid, his special "white lightening." He walked over to the coffee table, filled three mugs half-way, and passed them around.

"So, you think the missus done it?" Leon finally asked after Rusty sagged into the sofa next to him. Rusty motioned for him to keep his voice down.

"I do," Willy whispered. "Rich white women can get away with anything."

"I agree with Willy," Rusty said. "As I said, I saw her right afterwards and she was calm as a cucumber. I didn't tell no one. I need my job. But, I'm tellin' you boys, that girl just vanished."

"You done the right thing." Willy tapped his cane for emphasis. "If you start accusing the future Gov's wife of murder, before you know it, you'll be turning up on some riverbank yourself."

"But you're a witness," Leon said, sitting up. "We gotta go to the police for sure now."

"Shut up," Willy barked. "We ain't doin' no such thing."

"Willy's right, Leon. What I told that Air Force cat is all they need to know. Let them work the rest out on their own. You got what you come for. The wife did it. She pushed the girl overboard. Let it go."

"You didn't look into that girl's eyes," Leon said, shivering at the thought. "They'll haunt me until I do something 'bout it."

"And what would that be?"

Leon sat still, looking at his trembling hands. He turned, chugged his moonshine and appeared more sober than when he arrived, which after drinking Rusty's brew was a minor miracle.

About the time Leon was going to break down, Betsy walked into the room with a tray of crepes and coffee. The three men hushed up and acted as guilty as school kids caught smokin' in the boy's room.

39

The sun faded into the river like hot wax dripping into a pool of darkness. Vu tried to focus on his driving, but the sunset held him captive. Hill sat beside him in the rental car with the window down, sneezing periodically, not the least bit interested in the setting sun. He rolled up the window and an odor wafted from the back seat. He reached behind him and picked up the White Castle paper sack lying on the floorboard.

"This thing reeks. Pull over so I can toss it."

"I suggest you not do that," Vu said.

"Why?"

"You're holding a new sample of feces from the Seemore estate."

Hill cringed and gently returned the bag to the backseat floor. "Your recent fecal fascination with collecting horseshit worries me, Jack."

He wiped his hands on his pants. Then, he withdrew a map from the glove box and opened it on his lap.

"The place is called 'The Pine Meadow Trailer Park,' 101 Eden Street, Space 10. I'll find it on the map." He ran his finger over the paper. "Here it is."

"Which direction?"

"Go north, young man."

Both men were tired, edgy, and overworked. Hill saw the sign over the arched gate at Pine Meadow Trailer Park and pointed at the entrance. "It's on your left. See it?"

"Just point out where I should turn."

"Right."

All of a sudden, Vu veered right. Hill quickly looked up, startled. "Not here," he uttered, as he grabbed the steering wheel to pilot the car back onto the main road. "I'll let you know."

"You said, right."

Hill sighed. "I meant OK. I'll let you know where to turn. Don't be so literal."

"Then speak English." Vu watched the road. "We may want to park at the office and check in with the manager."

"Bad idea," Hill said. "We don't want to spook him. If the manager calls before we get to his front door, he's liable to do most anything. Let's drive through once. See the layout."

Vu reluctantly guided the car down the single-lane drive. Trailers were parked on both sides of the road, which didn't leave much room. The double-wides were near the back, where the recreation hall was located. Bright lights spilled out of the building as a number of residents seemed eager to enter.

"Must be Bingo night," Hill said.

"They look pretty dressed up for Bingo."

Hill rolled down his window and hailed a dapper looking gentleman sporting a checked jacket. "What's going on?" he asked.

"Dance contest. We got us some first rate Elvis impersonators. Come check 'em out."

Vu and Hill shot each other quick looks.

"When do they perform?"

The man checked his pocketwatch. "In a half-an-hour."

They had to park the car out of sight of Donny's trailer,

and behind the laundry building, was their only choice without blocking the street. It really didn't matter where they parked. Two strange men snooping through a trailer park attract enough attention, especially from a dog. This particular dog was the size of a football, wiry and nearly toothless. It was so old that it had thick cataracts over both eyes. It came barking out of its owner's yard and into the street. It bared its snaggletooth and nipped at the two men. Hill easily stepped out of its path and allowed Vu to deal with the terror. Vu calmly removed the wrapper on a packet of beef jerky he'd pulled from his pocket, snapped off a hunk, and tossed it down on the ground in front of the dog's nose. The diversion worked. The mutt sniffed around by its feet until he found the treat, lay down on its belly and began to chew.

"Sometimes, Jack, you impress the shit out of me."

Vu put the rest of the jerky back in his pocket. "Let's hope Mason is that easy."

Bursting into view like a naked girl prancing Park Avenue, the single-wide, hand-painted, turquoise trailer appeared ahead, a beacon of color in a bastion of drabness. A black Cadillac sat crooked in the drive and gold rimmed sunglasses sparkled on its dash.

From the driveway, Hill spotted a kitchen light on in Donny's trailer. He mentioned it to Vu who was focusing his attention on the Cadillac in the driveway. "Hill, come take a look at these glasses."

Hill stepped back to the car and peered inside. Vu drew his 9 mm. Hill drew his .38 S&W. They held their weapons out and cautiously approached the door. Hill knocked and waited. He knocked again. After no response, they backed down.

"We don't have a warrant," Vu said.

Hill frowned. "And we don't have jurisdiction."

"We've got guns and beef jerky," Vu countered.

"Good enough for me." Hill led the way.

40

"Mason!" Vu called out. "It's the police! We want to talk to you!"

No response came from anywhere inside the trailer. Vu searched the bedrooms, Hill the kitchen. The place was empty. They met up in the kitchen. Hill was staring at the wall, examining a massive collection of photographs and news clippings, some yellow with age. Donny Mason clearly had an obsession with Patti Knot.

"This is our guy. He catches Knot with Gates and snaps. I mean, look at this stuff."

"It's plausible."

"Sure as hell is," Hill said. "Let's go find Elvis."

The recreation hall was near capacity when the two detectives entered and stood near the back surveying the crowd. It was a mixed age group, mostly retired, some grandchildren, and a few sons and daughters sitting with their families. A toxic cloud of cologne and cigarette smoke hung above the crowd. Hill pointed toward the stage where a man in a dark suit appeared just as the lights dimmed.

"Welcome to Pine Meadow for our second annual Contest

Night. We got us some very special guests this evening. Please give a round of applause for the first of our five performers. Ladies and gentleman, the one, the only, Elvis Presley!"

The crowd roared its approval.

Vu nudged Hill and weaved down the narrow aisle toward the stage. A sweating obese Elvis lunged from behind the curtain, microphone in hand, and slid across the floor in polished boots belting the lyrics to Heart Break Hotel. The audience roared applause and jumped to their feet, clapping.

Several old-timers standing near the front blocked access to backstage. Vu slid by them gracefully and poked his head behind the curtain. Across the room, he saw three more Elvis impersonators hanging out, primping in a mirror. A few seconds later, Hill appeared. Behind him, the person in charge burst out from a backroom.

"Hey – what are you two doing backstage?"

Hill flashed his badge. "We need to speak to one of your impersonators. Donny Mason."

"You'll have to wait. He's up next."

The first Elvis burst through the curtains, puffing and out of breath. He shot a look at Vu who was sizing him up. "Hey man, how was I?"

"King size," Vu replied extending a double-thumbs-up.

Hill asked the man in charge. "There another way on stage?"

"Yeah. From over there."

The man pointed to a side door, which opened suddenly and Donny Mason appeared, bedecked in a glittering blue suit. He leapt through the curtain and onto the stage before they could stop him.

From the sidelines, Vu and Hill watched.

Donny grabbed a floor microphone and sang his heart out, crooning to the crowd with his polished lyrics and lonesome voice, silencing the room with a passionate rendition of "Blue Hawaii."

Grandmothers wept. Teenage girls cheered. The men rocked back and forth on polished heels. It was pandemonium.

Arresting Elvis in this crowd would be suicide.

While he was taking his bows, Donny, lost in his savior's persona, suddenly spied the two detectives near the stage. His eyes locked on them like silver-coated hollow points.

Donny bowed graciously and then darted behind the curtain on the far side of the stage. Vu and Hill fought their way through the backstage crowd to the far side of the room.

"Where'd he go?" Vu asked.

The stage door left exited onto the playground. Vu and Hill rushed out the door and glimpsed rhinestones sprinting away.

Donny's neighbor, George, had a small shed behind his double-wide. George liked to keep his tools and lawn equipment locked up inside. He also kept a 30-06 hidden there for emergencies. Donny knew this. He'd found it one day by accident while he was fixing a leak in the roof. He figured George wouldn't miss the rifle because George hadn't fired it in years.

But, Donny needed to pry the door open, which was why the stack of rusted fence posts came in handy. Donny looked around to make sure he had time, picked one from the pile, wedged the metal tip behind the hasp and snapped it off. He dashed inside, found a flashlight on the workbench, and turned it on. The shed smelled of gasoline from where George had been fiddling with his lawnmower. Donny shined the light along the wall, found the metal cabinet in back and opened it. The rifle was wrapped in a blanket, propped in the corner along with several boxes of old cartridges. Donny pocketed one box of ammo and removed the rifle. He set the stock down on the bench and unwrapped it. The barrel had rust spots. Donny inspected the chamber. It was empty with the exception of a dead spider. He shook the spider out onto the floor and began loading the old rifle.

Then, he heard something outside.

Donny lunged through the shed door and fired aimlessly. The bullet struck the neighbor's car and shattered the passenger window, setting off a dozen car alarms.

Hill and Vu dropped to the ground and drew their weapons. People were starting to run outside, making it impossible to return fire. Hill screamed for everyone to stay down.

They both heard the Caddie start up. Vu reached the front yard first, just in time to see the tail lights fade around the corner.

* * *

Detectives Buck and Smitty were enjoying a juicy hamburger at Rick's Drive-in when the call came over the car radio. "Shots fired in the vicinity of The Pine Meadow Trailer Park, 101 Eden Street. Any available unit, please respond."

Smitty put his burger down, licked his fingers and picked up the microphone. "Unit 13 responding, over."

"Go ahead 13. Backup is in route."

Smitty glanced at his partner. "That's where we were headed, right mate?"

Buck shoved his half-eaten burger back into the paper bag and switched on the motor. Smitty placed a flashing blue light on the roof. As they pulled into traffic, Donny's black Cadillac sped by.

"You see that?" Smitty asked.

Buck kept his eye on the road. "Pine Meadow, right?"

"Turn around. Let's go get him," Smitty insisted.

"First things first," Buck said and continued toward Pine Meadow.

What they found when they entered the turquoise trailer, besides broken glass and a stinking refrigerator, were Hill and Vu rifling Donny's personal belongings. Hill was in the bedroom searching a dresser. Vu was in the spare bedroom checking boxes in the closet. Vu heard the footsteps before he saw Buck's glaring face.

"What the hell are you doing, Detective?" Buck said disgustedly and holstered his .38.

Vu turned around and looked at him. "Mason shot at us then

fled the scene. We must have spooked him."

"Let me guess – you just happened to knock on his door and then he pulled a rifle?"

"Not actually, but close."

"Hill with you?"

"He's in the other bedroom. Where's Smitty?"

"Probably seconds from putting a slug in your friend."

Vu moved a box of baseball trophies aside and pulled down a heavy box from the top shelf. His legs were wobbly under the weight. Buck offered his help. "Here – move over."

Vu fought to hold control. "I got it," he uttered.

Buck yanked and the box slipped from both their hands and crashed to the floor. Stacks of unpaid hospital bills, legal notices and other official documents strewed across the carpet. Vu reached down and picked up a Marriage Certificate. He held it up to the light. It was made out to Donny Mason and Patti Knot, dated ten years prior. Vu handed it to Buck.

Buck stepped back from the mess on the floor.

"You got here too fast. Were you already on your way?" Vu asked.

"He assaulted you two, right? That's reason enough. And, we got a call of shots being fired."

Hill and Smitty walked into the room. Something on the floor caught Vu's attention. Buck told Smitty to radio in, inform them backup wasn't necessary, and to request an APB on Mason's black caddy.

"What is it, Jack?" Hill asked.

Vu reached down and picked up the photograph. He showed Hill the picture. It was a faded color photograph of Mason, Sanders and Knot posing with a prized Seemore colt at the 1997 Kentucky Derby. The picture must have been taken just hours before the rape, and before three lives were irrevocably changed.

Vu was hoping to find a copy of Knot's will. It would indicate Donny knew about his inheritance in advance. That would be motive for murdering Knot. If Donny didn't know, it'd be hard to prove

Vu said, "Mason is the beneficiary of Knot's estate."

"Have you seen her will?" Buck asked.

It was the same old cat and mouse game that his superiors in the Air Force liked to play. He wasn't going for it.

Smitty watched Hill search beneath the bed. "You find anything interesting? Perhaps a pair of dirty undies."

Buck frowned at his partner. "Mason had motive."

"Didn't the lad love her?"

"Is there a better motive for murder?"

41

On the drive back to Clarksville, Leon kept swerving onto the shoulder, not because he was drunk, but because he couldn't get the dead girl off his mind. It was even worse now knowing she may have been murdered. And, his friend Willy was no help at all. Willy said it was nature's way to deal with white folk – let 'em kill off their own. It only helped blacks. Kept things even.

"Maybe so, but it ain't right."

"And you always gotta do the right thing? Other people may think your right is their wrong."

"Don't confuse me."

"OK – let's go see that little Vietnamese cop. You can spill your guts to him."

"What about Rusty?"

"Make a choice. Rusty confided in us, now you wanna break his trust."

"It's your fault."

"My fault?"

"You told me to drive out to Rusty's."

"So you could find some answers and get some peace.

You keep losing sleep you're going to lose your job with the band. Then you won't be able to afford the gas for this piece of shit truck..."

"Don't knock my truck."

"Truck ... fuck ... you donkey dick."

"That's it!" Leon slammed on the brakes, pulled onto the shoulder and stopped. He leaned across the seat and pushed open Willy's door. "Get out!"

"My pleasure."

Willy stumbled drunkenly out of the truck and slammed the door. Leon stepped on the gas pedal and then slammed on the brake. The truck lurched forward, then came to a halt. The cab door opened and closed. Willy heard something tumble on the ground. Then, the truck sped off, kicking dust and gravel in his face. Willy listened to the tired old motor fade down the highway. He unfolded his cane and tapped the ground, eventually finding the baseball cap and empties Leon had pitched from the cab. He calmly brushed the cap off, slipped it on, straightened his shirt, stood tall and stuck out his thumb.

* * *

Donny's Cadillac sped down the asphalt. He glanced down at the rifle on the seat and figured he had about twenty rounds of ammunition to hold them off. What he needed was more time because things weren't all that clear to him. It'd happened so fast. He wasn't certain if he'd shot anyone or not. Still, he needed a plan, and he had to ditch the car. But where? And, where was he going to hide out with no money and nobody to talk to?

Through the front windshield Donny saw something up ahead. His headlights illuminated an old man in a baseball cap, standing on the shoulder of the road, holding a white cane, and thumbing a ride. Donny applied the brakes and slowed the ton of metal down to a crawl. The big block motor idled to a purr as he pulled off the highway and honked. The blind man hobbled up to the passenger door and climbed inside.

* * *

Leon had the heart of a lamb. Not five minutes after he kicked Willy from his pickup, he regretted the act and decided to turn around. Yet it served Willy's black ass right to stand out in the dark for awhile. He had no business talking to him like that. In the first place, what'd he ever done to deserve being called "donkey dick?" And another thing, it was his gas money, his pickup and his eyesight that got them around on four wheels. Willy couldn't do that. So why was he so damn argumentative all the time? It hurt his feelings.

Leon slowed, made a u-turn and started to pull back onto the highway when he slammed on his brakes, allowing a semi to blaze by.

"Idiot – slow your ass down!" he shouted.

Leon got hold of himself as he cranked the wheel hard to the left and started the drive back to where he'd dumped Willy.

Up ahead, Leon couldn't believe his eyes. Willy was climbing into a Cadillac driven by Elvis Presley himself.

* * *

It only took Willy about five minutes to figure out he'd screwed up. He had hitched a ride with a lunatic. And, the crazy SOB had a gun. He patted round the door for a handle and couldn't find one. The window and door handles were missing.

"This ride got a radio?" Willy asked, patting the seat beside him, but recoiling when he accidentally felt the rifle.

Donny took his hand off the wheel and tossed the rifle in the back seat. "It's broken."

"Broken? That's a sin, man. Got to have tunes to drive by.

How 'bout I sing us a few notes?"

"I can't really hear out of my right ear."

"Well, how 'bout the left one?"

"If I turn my good ear toward you, then I can't see to drive."

"That'd be OK. Pull over. We could just sit and sing 'cause you haven't asked me where I'm headed, which kind of troubles me."

"I'm not sure what you mean?"

"You pick up a blind man alongside the road and you don't bother asking how I got there or where I'm goin'."

Donny sighed, checked his rearview mirror. "OK, how'd you end up in the middle of the highway?"

"My crazy ass friend dumped me there. Where we going?"

"I'm taking care of business and I may need some help."

Willy looked out the window. "What kind of business, friend?"

"Show business."

Willy tried to relax. "Anyone ever tell you your voice kind of sounds like Elvis?"

Donny smiled. "Thank you, thank you very much."

"I'm not kidding. You have a gift, son."

Willy figured if the guy liked Elvis he might not be too sick in the head. Yet he couldn't be certain. Maybe he wasn't going to butt fuck him after all.

"There's a pint in the glove box. Why don't you crack it open."

OK … now he was talkin' Willy's language.

If things really turned south, Willy figured he could always get a few good licks in with his cane. Willy opened the glove box and shuffled under some papers until he found the bourbon bottle. He opened it and took a long drink. The whiskey was cheap, but tasted better than Rusty's rock-gut. God damn Leon, it was his fault he was stuck in the car with this maniac.

"You want a nip?"

"Sure."

Willy passed him the bottle. Donny threw back a swig, then

stuck the bottle between his legs.

"You going huntin' or somethin'?"

"Might be."

"It ain't season."

"Depends on what you're hunting."

"I don't like the sound of that."

Donny's face reddened. "I wasn't planning on shooting you, but if you keep talking that way, I just might."

Willy realized then that maybe it was his mouth that always got he and Leon into trouble. Maybe it never was Leon's fault after all. How come he just now figured that out? Hell, he began to regret being so damn hard on his friend.

The Cadillac continued barreling down the road. Willy listened to the noise through the window as the varied sounds painted a picture that they were heading out of the city, but not toward Clarksville. Maybe Highway 64 toward Lexington, he thought. One thing Willy could do was distinguish road noises. Highway 71 sounded different than Highway 64. More grooves in the pavement gave a different pitch to the sound the tires made.

After ten minutes of silence, Willy could no longer take it. "Man – I gotta right to know where we're headed."

"We're going to Graceland."

42

Patti Knot always kept a spare key hidden in an elm tree on the south side of the property. Donny got out of the car and retrieved it, then entered the code in the gate and drove up to the house. He opened Willy's door and helped him out of the car. Willy kept his mouth shut and listened. He heard crickets chirping, could smell the scent of trees, pinecones, and manure. He also heard horses trotting in a pasture. He could smell moisture in the air and knew it was dark. What he couldn't smell was freedom.

Donny led him by the arm to the stables and into the tack room. The room was cluttered with feed, tools and gear. The door was made of solid wood. "Man, where are we?"

"I already told you. Graceland, but Priscilla's gone. I'm alone here." Donny's voice suddenly got small and quiet, childlike. "I've been thinking – trying to figure it all out."

"Figure what out?"

"See, in a way you and me are a lot alike." Donny scrunched up his face in thought. "There are things I can't see either. But still, I know things. Like you develop your other senses to make up for not seeing."

243

"Nothin' makes up for that," Willy said quietly.

"But two heads are better than one, right?"

"That's what folks say. Maybe if I can help you, you'll help me get where I need to go?"

"Sounds fair."

"I'm gonna lock you in here while I go change my clothes. Then we are going to try to figure it all out together."

"I'll go with you." Willy stood up, but Donny pushed him firmly back on a feed sack.

"If you need to pee, there's a bucket to your right. There's also a jug of water. I'll be back later."

The door slammed. He heard a lock click.

Willy sat down. He listened to the stable sounds which were somewhat muted by his beating heart. He figured if it all ended now – the only regret he had was not telling his friend Leon he was sorry. He was an asshole and Leon had put up with plenty lately. He owed his friend an apology before he died and this gave him renewed strength not to give up, to keep his head in the game.

After thirty shivering minutes sitting in the cold room, he heard footsteps.

"Who's there?" he called out.

"Willy? It's me, Leon."

Willy jumped up. "Leon? What the hell … how'd you find me?"

Leon pressed his body against the door. "I followed you."

"God damnit, I could kiss you. Get me out of here."

"The door's got a padlock on it."

A porch light came on. Leon jumped. "Damn – someone's coming."

"Hide for Christ sake. Wait. I'm sorry."

"Not now."

* * *

Donny stormed out of the house packing the rifle. He found

Leon's truck near the gate. He checked the cab, found it empty, went over to the hood and popped the latch. The engine was still warm.

He'd show them...

* * *

Willy heard rustling nearby and then all went quiet again. A few moments later, Willy heard Donny searching the stables.

Donny opened the door. "Who were you talking to?"

"I was just practicing a song. I'm a musician, man."

"Didn't sound like no song?"

Willy shrugged. "Give me a drum set and it might."

Donny heaved a sigh. "I'm moving you. I'm gonna have to tie you up."

"Don't tie my hands. I need my cane and I need my hands to touch things. My hands are my eyes."

Donny put down the rifle, cinched a rope around Willy's waist, and led him like a pig to slaughter out of the tack room, stumbling, cursing and fighting each step. When he reached the stall where Patti was killed, Donny slowly pushed the door open.

"Concentrate now," Donny snapped, and pulled Willy up closer. "Help me figure out what happened in there."

Donny nudged Willy to the edge of the stall, but wouldn't allow him to go any further. Willy sensed something horrible had happened here and wanted no part of it.

Donny stood stock still, peering into the stall, into the cavernous pit of his memory. The straw was black and hard, the blood long dried. He heard muffled screams, grunts from a desperate struggle, heavy breathing, heels kicking the floor and pleas for help.

"Did you hear that?" Donny grabbed his head in his hands, and stumbled back. "Stop it!" he screamed.

Everything froze. The body was a motionless bloody hulk, a pitchfork stuck straight up like a cross marking a grave. A figure rose from the floor and advanced. Donny held his arm up to block the blow, scattering flowers across the room.

A light hit the approaching attacker's face just as he lost consciousness.

Brad...

Leon used a knife to cut Willy free of Donny, who was drooling moanfully on the floor.

"What'd you hit him with, Leon?" Willy asked.

"Nothin'. He had a fit or something. Let's get out of here while we still can."

"Get the rifle."

"What rifle?"

"He must have left it behind. Maybe you should try to knock him out or something." Willy searched the floor frantically for his cane. His hand latched onto a silver spur. He tried to hand it to Leon. "This should do the trick."

"I ain't beating an unconscious man," Leon said.

He was getting ready to hand it back to Leon when he noticed something. "There's an engraving. Can you read it?"

Leon tried in the dim light. "It's got mud on it"

Willy ran his fingers over the bumpy surface. "What's BB stand for?"

"Blind Buttfucker," Leon shot back. "You comin', or do I have to leave your ass behind again?"

"I'm taking back my apology," Willy sniped, already on the move.

* * *

It'd been a busy night for everyone, yet a light was still burning in the Medical Examiner's office. Vu walked in and looked around for Frank Ruttle, didn't see him in the cluttered area, and entered the laboratory. Ruttle sat with his back to the door, grumbling as he examined evidence under a microscope.

Vu cleared his throat. Ruttle craned his head around, his eyes bloodshot from working overtime. It seemed perfectly natural to him that Vu would show up at this late hour. Vu sat a paper bag on the counter.

"You bring me dinner?" Ruttle asked.

"Not exactly."

Vu opened the bag and took out a plastic bag containing horse manure. Ruttle studied the item.

"You're not going to ask me to analyze this are you?"

"I'm afraid so," said Vu.

"From a quick glance, I'd say it's horse droppings." Ruttle frowned and handed the bag back to Vu. "I'm booked solid for two months. Wait your turn."

"It's very important."

"Last year our budget was cut by thirty percent. Of the three hundred thousand people that were arrested in Kentucky, one hundred and fifty thousand of those were released without fingerprinting. You think I care about a sample of shit?"

Vu weighed his options. Only one thing would work on this hardened ME. "I can't appeal to your pocketbook, so I might as well appeal to your sense of justice. Two innocent women are dead, and you hold the key to their murders. It's your call."

"To which case does this excrement refer again? Knots' or Sanders'?"

"As I said – both."

"Well then, I suppose I shouldn't waste any time." Ruttle stood up and crossed the room. He took a plastic specimen tray from the cupboard and returned. He placed the tray on the counter.

"What is it you'd like to know about this shit, sergeant?"

"I'd like to know if the sample matches either of these."

Vu pulled out the lab sheets Betty had faxed to the hotel less than an hour earlier and handed them over. Her results concluded that the two samples collected from Patti Knot's ranch were quite different.

"Your friend detailed the tests she ran, which is a big help. It should be rather simple to verify. I suppose you aren't leaving here without an answer, are you?"

"If it's not too much to ask."

"As I said before, I've got nothing better to do." Ruttle chuckled at his own joke. While Ruttle did his job, Vu wandered around the laboratory. Being there made him think of Betty in her own lab. She'd come through for him once again. He loved her. Despite his fatigue, he felt his dick load one into the chamber.

Vu went down the hall to walk off the woody and eventually found a vending machine where he bought a Snickers bar. As he chewed, it oddly began to remind him of the horse apples. He might have to give up eating anything round and brown for awhile, or at least until he reprogramed his mind.

Back in Ruttle's office, Vu thumbed the latest edition of *The Journal of Forensic Medicine*. After about an hour, Ruttle entered. He peeled off his rubber gloves and tossed them in the garbage can by his desk.

"You have matching crap."

Vu sat up straight. "Conclusively?"

"Close enough for government work," Ruttle continued. "Race horses have unique diets that contain vitamins, minerals and anything else that will make them run like the wind. Their diets are as individual as fingerprints."

Vu jumped up. His sagging expression vanished. "Would you please treat the feces as evidence?"

"Sure – how you want it marked?"

Vu reached into his pocket and pulled out a sheet of paper. On it, he'd written dates and locations.

"Next time, Jack, would you bring me a double-cheese burger with fries?"

43

Detective Buck was in his shorts playing his guitar when he heard someone knock. Reluctantly, he put the instrument down and opened the front door.

Sergeant Vu stood on the porch in an overcoat and stocking cap warming his hands. He smiled up at him.

"Good evening," Vu said. "I'm glad I didn't wake you."

"Haven't you two done enough damage for one day?"

Buck crossed his arms impatiently and appeared pissed. His hairy arms reminded Vu of thick pine planks, barring an entrance.

"I have determined one or both of the Seemores are lying."

"They are Southern politicians. Of course they're liars. You came all this way to tell me that? You can go back to your hotel and sleep tight now," Buck grumbled and stepped back from the door. Over Vu's shoulder he saw Detective Hill sitting in the rental car at the curb. Hill had the passenger window rolled down and was staring up at the house.

"There is no way in hell I'm going to wake up the future governor just to ask him a few questions that can wait until morning." Buck started to close the door. Vu reached out and grabbed it.

"Detective Hill and I are going to visit the Seemores this evening, with or without you," Vu said firmly.

Buck glanced at his wrist as if he expected to see a watch. "OK, what's the evidence?"

"Feces."

"You have shit?"

"That's right. And it's conclusive shit."

Despite himself, Buck smiled.

"I'll explain in the car." Vu felt Buck shift in his direction.

Buck studied the earnestness on Vu's face and realized he would not take no for an answer. If he went with Vu and Hill, he could at least smooth things out with the Seemores if the inquiry went south.

* * *

The dark pasture was silent. A cool breeze had picked up out of the east. Stars flickered in the big open sky. The two black men fled the stable and hustled out to the cars. As Leon approached his pickup, he noticed the hood was up. A closer inspection revealed the distributor cap was off and the rotor was missing.

"We can't take the truck," Leon said. "Elvis fucked with it."

"Well, let's hotwire his car."

"All niggers don't know how to hotwire cars. Do you?"

"No."

Leon looked around the perimeter and saw lights burning about a mile away. "Follow me," he announced, and latched onto Willy's arm. "We're gonna get help."

"Do I have a choice?"

The two men hustled off across the open field where horses had worn a path. Suddenly, Willy stumbled. "Leon – damnit! Slow down."

Willy stopped and rubbed his sore leg. The two men caught their breath. Out over the vista only insects moved under the twilight.

Leon snapped his head around, staring back at the house, now just a luminous haze in the distance. "You hear somethin'?"

"Yes – my heart pumping."

"I think he's coming after us!"

Willy looked in the general direction. He could hear sounds. Yet the movement was far away, like a horse trotting over hard ground. "We got a pretty good head start. Let's keep going."

The two men trekked along through the wet field, stumbling a few times over potholes and dead branches in their path. Up ahead the Seemore estate came into view. A few outside lights burned through the dark sky. Leon squeezed his friend's arm. "We're gettin' close."

He blamed himself for this whole mess. If he hadn't lost his temper earlier in the car, none of this would have happened. Willy wouldn't have jumped out of the car. Willy wouldn't have gotten kidnapped. And, he wouldn't have had to follow them.

"Willy," Leon whispered. "I'm sorry. This is my fault."

Willy slapped his friend's shoulder. "Just get us the hell out of here."

"You think the dead girl is the cause of all this? Maybe we're cursed now."

"The only cursing goin' down is the curse on you if you don't keep your voice down."

"Sorry."

"If you say sorry one more time, so help me Jesus."

"Sorry."

"That's it."

Willy stopped suddenly. He took his cane and swung it hard. The end slapped against Leon's cheek. Leon let out a yelp, clutching his jaw.

"What'd you do that for?" Leon uttered, rubbing the pain in his face.

"That was for leaving me behind."

"I said I was –"

Willy interrupted. "Don't even say it. Now pull yourself

together and get us out of here."

"Why you have to be so nasty all the time?"

"It's my nature," Willy said, beaming with pride. But, it wasn't true. Leon knew it, too.

A couple hundred yards away they came to a fence. Leon had lost sight of the trail. It just ended, or he had missed it. "Hold up, Willy. We're here, except there's a fence."

"There's no gate?"

"Here – give me your hand."

Willy refused help. He pawed the dark until he touched the fence post. Both men heard shouts coming from the direction of Knot's ranch. Donny was stomping through the field toward them screaming Brad's name. He was getting closer. They had to hurry...

"C'mon, he's coming."

"I can hear."

"Willy – don't start in again."

"We're finished."

Leon checked the ground. There were no branches, rocks or objects to throw. They had to get over the fence one way or another.

"Come on Willy. I'll give you a boost over."

"Just watch where you're grabbin'."

44

John Seemore got up from his desk and paced back across the floor. He was on his third single malt scotch of the evening. The liquor had taken the edge off his anger, but he still couldn't sleep. His mind was whirling.

He pulled the .32 from the drawer, dropped it into his pocket, and checked the clock again.

Where was the son-of-a-bitch?

As he walked from the room, he played it all back in his head, a recording that would later haunt him. Earlier, he had called Brad Black at home. He said he wanted to see him at once. No it couldn't wait until morning. No it didn't involve the upcoming Derby. Yes, it was personal, and they had to talk now.

Mona came walking down the stairs in her silk nightgown. She met her husband in the hall.

"What are you doing up?" John asked.

"One might ask the same of you."

John chugged the last of the scotch from his glass and wiped his lips. "Go back to bed."

"Don't tell me what to do, John," she said coldly.

John pushed by her and headed toward the kitchen to refill his glass. Mona went into the restroom and later he heard her pacing upstairs. As long as she didn't interfere, he didn't give a shit how many pills she took tonight.

The doorbell rang. John answered it. Brad Black was standing on the front step staring out toward the driveway. He had on a new Ralph Lauren dinner jacket, Tony Lama cowboy boots and fresh expensive cologne. His breath smelled of alcohol. John closed the door and told Brad to follow him outside.

"What's this about, John?" Brad said on the walk.

"Mona."

Brad's eyes darkened. He slowed his walk. "So that's why the guards weren't at the gate when I drove in. Is she all right?"

"She's in bed."

"Maybe she should hear this?"

"Hear what, Brad? This is between men. She doesn't need to hear it."

The area was quiet with the exception of a few horses stirring in the pasture.

John turned on the office lights and told Brad to take a seat across the room. John walked over to the liquor cabinet and poured two stiff drinks. He handed Brad one of the glasses and then sat down behind his desk.

"I told you to sit down."

Brad reluctantly sat and unbuttoned his jacket. He took a sip of bourbon and waited. John sipped his drink, staring at Brad across the immaculate desk.

"How long have you been sleeping with my wife?" John finally asked.

"Does it really matter?"

John clenched his jaw. "Are you planning on riding in the Derby?"

Brad swallowed. "Yes."

"For whom?"

"That should be obvious."

"I've spoken with Mona about this. You're fired."

Brad reclined and studied the hardened expression glaring at him from across the desk. "You're lying. I called her on my cell, not more than thirty minutes ago."

John reached into his pocket and pulled out the .32. He pointed it at Brad's head. Brad put his drink down and warily kept an eye on him. "Put that away," he uttered.

"I'd put a bullet between your eyes right now if I thought it'd change things between Mona and me."

"Then put the gun down!"

"I'm not finished." His grip tightened. "If I find out you had anything to do with Patti's death, so help me I'll see to it that you rot in jail. I didn't believe Bevy at first when she came to me last week, but I did some checking of my own. Now I know she was telling the truth. So, I'm going to give you an option. Either leave town, or I'm going to call the Racing Commissioner and have him jerk your license. Then, I'm going to the police and have you charged with statutory rape and attempted murder. Which is it going to be?"

"You don't give a damn about Mona. That's why she chose me. I wasn't the first, you know. And I won't be the last."

John put his finger on the trigger. "What's your answer?"

Brad looked for a way out. John watched him study the door twenty feet away.

No, Brad, you'll never make it...

All of a sudden, the same door burst open and two frightened black men barged in. John's nerves were already edgy and the noise startled him, nearly causing him to squeeze off a round by mistake. He turned the gun on the two strangers, but before they could get a word in, Brad reached into his jacket and pulled out a handgun of his own, a 9 mm Beretta.

"What the hell is going on, Leon? Who are these people?"

Brad kept the gun pointed on John and backed toward the door. "Good timing, gentlemen."

Leon was shaking. He nervously said, "I wouldn't go out there. There's a lunatic with a rifle. Call the police!"

John asked. "Who the hell are you?"

"Your lunatic neighbor chased us here. He's looking for somebody named Brad."

"That's preposterous." John narrowed his eyes. "Who put you up to this? Mona?"

John glared at Brad and lowered his weapon. "Why don't you lower your gun and sit back down."

"We'll finish this conversation later," Brad informed him, and motioned for the two men to move out of his way.

Leon looked at Willy. "They have guns, Willy, step aside."

Willy planted his feet. "Either take those guns and defend us, or call the damn police. But we ain't going back outside."

Brad knocked Willy back against the wall and into the light switch. The room went dark.

The men heard the door open and slam closed.

45

onny fought his way through the thick brush. The heavy wet branches slapped his body like lead clubs while the bristly ends tore holes in his silk shirt. It was cold, dark, unfamiliar territory. The muddy earth swallowed him. He visualized bats swooping down out of the trees, attacking him. Finally, suppressing his demons, he pushed through to a clearing and stopped, winded and confused, blood oozing from fresh cuts on his hands where they clutched the rifle.

Resting the rifle against a tree, he tried warming his hands. But his damp clothing chilled him through and he began to shiver uncontrollably.

Where the hell were they?

Then, he saw an office light burning up ahead and heard voices. He picked up the scoped rifle and moved closer.

Positioning himself near the office window, he could make out four people inside. He recognized the two black men from the ranch. Mr. Seemore he recognized from the track. The fourth man, who had his back to the window, held a gun on the others. As the man moved toward the door, Donny got a good look at his face.

Donny's hands began shaking. His heart pounded. Tremors cascaded through his legs. His breathing became rapid. He was a drowning man gasping for his last breath. A searing pain roared through his head and escaped, like an arrow leaving a clean exit wound. Yet it was no arrow, it was a pitchfork.

He gathered all of his strength and steadied himself against a fence rail, pointed the rifle and waited.

It all rushed back to him in those final moments before he squeezed the trigger....

As the door closed, Brad dashed out into the night. *The stupid bastards. He'd showed 'em...*

He lunged into the open and heard what sounded like a twig snap. Ignoring it at first, he then heard what sounded like heavy breathing – a large animal perhaps. Brad froze, intuiting danger, yet he couldn't make out its source. What was out there?

He stared toward the dark field. Then his eye followed the fence line before landing upon the large oak. He saw movement behind it, but it was too dark to make out. Definitely, someone was out there. He raised his weapon just as Donny's haunting face appeared from behind the tree....

* * *

The gunshot sounded like it had come from a long-barrel rifle. John crawled over to the door and quickly peered out, only to lock the door and crawl back over to his desk. He reached for the telephone. A second gunshot went off. It struck the office window and shattered the glass. He crawled over to the broken window clutching his .32. He didn't see movement outside, but he heard the horses in the stable getting spooked. Wild hooves pounded the doors. Then, a light in the upstairs bedroom of the house came on. Mona came running frantically out the back door in her nightgown.

46

From inside the car they heard shots fired. Sergeant Vu jammed on the brakes and pulled the car over.

All three men jumped out, guns drawn, and took cover in the trees. None of the men could tell from which direction the shots had come. They were taking no chances.

"Hill!" Vu ordered. "Spread out. I'll take the rear entry, you two take the front."

"The shots might have come from the barn," Hill said, from behind a tree.

"Sounded like the woods to me," Buck added.

All three men could hear the frightened horses in the stables.

The men dispersed through the woods. Vu watched the trees and the area toward the rear of the house. He could hear voices out near the stable area. As he rounded the corner, he saw a woman's shadowy figure dart across the grounds. He thought he saw a man run across the field – a skinny guy packing a rifle. He waded through the thick, damp brush, as quietly as possible. He made it to a clearing, but the man was gone.

So was the woman.

* * *

Inside the office, John said to Leon, "Stay here." He passed him the handgun. "You might need this."

"What about me?" Willy asked.

"Use your cane."

John peered out the door. Mona was running wildly around the yard, screaming Brad's name.

"You're going outside without a weapon?" Leon asked.

"There's one on the ground."

"Is the boy dead?"

"He's been shot."

"Is he moving?"

"No."

Leon squeezed the .32 in his trembling hand. He was too old for this shit. Way too old.

After John ran out, Leon locked the door and flopped back down on the floor beside his friend.

Willy scooted next to him and whispered, "If we make it out alive, I promise to be nicer to you."

"Just let some son-bitch come in here," Leon mocked. "I'll shoot 'em between the eyes."

Willy attempted to laugh.

Outside, John remembered he'd hidden an old shotgun in the tool shed behind the garage, if he could just get to it in time. He took off running in that general direction, hoping to grab Mona on the way.

Mona was wandering round in the dark, screaming nonsense. She'd taken more pills, John thought, as he appeared from the shadows. A man scurried into the trees. Another shot rang out. He tackled Mona to the ground.

"Let go of me," she squirmed, swinging her fists wildly.

"Mona! Knock it off!" She slugged him in the face. "What have you done to Brad?"

"He's been shot."

"You bastard." Mona spit in his face "I risked everything for him."

John released her. Mona jumped to her feet and started running aimlessly. John lay, stunned. His wife was in love with another man. He slowly got up and no longer cared about saving her. His thoughts were on his horses. Their frantic whinnying and pounding could result in many being injured severely enough that they would have to be destroyed. Calmly, he walked to the shed where the shotgun was waiting.

John found a box of shotgun shells on a dusty ledge. He loaded the chamber and then shoved a handful in his pockets and left.

The door to the thoroughbred stables swung back and forth in the wind. John crept inside. He heard something scurry down the aisle. He kept low, slowly inched along, and listened to the frightened sounds of horses rustling about in their stalls.

He released the locks on the stalls, allowing the horses to escape. One by one, the powerful horses pushed open the doors and rushed the aisle. John was overwhelmed by the presence of so many disorientated animals. He backed towards the door, keeping his gun pointed upward. Firing a shot now would cause the horses to stampede. He kept his finger off the trigger. But, at the back of the building, a shot was fired. Its deafening roar in the confined area shattered the silence. The horses charged the large bay doors in panic. John fell to the ground. The raging horses divided, missing his body by mere inches as they thundered from the building. Donny ran out behind them, wielding his rifle.

Out on the grounds, Mona knelt beside Brad's body, cradling his head, rocking back and forth on her heels. The wind carried her sobs across the field as she stroked the man's forehead like a mother would for her child. She pulled his limp body against hers, though it was too late. Brad was dead.

The thoroughbreds sped wildly. Sergeant Vu ran out of the trees shouting.

Mona looked up in horror. Ten feet away the horses thundered toward her. In a futile attempt to save herself, she pulled Brad's body against her chest as the horses stampeded. The sound of pounding hooves silenced a lone painful cry amid the pulverizing sounds of breaking bones.

Vu had not reached her in time. He knelt beside her mangled body. Mona's eyes were hollow, lifeless orbs. He checked for a pulse in futility.

Detective Hill ran up, breathless. After the dust cleared, Buck also appeared. He was packing a rifle and escorting Donny who was handcuffed. Beside him was John, a broken, limping man. The two black men walked out of the office and joined the others.

Willy said nothing, just stood with his friend while Leon stared at the bodies on the ground. No one spoke. Not even John, who remained taciturn, eventually collapsing to his knees by his dead wife.

47

As the chaotic night surrendered to the watery light of dawn, the events at the Seemore Estate were methodically sorted, categorized, and evaluated. The horses were rounded up, the bodies removed and witnesses interviewed. John Seemore was sedated and reported to be recovering under care of his private physician. About mid-morning, Leon's truck was restored and the two bantering jazz musicians were sent on their merry way. By noon, the Racing Commissioner, Mayor, Chamber of Commerce and Police Chief had all assembled to orchestrate the spin. With the Seemore estate in the background, the cameras rolled on an expertly choreographed press conference. While heads talked and photos flashed to extoll the virtues of the dead, crawling banners scrolled across the bottom of the screen, announcing, *"Future Governor, Now Grieving Widower," "Brad Black, Louisville's Derby Favorite, Snatched In His Prime," "Plucky Musicians Risk Lives To Save Their Patrons."* Back at the Galt, Jack Vu and Bruce Hill sat in the bar and watched it all unfold. Louisville was promoted as a town of strong traditions and deep faith. Patti Knot's murder was never even mentioned, eclipsed by the glare of this new southern tragedy.

Across town at Police Headquarters, Captain Lazarus hung up the phone and turned his attention to Sam Buck.

"First, let me say that I've read your report on the Beverly Sanders' drowning and am glad you concur that this was a tragic accident."

Buck's gaze drifted out the window and squinted into the brilliant sun.

"I am putting the Knott murder on the back burner for now. The Commissioner has convinced me that with Brad Black dead, nothing is to be gained by pursuing this line of inquiry."

Buck opened his mouth to speak, but Lazarus held up his hand to check him.

"I've read about the spur and the horse shit, but it's all circumstantial. With both Mona Seemore and Black dead, we could never get a conviction anyway."

"What about Donny Mason?"

Lazarus ticked off the list, "Kidnapping, murder, assaulting an officer…"

Buck cut in. "A homegrown hero who was injured attempting to save a child from rape…"

Lazarus finished the sentence, "Does not make a good defendant. I agree, Detective. The police will rule his shooting at the Seemore Estate as self-defense since Black was found with a 9 mm in his hand. And, I just got off the phone with the blind musician, what was his name?"

"Willy."

"Yes." Lazarus flipped through his papers. "He has agreed to drop any kidnapping charges. In exchange for his cooperation in this matter, the mayor has made the Brother Hooch Band the Official Musical Ambassadors of the City, with all the benefits that come with such a title."

Buck recalled an afternoon playing music with his sister.

"I'm placing you on medical leave for the next month. I would suggest you leave town during this time to heal your knee."

"Which knee would that be, sir?"

"The one you injured last night." Lazarus gave him a pointed look.

"And just how am I supposed to pay for this "suggested" vacation?"

"The Racing Commissioner has a special fund for police officers injured in the line of duty while rescuing animals." Lazarus looked down at his desk, unable to face Buck. "Your work in rounding up the frightened horses qualifies. Ben Hurt specifically mentioned you as recipient of said funds to facilitate any travel necessary for you to receive the best rehabilitation available."

Buck figured staring at the bottom of a bourbon bottle sounded like effective rehab. "Is there anything else?"

"Yes. I would like you to personally handle the release of Detective Gates. You are to escort Ms. Gates, and the two detectives, to the airport taking their leave. And, I would like you to impress upon them the importance of not engaging the press before departing our fine city."

"Yes, sir." Buck rose to leave.

"And one more thing, Sam." Lazarus stood up. "I am going to recommend you for the Lieutenant's exam."

Buck now knew what a street hooker accepted when she finally graduated to call girl – still a whore, but with better pay.

48

D orene waited as the officer catalogued her personal effects.
"Watch ... change ... wallet ... shield," he monotoned.
She numbly watched the detritus of her life splayed
across the counter. Her eyes widened as she recognized Patti's
lucky coin among her change. Had taking that coin changed
Patti's destiny? She squelched the thought. This was no time
for useless musing. She signed the receipt and scooped it all
into her purse, acutely aware of the missing items. As the
electric door lock released at the exit, she resisted the urge to
wrench it open and run. She took a deep breath and strode
through the exit toward the sunlight. Near the end of the hall,
and the glass doors separating her from the first fresh air she'd
had in nearly two weeks, a man stepped into view.

"You'll want to leave through a different door," Buck
took a hold of Gates' elbow."

She jerked her arm out of Buck's grasp and backed
away.

"Look, there's a ton of press out there."

Gates hesitated, weighing her options.

"Your buddies are waiting for you back at the hotel. I've

been instructed to escort the three of you to the airport later this afternoon."

"Good. I don't want to spend another night in this measly town." She turned and looked directly into Buck's eyes. "Get me out of here."

Buck unlocked the passenger side door. As Dorene got in, she spied boxes of files, army duffel bags, sacks of food and a case of beer piled in the back seat.

"Is my suitcase under all that crap?"

Buck swung into the front seat and slammed the door. "Naw, your gear's in the trunk."

"Looks like you might be taking a little trip yourself?"

"I've wanted to take a break for awhile now, and this seems like as good a time as any."

Gates grunted and said nothing more. Instead, she concentrated on the city out the window and remembered her last time down that street, headed toward the reunion – and Patti.

The drive took about ten minutes. According to the clock on the dash, they pulled into the parking structure at 2 p.m.

As Buck unlocked the trunk, Gates joined him. She recognized her luggage, but not the bag on top. It was a police evidence bag, marked "Knot Homicide." Buck cleared his throat and absently patted his pockets.

"Looks like I forgot my notebook inside the car. It may take me a minute to find it. Go ahead and get your suitcase and I'll meet you at the elevator."

Without a backward glance or visual hint, Buck turned and moved out of sight.

Dorene knew a set-up when she saw one, but her instincts overrode her training. She reached inside the trunk, unzipped the outside pouch on her suitcase and slipped the bag inside. When her arm emerged she was gripping only her luggage.

Buck rejoined her as they walked together to the elevator.

"You're staying in the same room as your friends. It's in the basement."

Buck pushed the up button. As the doors opened, he turned and shook her hand, placing a room key inside. "You've got the place to yourself. When you're ready, we'll be in the bar." Buck stepped back and the doors swallowed him whole.

Dorene remained there for a lost period of time before pushing the elevator button to go down and stepping inside.

Buck entered the lounge and recognized the familiar back and shoulders of Hill at the bar. He slid onto the stool next to him.

"What's on?" he asked casually.

"Same shit, different town." Hill turned away from the TV. "How is she?"

"Quiet." Buck's eyes went inward. "It'll take her awhile to sort it all. I told her to join us when she was ready."

Business was slow in the bar on this bright afternoon. Sally, right on schedule, walked up with Buck's scotch and water.

"I believe you've met Detective Hill, Sally."

Sally nodded, her face neutral. "You boys need anything else?"

"Maybe later. We're expecting company."

"Just let me know." Sally moved back down the bar, lit a cigarette and leaned against the cash register. Hill and Buck fired up, too, and together the trio watched the nearly continuous coverage at the Seemore Ranch.

The bed had the information laid out in neat piles. The police files, the personal effects taken from Patti's home, newspaper reports, autopsy photos and copies of both Vu's and Hill's personal notes.

Gates locked the door and sat down on the bed. She removed the evidence folder from her bag and laid it next to the others. She decided to start with the facts. She placed the case file on her lap, and cloaked in her police façade, opened Pandora's Box.

It felt like a personal assault: the sequence of events, murder scene photographs, witness statements, the mounting evidence suggesting she had killed her girlfriend in cold blood. Lies, conclusions and strategies in black and white. She lowered her head, took a few deep breaths, and read on.

She read Hill's and Vu's notes. Their thoughts and judgments. Vu's shit samples. Their personal accounts of the Elvis attack. Despite herself, she laughed out loud at what sounded like a Three Stooge's shtick. She read of Hill's frustrations and Vu's dedication to free her. And, as she absorbed the minutia, a faint seed of hope took root, allowing a tiny crack in the impenetrable seal surrounding her heart.

She had never felt loved. She had settled for respect. But, respect was an emotion that didn't spark a passion fierce enough to burn its way to the truth.

There was more.

She picked up Hill's items from the house. She held the faded photo strip from the booth at the fair and stared at the happy faces of the two of them mugging into the lens. Patti had kept it all these years. She read about Patti and Donny Mason, a woman she knew only as a teenager. Patti had supported Donny financially to such an extent that she nearly lost her ranch. It seemed fitting Mason had shot Patti's murderer. One can only chalk it up as karma. Gates flinched at even the thought of karma. Maybe Vu was affecting her.

She sat there for what seemed like hours before opening the last envelope. She pulled out the silk handkerchief, pressed the soft material to her face. Patti's sweet scent had survived lockup, as had she.

She slowly unveiled the contents, the precious snip of hair. She realized that this was not a photo, or a letter, or a memory. This was the last tangible piece of Patti. She remembered the last time she held them in her hands. She leaned close and sniffed their essence. "Sweet baby," she crooned softly.

Later, in the shower, after tears and water left her cleansed and empty, she snipped her own ebony mound and placed it in the handkerchief with the flaxen curls, watching as they once again entwined. Bidding one final goodbye, she placed their photo inside. As she pulled the silken ends into a knot, she tied off entrance to this hidden chamber of her heart.

Gates left the room and headed to the Riverwalk, allowing herself just one more wonder as to what might have been. Then, she said goodbye, tossed the scarf into the water, and headed to the bar.

As Vu pulled off the road and parked behind the old pickup, he experienced a range of emotions. Water always stirred his thoughts. From the moment he had been delivered from his warm bath inside his mother's womb until now, the flow of water, with its currents and eddies, could bring life or death. Vu had experienced both many times while held in its liquid embrace. It was on water he had floated to rescue from the Killing Fields, and on water where his love for Betty had swelled. Sadly, it was in water that Beverly Sanders lost her life.

Vu listened to the waves slapping the mud bank, as he followed the sticks down to the shoreline.

Sanders had survived a brutal rape, estrangement from family and friends, and still had remarkably gone on to become a respected young woman whose Air Force career appeared unlimited. In the end, her need for closure and some measure of justice led to her death. Though she never saw her assailant brought to justice, her death triggered events that settled the score. Her karmic path had not been in vain.

"Jesus H, Leon, would you stop that infernal smacking? You're gonna scare the fish," Willy said.

Leon just smiled, tore off another piece of tobacco, and continued chewing while he hummed.

"I thought I'd find you two here." Vu walked into the clearing and sat down on a flat stump.

"We don't gotta give the money back, do we?" Leon asked, and then mumbled more to himself than anyone, "I just knew there'd be a catch."

"Shut up, Leon. He don't know nothin about no money, do you, Jack?" Willy turned his head toward Vu.

"No. I just wanted to tell you two about the Sanders case."

"Did you figure out for sure who killed the soldier girl?" Leon asked hopefully.

"As close as we'll ever know. Beverly was assaulted and raped as a teenager by Brad Black. She had no clear memory of the attack because of the physical injuries she suffered then."

"Lord, to think men'd do that to a white girl," Willy wagged his head sorrowfully.

Vu ignored the implication and continued. "According to her own notes, another track worker, a groom named Frank DeMarks, saw the whole thing. To make a long story short, DeMarks ended up in a Florida penitentiary on different charges, spilled the story to a cellmate and the cellmate contacted Sanders, figuring he could cash in."

"Even though Beverly never got the name, it was enough for her to begin trying to find her assailant. When she got invited to the party, she decided it was a sign. By the time she arrived at the party aboard the Belle of Louisville, she knew most of the story. She asked the Seemores for their help. Mona convinced John Seemore it couldn't be true. As we now know, she had plenty of reason to keep things quiet, so she invited Beverly to the foredeck for a private chat."

"Rusty seen them there all right," Willy added.

Vu continued. "The river conditions were rough that night and the large ship struck some flotsam in the water. The impact caused several passengers to fall. No one knew for certain what really happened. But, based on the testimony of the cook and others aboard, it was determined that Beverly lost her footing and was at a precariously dangerous point of going overboard. Mona either finished the process by pushing her or not seeking help after she fell."

"Poor child, to die out there alone on that river after all she'd been through." Leon hung his head.

"That's some story," Willy said. "At least the guy who did the deed and the woman who protected him are both dead, too."

"I suppose so," Vu said.

Leon perked up. "What's goin' to happen to that crazy guy?"

"Shit Leon, you already know the answer to that one," Willy sniped. "Why you think they gave us the gigs and money?"

"We ain't ever supposed to talk about that, remember?" Leon retorted. "They could come and take it away."

Willy ignored Leon and spoke directly to Vu, "I suppose you're headed home now?"

"In about an hour, but I wanted you two to do me a favor before I go." Vu reached into his jacket pocket.

"As long as it don't involve sharing my whiskey," Willy laughed.

"Just your signature, Willy." Vu pulled a CD from his pocket. On the cover were a much younger Willy and Leon, standing with other members of the Brother Hooch Band.

"Where in the world did you dig up that thing?" Leon squealed.

"What's he got?"

"Look at them red leather pants," Leon laughed, "and that Afro. Willy, you ain't had that much hair in years."

"It's a CD I had burned from one of your old albums. A store here in Louisville specializes in transferring LP tracks onto CD's. They carry all types of regional music. Could I have your autographs?"

"Mine'll cost you," Willy smiled.

The boys signed the cover with the Sharpie Vu produced.

"This calls for a drink," Willy enthused.

The three leaned back into the bank, sharing sips of Willy's whiskey and basking toward the river in the afternoon sun.

In the distance, the sun glistened off a shiny piece of silken cloth as it floated past.

Author's Note

At some point during the writing, I felt a heavy sadness weighing on me from the many stories I'd heard following Katrina's aftermath. New Orleans had been the setting for both earlier books. Since this story involved the death of a famous Jockey, I opted to instead set it in Louisville, Kentucky, the home of the Derby. Yet, I still had this need to pay tribute to all the courageous and self-sacrificing individuals, those who had been involved in clean-up or lifesaving efforts. Ultimately, it was because of their early commitments that spurred an entire community forward to do whatever was necessary to survive. New Orleans is still rebuilding, finding its way again. I both respect and admire that. So, this tribute goes to the honorable citizens, the volunteers, the governmental agencies, the famous and not so famous actors, actresses, artists, labors, poets, musicians, street rats, police, cooks, churches, and of course the military, Portland's own Oregon Air National Guard unit, the 125 STS, that provided assistance. Although lives were lost, lives were saved. In the end, the spirit of the people never faltered. These are trying times in which we live, even without calamities of this magnitude, it's not always easy to stay on tack, with or without a moral compass to guide us through our journeys. At times, the path can get a little treacherous. It is in disasters like Katrina where the true spirit of a people shines. So to all of you heroes, I hope you find some satisfaction in knowing that I'm your biggest fan.

About The Author

Doc Macomber is a native Northwesterner. His previous books include: *The Killer Coin* and *Wolf's Remedy.* He is a contributor to various national and international publications. Doc divides his time between wrenching on Harley-Davidsons and serving in a Special Ops unit. He currently lives aboard a sailboat on the Columbia River.

(Author photograph by Serge A. McCabe)

Also by Doc Macomber

"As addictive and satisfying as my first tattoo, Wolf's Remedy left me craving more."
– Lyle Tuttle, Tattoo Legend and Historian

Wolf's Remedy

What secrets lie hidden in the WWII Harley-Davidson motorcycles? Why was a harmless young soldier assassinated in a crowded train depot? And when do avenging angels cross the line to become killers? Follow Air Force investigator Jack Vu as his hunt for a murderer uncovers an aged cadre of veterans set on making one final attempt to redeem themselves by recovering and returning cached treasures to Holocaust survivors. As time runs out, and the true wounds of war are revealed, a sense of urgency propels these modern day Robin Hoods forward. This historically accurate tale forces moral choices by unforgettable characters that will stay with you long after the satisfying conclusion.

Fiction/Mystery/978-0-9785717-0-2.

Floating Word Press, LLC.
Available at your local bookstore, or visit
www.floatingwordpress.com